Not Forgotten

A Harbour Bay Novel

Camille Taylor

Not Forgotten

Limitless Publishing, LLC
Kailua, HI 96734
www.limitlesspublishing.com

Formatting: Limitless Publishing

ISBN-13: 978-1-68058-289-5
ISBN-10: 1-68058-289-5

Dedication

For my sister, Bec.

Prologue

The tyres skidded against the cold bitumen of the deserted old highway as Hallie Walker's father braked for the lone man who appeared out of the heavy fog dead ahead. The car protested, the tyres squealing and buckling beneath them from the strain. Hallie screamed as the sharp smell of burnt rubber wafted up to fill her nostrils.

The car jerked as her father lost control. The car spun and her heart thudded in her chest. The sudden impact as the Ford Fairlane hit the thick, dense tree truck sent her twelve-year-old body tumbling into the foot-well between the front and back seats with a thud. She'd stupidly released the seatbelt to find a more comfortable position in an effort to fall asleep, the trip long and tedious and now regretted the decision. She lay frozen on the floor for a moment, stunned before sitting up, slowly registering the minor aches and pains that would later leave bruises. Smoke escaped from beneath the hood and a sizzling sound reverberated through the semi-

1

silent night. The only sound other than their harsh breathing was Slim Dusty playing lightly on the stereo.

Her breath came in white puffs as the heat from her mouth met the frigid pre-dawn August air which poured into the car through the cracked and splintered windscreen.

Her father's head lay against the steering wheel and he slowly lifted it, turning towards her mother whose eyes were closed, her head resting against the back of her seat but thankfully otherwise uninjured. He turned his attention to her. "Hallie, baby, are you—"

Her father's words were cut off as his window shattered and two large hands reached in and pulled him roughly from the car's interior. She thought she screamed but she couldn't be sure. Her father struggled against the man who had appeared out of nowhere and threw him roughly to the road. She heard her father grunt. Her breath caught in her throat as she watched in horror as the man stabbed her father repeatedly. Black dots danced in her vision and she swallowed hard, almost passing out at the gory image in front of her.

Her mother scrambled from her seat and started running back the way they'd driven, the sound of her heels on the asphalt echoing in the night. Hallie froze for the second time that night, terrified. She was alone. She wanted to call out to her father but knew it was too late. He lay unmoving on the dark, pockmarked road. Screaming for help would be useless. She hadn't seen another car for hours.

She trembled. Tears burned her eyes as fear

cooled her blood. She had no idea what to do. It didn't matter, she couldn't get her limbs to move anyway. She shook as she held the tears in check. Her whole world was disappearing before her eyes. The man raised his head and started after her mother, his long legs eating up the distance between them, his footsteps thundering against the road.

The man reached out and grabbed her mother's blonde hair, jerking her back into his chest. She screamed, the sound piercing Hallie's eardrums as her mother kicked and struggled against him.

Hallie ducked back into her hiding place in the foot-well as the man dragged her mother back toward her. She chewed on her nails, a horrible habit and her fingers bled when she bit past the quick. Hallie's gaze found the man's face and remained there. As hard as she tried, she could not look away. As he moved closer, the moon's bright rays bounced off his long, dark, greasy hair, illuminating him in the night almost like a spotlight, highlighting his features. The man's lower face was covered with several days' worth of growth. His heartless brown eyes glowed almost demonically in the light and she felt her bladder release, filling the car with the scent of ammonia.

Her mind ran riot with thoughts. Why was he doing this? She wondered as she thought of several scenarios. None ended favourably. She felt the first stages of a panic attack and tried to calm herself, taking long, deep breaths even as she cowered back into the small space as the man's shadow cast over her.

From the short distance dividing them, Hallie

could see the well-worn jeans encasing strong well-developed legs. The jeans themselves were threadbare. The left back pocket dangled down, held on only by a few measly threads. Tears fell unabashedly down her cheeks. Her nose ran and she watched everything through misty eyes.

She was a coward, useless and scared. The man had just killed her father and was now about to send her mother to the same fate. But still her body felt heavy, unable to move except to push herself farther into the floor. A sob escaped her mouth and she quickly stuffed her fist in the gaping hole to muffle any further sounds. Her teeth bit into her hand, her mind numb against the horrors she had already witnessed this night. She shivered, the warm air from the heater long since evaporated and replaced with the icy breeze outside. She curled up into a ball as much as the car would allow.

Hallie heard her mother's pleading voice as she was shoved none too gently onto her recently vacated seat. Hallie knew she would never forget the pungent scent of the man for as long as she lived, a combination of blood and bad hygiene. A thought kept repeating inside her head.

We're going to die.

Her mother made a sound of despair and Hallie's gaze shot back to her mother and their eyes met and held. She watched helplessly as the man brought his knife up to her mother's throat and pressed it deeply into the soft delicate flesh of her neck. Blood spilled from her body, flowing onto the seat and ruining the careful detail of the vehicle.

A scream, muffled around her fist, escaped

Hallie's throat as she watched her mother's body go limp and lifeless. The man looked straight into her eyes and once again she felt frozen, as if the ice in his veins jumped from his eyes into her. She shivered uncontrollably.

Hallie had the car door open and was racing towards the tree line before the man could react. Her tiny frame and short stature allowed her to blend into the woods as she sprinted for her life. Her vision blurred black as she ran faster, the darkness swelling around her. She could only just make out where there were gaps in the thick trees and bushes. The fog hindered her even more as she made her way farther into the dense growth.

Her heart jumped to her throat and she was having trouble breathing. Her feet landed heavily on the ground and every so often she heard a twig snap under the pressure of her weight. She could hear the man behind her covering twice as much ground with his much longer and stronger legs. She strained to hear his breathing and desperately wanted to know if he was winded in hopes he would give up the chase. She didn't dare look back for fear of tripping. She was already having trouble with that, her focus on the ground.

Hallie knew he was closing in fast behind her. She pushed herself to go faster even though she was exhausted and her body was ready to collapse. Her nose twitched as her feet kicked up the undergrowth. The scent of mouldy leaves and damp soil assaulted her senses. The sound of heavy stomping behind her terrified her but she didn't allow it to immobilise her. Her brain had long ago kicked into survival mode and didn't let her dwell on anything but getting to safety.

Hallie had no illusions. She knew if the man behind her caught up with her, he would kill her just like he had done to her mother and father. She breathed in through her nose and out her mouth as she had been taught. Her whole body ached with fatigue and fear and she wanted so much to curl up and cry in despair. She whimpered uncontrollably, knowing she was almost beaten.

She pressed her right arm against her side as a stitch made her uncomfortable. She pushed on. She had to keep going. Hopefully soon she would be out of the woods and into a clearing. Maybe then she could find a busy road or a house. She was well within the forest now. In every direction stood more trees and even more bushes, both furry and prickly.

Hallie heard the sound of tearing right before she was jerked back. She panicked, striking out trying to hit her target. It took her a few full seconds to realise she was still alone and that she was caught on a branch sticking out of an old flaky tree. She yanked at her winter jacket vigorously, the fabric well entwined with the branch. Desperate, she quickly unzipped the garment, shivering as the cool air hit her bare arms but soon she completely forgot about the cold.

Little mewling sounds came from her throat as she imagined she could feel her pursuer's horrid breath on her neck, his hands on her pulling him to her, the feel of his knife against her own throat. Distracted she tripped over a group of raised roots and scratched her face on the bark of the closest tree as she tried to steady herself.

Hallie headed straight, the trees not so dense up ahead to what she considered north. Her legs gave way as she came across a small dip in the ground and her body landed heavily with a thud on the leaf-covered floor. Without sparing a moment to wallow in self-pity she climbed to her feet, feeling her ankle buckle beneath her before crashing once more to the ground. She bit her bottom lip to stop from crying out and alerting the man to her location and started crawling, her pants soaking up the damp ground. She barely made it a metre before she felt the ground beneath her give way to a sharp decline.

Hallie's hand flayed about in mid-air for a moment right before her body slipped and she tumbled down into the river resting at the base of the decline. Her head went under the water and she struggled not to breathe. She kicked her feet and tried to swim as she resurfaced. Her waterlogged clothes tugged at her, determined to send her to a watery grave. The current proved to be too strong and pulled her light weight away from the edge and into the whirling centre before she was once more dragged under, down into the murky depths.

Chapter 1

Detective Inspector Matt Murphy sat at his desk and looked down at the folder his partner just handed him. He warily opened the manila folder he knew contained graphic pictures of another life that had been abruptly taken. He took a deep breath which immediately caught in his throat as he examined the colour photos of a butchered woman. His hands automatically became fists, crumpling the folder inside them.

One crime he despised more than all others was crime against women and children. He had been raised singlehandedly by his mother since his younger sister, Kendall, had been a baby. His father had been an unfortunate causality in a liquor store robbery. After drying the many tears spilled over the years by his mother and sister, he had learned to respect the softer gender and could pick up on the slightest hormonal change in a female.

According to his fellow policemen, he had a superpower. One they would love to have themselves. One officer had even said it would make his life easier knowing whether to fight or flee.

Matt could never imagine raising a hand to any woman and despised those who did. He worked those cases extra hard. Never resting until the perpetrator was arrested and behind bars.

Matt ground his teeth together and threw back the last of his coffee that had gone cold and started to congeal in the bottom of the mug. He took in the sight of the beautiful young woman who now sported several stab wounds and a gaping hole that had once been her throat. He never realised just how much he could come to hate the colour red.

Just looking at the photo, Matt could smell the crime scene. Years of working homicide cases will do that to you. All a cop had to do was to look at a photo to imagine all sort of things. He scanned the photos with a critical and analytical eye, cataloguing what might prove useful in nailing the bastard who had brutalised and then murdered the innocent woman.

"Jesus." He let the exclamation escape beneath his breath, disgusted.

Matt jotted down a few notes in point form. Questions he wanted to ask the first-on-scene officer or evidence he wanted to inspect closer. As he put his pen down, he looked up at his new partner, Darryl Hill, and squinted against the bright sunlight streaming through the large glass window directly behind Darryl.

It was such a beautiful day outside. It seemed ghastly to be reviewing such a horrible murder. It was the time for kids and adults alike to run around amongst the daffodils and daisies. For the sweet smell of jasmine and lavender to fill their noses and for the light breeze to tease at women's dresses. Matt certainly wouldn't be appreciating it any time soon. He sneezed as the dust particles wafting about the room settled in his nostrils from the ancient air-con as it vigorously pumped out stale air.

As much as Matt liked spring—the warmer days, the flowers blooming and the promise of summer coming—he hated the fact that his nose tended to look like Rudolph's as he was assaulted with hay fever. Matt popped two tablets from the collection in his top desk drawer and washed it down with a gulp of water from a bottle he found tucked away behind the stapler. His lips curled in distaste as the stagnant water ran down his throat.

He coughed, clearing his throat from the almost toxic taste and threw the empty bottle in the small circular bin beside his desk before once more focusing on his partner. Darryl Hill was new to Harbour Bay after recently passing his detective's exam and landing the job after Matt's last partner retired.

Darryl was six-foot and lean. Any weight on him was pure muscle. A regular down in the gym. Matt briefly wondered if Darryl was married or divorced. It wasn't something they had discussed during their short acquaintance. He leaned more towards single since he hadn't seen Darryl rush out in the middle of a case as many did to placate their women when they pointed out how much time the men were spending at the office. Matt had seen many marriages fail. Wives never seemed to understand the importance of what they were striving to achieve. They only saw junior's missed soccer game or a family barbeque they turned up late for or had to leave early.

Matt himself had never had this issue and sure as hell planned to put it off as long as he could. His career was his life at the moment and he wasn't looking for anything long-term. He certainly didn't want something that started with love to end in hatred. He had known very few cops who had actually made their marriages work.

He and Darryl had never talked about anything personal. Matt sensed Darryl was much like him and preferred to keep his own counsel. When they were together, they spoke about cases and brainstormed ideas. One thing Matt did know was that Darryl was meticulous with his files and was the type of man who always strived for excellence. A real go-getter who didn't need to be told when or how to do his job.

Matt had heard similar stories from officers who had worked with the detective. The top of his class at the Police College in Goulburn. He got the job done and rarely let any case go cold. Matt felt reassured at the knowledge. He didn't like guys who kissed arse to get ahead. He wanted dedicated people. Those who would happily give up dinner at home and sweat blood for results. Because of that, Matt knew he could trust Darryl with his life and in the future there would be times he would need to.

Below his clean pressed shirt, Darryl's pants were creased and drops of spilt coffee marred the shiny polish on his brown leather shoes. His naturally tanned face was clean shaven and had it not been for the bloodshot light brown eyes, one would have thought him well-rested. His skin held a slight green tinge and beads of sweat dampened his light brown crew cut. The rookie had obviously seen the pictures prior to passing them over and was probably wishing right about now he hadn't. Matt waited a moment just in case his partner needed to make a quick trip to the head. He watched as Darryl's Adam apple bobbed up and down as he swallowed in an effort to keep his breakfast down.

Matt remembered his first bloody scene and the struggle he had not to let his dinner repeat itself. He had been ready to right the world's wrongs. Now, at thirty-five, he wasn't as stupid as to believe he could save everyone. It had been a hard lesson to learn but in the end after the countless heartbreaks and guilt trips he had finally accepted it. But not without cost.

He was as physically fit as someone could get without being a bodybuilder, spending his downtime in the gym downstairs, unwinding after long hard days like these. His hair, sporting a few stray greys, was longer than regulation allowed but he could never find the time to have it cut.

Darryl nodded stonily at Matt's assessment of the case. "Marie Stanton, twenty-seven-year-old med graduate. The perp took his time with her before he cut her throat ear to ear."

Matt shuddered. He had seen this work before and knew exactly who was responsible. The only problem was finding the man. He was as elusive as a four leaf clover and had been wanted by law enforcement for years. His capture would be paramount to that of Ivan Milat's.

"The Butcher," he said through his teeth. His face was a mask of pure rage at not being able to prevent the victim's unfortunate and unnecessary death.

Darryl's face screwed up in disgust. "It's been confirmed."

Matt felt the wariness in his body deepen. He had already been up for seventeen hours and he figured he'd be up for another seventeen at least. He ran his long thin fingers through his hair, in agitation, no doubt making the almost black tufts stick straight up in the air. He mentally shrugged. Appearance wasn't high on his list of concerns.

Matt took in the room. There were five detectives in Harbour Bay's DU—Detective Unit—including himself and Darryl. Thankfully the city was fairly quiet when it came to murder, at least until now, and he and Darryl along with the other detectives in the unit worked a variety of cases across all of the divisions within the LAC, Local Area Command: Dean Matthews, Nicholas Doyle, and Amelia Donovan, the only woman on the team.

Amelia was neither fat nor thin, her physical type tough rather than fragile and could take down any man in a fight—including him one time when she had goaded him into a knock-down all-in wrestle. He had walked away red-faced and from that moment on he had admired the spunky woman. Her raven hair was just long enough to be tied into a ponytail and she sported light brown almond shaped eyes. She never hid her femininity from the men she worked with. Her clothes often hugged her body but not enough to distract them from a case. She was all business and didn't take any shit from anybody, least of all 'scum-sucking criminals' and they all had tremendous respect for her. She was one hell of a detective, ambitious too. Matt knew, as he knew the sun would rise again tomorrow, that one day she would be his boss.

"And the last two victims?" he asked, dreading the answer he knew was coming. Marie Stanton hadn't been the first, not by a long shot. Since the early nineties, the Butcher had been killing, moving from state to state leaving a trail of bodies in his wake. For some reason which Matt couldn't fathom, the Butcher had come back to Harbour Bay and apparently he planned to stay.

His gaze drifted over to the large bulletin board opposite his desk. Multiple photos of smiling women were pinned to the board. Below the snapshots were the corresponding crime scene photos. Each mutilated body stared back at him, condemning him for allowing them to die. Darryl's stare followed his.

"The boys in forensics say they're all the work of the Butcher."

Matt nodded. It had been five years since the Butcher had last reaped havoc in Harbour Bay. At that time he had not yet been labelled a serial killer. He had moved on after inadvertently leaving his last victim alive and in police custody.

Matt stood, running his hands over his wrinkled forest green shirt, as if to magically iron out the creases. His tie was loose and hung haphazardly around his neck. He started making his way down the corridor of the LAC, Darryl easily keeping up with his long strides.

"I hear back in 2005 with the Walker double homicide, there was a survivor," Darryl said, looking for new angles in which to tackle the case.

Matt nodded, remembering it like it was yesterday. It had been his first case as a detective, and the crime scene was forever burned in his memory. The Ford Fairlane parked into a tree. The body of Senator Ian Walker left on the highway, his throat slit, his head barely attached to his neck. His wife, Missy, half inside the car and half out. Both their bodies had been stabbed multiple times close to or not long after death.

It had still been dark when he and his partner, Ed Graham, a seasoned veteran with over twenty years' experience, had entered the LAC. The sight of the little girl huddled beneath a mountain of blankets had broken his heart and gave him nightmares for months afterward. He was surprised at the strength of will to survive the girl had showed. After pulling herself free of the nearby river that flowed adjacent to the town she had ran towards the nearest civilisation she could find, which happened to be a house roughly thirty kilometres outside of Harbour Bay. She'd banged on the door until it had opened to reveal two sleepy farmers. The owners had bundled her up in a blanket and had immediately taken her into town.

When children her age would have collapsed in tears and closed themselves up, Hallie Walker had talked and hadn't stopped until she had told her entire story. Not only had she told her story but she had kept on telling it to whomever asked. Matt figured it was due to the fact the girl was running on pure adrenaline.

Later, she had sat there still as a statue, the only sign of life her active eyes shifting about the room as they took in the commotion around her. He and Ed had walked over to her and her solemn amber eyes, red from crying, watched them warily. Her short shoulder length red-brown hair was knotted from the events of the night, her clothes still damp beneath the blanket and her skin smelled of the river.

She'd been terrified, her slight body shaking slightly. He imagined all that she'd experienced, all that she'd witnessed. How scared and alone she'd felt, knowing help was too far away, the highway rarely used other than by locals as travelling motorists preferred to use the newly built freeway that bypassed the smaller towns along the coast.

When he and Ed had started questioning Hallie, she repeated her story once again, giving them the cold facts not even a traumatised cop might recount with such detailed efficiency. She was extremely remarkable, Matt had noted at the time, and noticed her reluctance to steer towards anything emotional. He understood the need to close that part of oneself off. Anyone in her situation would do the same. Later he learned the young girl had been admitted into a rehabilitation centre that specialised in the mentally unbalanced for observation and eventually incarcerated. A sad ending for such a brave girl, Matt had thought at the time.

"There was the daughter. Hallie Walker was twelve years old and was able to give us a detailed description. We ran the sketch through the media— newspapers, TV, internet—but came up empty."

"He was considered a transient?" Darryl asked.

"Yes, but a very smart, methodical one. His attacks are well organised so he has the means to stalk them for a considerable amount of time. He's been doing this for almost twenty years and the only time he ever messed up was when he left Hallie Walker alive."

"Can she help?"

Matt shrugged. "She did once. Whether or not she can now is a different story. A couple of months after the Walker murders, Hallie was incarcerated in Paradise Valley."

"That's rough," Darryl commented.

"It is," Matt agreed. In his mind's eye he saw Hallie Walker as she had been—formidable. A force to be reckoned with even when she was hurting. There was no guessing as to who the young woman in Paradise Valley was. For some reason he couldn't imagine her as a little girl lost somewhere within her own mind. Hallie had seemed so capable to him, so brave and sure of herself that he couldn't believe she would allow herself to be beaten down.

He wondered if she still had those intelligent, almost gold eyes. The ones that saw and understood too much. He sighed, knowing full well he would find out soon enough. But this was a delicate situation. One in which he was clearly out of his depth. He was going to need help.

He was going to need a professional.

Chapter 2

Doctor Natalie Miller sat in the leather bound chair that faced the couch. Her office, decorated in soft pastels and soothing tones, was on the fourth floor of a building in the CBD of Harbour Bay. It had taken her years to afford the sleek office in its prime location but whenever she looked around she felt such a sense of accomplishment. After all her hard work, she had finally made it in her profession. She was one of the most sought out psychologists in the city and the surrounding areas and was now earning a healthy wage.

Yet, for all her talent in the field, she had never once turned her insight on herself to heal her old wounds. Natalie knew she was emotionally stunted and often felt ice cold inside. She had dated some over the years but had never allowed anyone to see the other side of her—the vulnerable side, afraid of having someone exploit it. It all came down to trust. Her trusting others, and she just couldn't do that.

Fear was a powerful immobiliser.

She made notes on her notepad as her shy,

awkward teenage patient spoke. He tried—and failed miserably—to keep his eyes off her body. His gaze ping-ponged between her breasts that rose and fell with each of her breaths and her silk encased legs, exposed by the knee length hem of her navy fitted dress.

Billy had been seeing her now once a week for almost a month since he had set off the fire alarm at his high school and had subsequently been suspended in a cry for help. His parents thankfully heard the cry and had sent him to her. He was a good kid, a little high strung from the daily pressures of bringing home good grades and the stress of making his parents proud.

Poor Billy, she thought. During these turbulent teenage years it had to be torture to be stuck in a room with someone you found attractive. He was trying so hard to pretend otherwise. She had thankfully been spared such awkwardness. Natalie may spend her time watching the males of the species but never in attraction. No, from a young age, she had found herself looking at a man and assessing his strength, wondering what lurked beneath the surface. Later, when she had begun dating and a man ordered an alcoholic beverage, she would wonder whether he was a happy or a mean drunk but never stuck around long enough to find out.

The study of the people around her, while it had been in fear, had been what had first interested her in psychology. She wondered if she could read someone so accurately that she would never be surprised by their actions. After four years of psychology classes she had come out of university with a bachelor's degree and a masters in clinical psychology.

She took a deep breath. Billy's eyes were instantly upon her breasts like heat seeking missiles. She would need to rethink her business attire for the days she counselled the teenager. Not that she ever dressed provocatively. Natalie hated being on display and much preferred to melt into the background, her back against the wall, protecting herself.

She made herself silently count to ten. Billy was beginning to make her feel uncomfortable. He was a sweet kid but he was also a male and Natalie didn't trust the male gender. She was always wary of them and their intentions and never once allowed her guard down in their presence. Even Billy, who was tall and lanky and seemed as soft as a marshmallow.

She pushed away her issues and focused on her patient. He deserved her full attention. She made several more notations on the page and asked him how he felt, listening not only to his words, but his tone and watched the expressions play across his face to determine his truthfulness. A buzzer sent out a low hum from her desk, alerting her to the hour.

"It appears our time is up Billy," she said, standing. He rose also in one limber motion. "Have you spoken to your parents about how you feel?"

He swallowed hard. "No. I don't want to disappoint them."

"Your parents love you, Billy. You could never disappoint them. I'm sure they'll be shocked to hear their pushing has caused this breakdown."

"I guess," he said, his tone conveying he was not convinced.

"Would it give you courage if I was there also? Perhaps at your next session, they could attend as well? We can tell them together. Help them to understand what it is you're feeling and why."

"Yeah. I think that could work."

"All right. I'll have my receptionist arrange a time that's suitable for all and we'll work this out. Are you going to be okay? Are you still stressed?"

"I don't know." He gave her a once over.

"Billy," she said softly. His gaze jumped to hers guiltily. "I have a suggestion. Why don't you ask one of the girls from your school to the movies? That'll be fun and stress free and it'll get you out of the house."

He blushed. "I like my women to have meat on their bones and a nice round figure. The girls at school are too skinny."

Natalie wasn't sure if she should feel complimented or insulted. She maintained a healthy weight, but she would never fit into a size eight.

"I'm not asking you to marry her, Billy, just take her out as friends. Have a few laughs. It really is the best medicine."

"Okay, Doctor Miller."

She wasn't sure from the teenager's tone if that meant he was going to comply with her suggestion or ignore it. There wasn't anything more she could do. The patient had to be willing to help themselves before she even had a chance. Which probably explained her own reluctance.

She waved off that thought as she walked Billy

to the door. "Remember, when you feel like it's all too much, just let go. Get up and go outside. Breathe and get some fresh air into those lungs, okay?"

"Yeah, I know. Don't let it get to me."

"Exactly. I'll see you next week."

Billy nodded before slipping through the door. When it was closed behind him, Natalie sank into the chair at her desk. She glanced at the clock. It was still morning and she had hours to go before she could retire. Today was just dragging on. She closed Billy Duncan's file before tucking the red folder away in her desk drawer. She stole a look at the pile of manila file folders on her desk. Sometime soon she would have to go through and review each case. It was something she was not looking forward to. Natalie didn't like seeing her failures, of those she couldn't help, the ones referred elsewhere or institutionalised. No she never liked knowing the statistics on her work, just as she never liked to hear criticism, constructive or otherwise.

She walked over to her side table where her coffee maker sat and measured out the coffee and pressed the button on the side. The coffee maker sprang to life and made delicious sounds as the scent of coffee filled the room and revived her weary body. She stood there watching the coffee slowly pour into the carafe and when it was done, poured the strong coffee into her favourite "I Love Psychology" mug her aunt had given her when she had graduated.

When she returned to her desk, she set her cup

down and waited for it to cool. Rather than waste time, she switched on her computer and brought up the local news website. She had planned to check her emails but didn't see the harm in playing five minutes of hooky as she caught up with what was happening around the world. The front page of the website caught her attention. Under the heading of *Breaking News* was *Murder in Harbour Bay*.

Curiosity edging her on, Natalie clicked on the photograph of a young, beautiful woman with a brunette bob and hazel eyes. The caption said her name was Marie Stanton, a med student at the local university. The article was short but to the point:

`Marie Stanton has been brutally murdered in Harbour Bay. While reports are sketchy, the police are saying citizens should be vigilant. Anyone who was in the area at the time of the murder should come forward for questioning. Detectives are keeping quiet about the exact details of Ms Stanton's death but what is known is she was found in a downtown parking garage off Charles early yesterday morning. If you can shed any light on this crime please call local officials or Crime Stoppers.`

The reporter went on to speculate that the murder was one of many attributed to the Butcher, the man who'd killed Senator Ian Walker and his wife Missy just outside of town on the King George Highway in August of 2005.

Natalie shivered despite the warm temperature.

The thought someone had been murdered in her town gave her the creeps. Someone walking about outside her office doors was a murderer. She hoped the police would catch the bastard quickly. A man like that did not deserve to be out in the world free while women like Marie Stanton would never live again.

She clicked on the email icon on her taskbar and scanned her emails, relieved to find nothing required immediate attention. She answered a few about rescheduling appointments and deleted the junk. She closed her inbox and decided to get on with her work. Maybe that would clear her mind of the recent article and thoughts of a murderer free in her beloved city. She glanced over at her appointments book and took in the name of her next patient. Natalie swivelled her chair around and opened her desk drawer to pull out his file. She then turned her full attention to the file.

The name *Henry Rellet* was printed in capitals on the top of the page. Natalie took another deep sip of her coffee and let the liquid trail down her throat and into her stomach. She caught herself just moments before she moaned in pleasure. She was so caught up in her nirvana that she didn't hear the man enter her office and come to stand beside her desk. One minute she was alone with her delicious and desired coffee and the next a man with brown hair and sparkling green eyes was standing beside her, casting a shadow over her desk and paperwork.

"Doctor Natalie Miller," he said in greeting.

He was a tall man, good-looking too, and she was surprised that these were her first thoughts about the stranger invading her privacy. Natalie felt the burn of desire low in her belly and was startled at her response. She had heard of instant desire but had never experienced it herself. She was by no means a virgin but not one of the few men she had invited into her bed had ever made her feel this wanton. She realised she was undressing him with her eyes and immediately squashed the imagery, delightful though it was.

She studied him with analytical eyes as she would any other stranger. His body was hard and strong from working out. He probably did it often, unlike her whose current fitness regime was walking up and down the stairs in her house on the way to and from work. Strangely, she did not fear the threat he posed to her with his brute strength that would easily be no match against her. Bizarre. He held a folder in his big hand and when he smiled at her, wrinkles appeared around his eyes. She judged him to be in his mid-thirties and not married, if his bare finger was anything to go by, not that she planned on doing anything about that.

Natalie closed the file and placed it on her desk for easy access later. She turned and gave the intruder her undivided attention, her eyebrow slightly arched.

"Yes. What can I do for you?"

Her gaze once again travelled the length of him, this time taking in the creased shirt, five o'clock shadow and the coffee stains on his cream tie. Her eyes widened, seeing the badge and gun attached to his hip which she had clearly overlooked during her first perusal. Her mind—and libido—obviously engaged elsewhere. She had been lusting over a law enforcement officer. If only he knew what she had been imagining. He would have arrested her, or being that he was male and breathing would have eagerly accepted her offer. Why did that thought give her such a rush?

"Detective?"

The man gave her a brief nod, answering the question in her voice. He pulled out his identification and showed it to her. Natalie could see the hologram imbedded on the card as it played in the light, proving its authenticity.

"Detective Inspector Matt Murphy, Harbour Bay LAC," he said.

"What can I do for you, Detective?"

She offered her visitor chair to him and he moved around to the chair facing her across the desk. She watched as he stretched out his long legs and shifted to find a comfortable position.

"I have a case for you, if you're interested. A delicate one."

Natalie nodded. "All my cases are delicate, Detective."

Matt handed her the file and she took it from him. He held her gaze for longer than necessary as he said, "I can guarantee this is more so."

Natalie licked her lips, her palms suddenly slick with sweat. His stare followed the movement of her tongue as it glided over her dry lips. Her body heated to the point of boiling and once more she was surprised at herself. When normally she would lash out at his obvious interest, she found herself wanting more of his attention. She tore her eyes away from the gorgeous detective and opened the file. As she regulated her suddenly fast breathing, she glanced down at the name on the top.

"Hallie Walker?"

"A very distraught young lady," he added.

"Any relation to Ian and Missy Walker?" she asked, recalling the article she had just read, the name popping out at her.

"Daughter," he replied simply.

"Is the girl in danger?"

"She's in a padded room. It's not her I'm worried about."

No, Natalie decided, he was more worried about the Marie Stantons of the world. She didn't envy him in the slightest. His was a hard and unappreciative job, much like hers, but she didn't put her life on the line every day as he did. She took a deep breath and was immediately assaulted with the unique scent of Detective Murphy, a combination of pure raw male and perspiration. The mixture was currently wreaking havoc on her senses. Her leg began to bounce up and down beneath the desk, a sure sign of her frustration.

"Has she been susceptible to previous counselling?"

Matt leaned forward in the chair, placing his arms over his thighs. "According to the Director of Paradise Valley, no. In fact, she can be downright antagonistic."

"That's not surprising. Not everyone is interested in spilling their innermost thoughts to a stranger." The very idea of verbalising her violent past had her quivering slightly. It was her pain alone and not meant to be shared. Natalie leaned back in her seat and regarded him. "What is it you want from her? Surely the police interviewed her back then. What more do you hope to gain from her?"

Matt held her gaze. "To be honest, the case has gone cold, despite the recent murder. I'd just like to hear her recount the night once more. See if any new information can be had."

"I see."

Natalie quickly read through the first page, absorbing the text and filtering out the important information and disregarding the nonsense and doctor babble.

"It's not unusual for a girl so young to be institutionalised after such an event," she commented, more to herself than to her audience. "But there are other treatments available, ones that should've been attempted before such an extreme measure." She looked over at him from above the folder. "I notice her file doesn't mention any of them."

"You'll have to discuss that with the Director of PV, should you take the case."

"Why me, Detective?" she asked, eager for the answer. She wasn't sure why it mattered to her. "There are many other psychologists."

Matt shrugged. "I heard that you were the best in town and this girl deserves the best."

Natalie raised an eyebrow at his comment and wondered who the girl was to him that he would seek out a private psychologist rather than just a government appointed one. While she wouldn't say she was the *best*, she was certainly up there in the top ten and she would need every ounce of that ability to help Hallie.

It was no wonder the girl had been taken to hospital. After skimming through the rest of her file, Natalie thought Hallie was lucky she hadn't ended up insane. Although the jury was still out on that one, and Natalie wouldn't know for sure what she was dealing with until she had had a chance to speak with the girl and determine for herself just how bad of shape Hallie was in.

She thought back to when she was twelve, still trying to figure who she was and what she would be. She even admitted to herself that in her earlier years she'd been a dreamer all the way. But that was all she had back then—dreams. She tried to imagine witnessing such a violent double homicide, as Hallie Walker had, and she shivered. While her childhood hadn't been a walk in the park, Natalie seriously doubted her ability to survive and thrive after such an event.

She knew she'd been weak, but the truth was she hadn't known any better, hadn't known what laid beyond the farm gates. Her ignorance had almost been her downfall. She shook her head in an effort to clear the memories she had tried so hard to repress and turned her attention to the detective.

"Who is Hallie Walker to you, Detective? Surely she is more than just a witness or a survivor?"

"No, you're right, she's more. She's remarkable. The first time I saw her was that night and I was so impressed by her courage, her veracity, that if I can do something now to help her, I will," Matt declared.

Natalie tapped her manicured finger gently against the folder while she thought. It would be a tough case. She wasn't completely certain she could do anything to help. Cases like Hallie's were difficult, especially if the patient didn't want to help herself. Natalie wasn't sure but she suspected this was the reason Hallie was still at Paradise Valley.

Having made her decision, she glanced over her desk to the sinful looking man who despite his grungy appearance set her heart pounding and her stomach fluttering. She took a moment to soak in this new experience before speaking. She realised she must have taken more than a moment when she saw Matt raise an eyebrow at the same time one side of his mouth lifted. She blushed profusely and Matt laughed. The sound sent a thrill of pleasure through her body. She frowned at the unexpected discovery and cleared her voice before rushing on.

"Leave me the file, Detective, and I'll take it home and study it. If it's convenient for you, I'd like to meet with Miss Walker tomorrow."

Matt nodded his assent. "Thank you. There is a complete work up on her, her parents, and the murders along with some photos and a few pictures the hospital thought you might like to see."

Natalie stood and made her way around her desk to sit on the edge of the dark stained wood. Her navy skirt tightly closing around her thighs as she crossed her ankles.

"You do realise that with trauma such as Miss Walker has experienced, the chances she will remember anything is slim to none. When the brain goes into shock, it will protect itself usually with loss of memory," she warned, making sure he knew the risks. She was good at her job but wasn't a miracle worker.

"I understand. She gave us an explicit account last time around. We're just hoping for some information and clarification. Even if she can't help us, she needs to be helped. I owe her that."

Natalie let out a deep breath. "I hope I can be of some assistance, Detective, and I hope you get your man."

"I'm sure you'll do all you can, Doctor, and that's all anyone can ask."

He stood, bringing his body closer to her, filling the small gap between them. Natalie felt the heat before she promptly stepped away, making the action seem more like courtesy rather than anxiety. She may be experiencing some serious attraction to him but that didn't mean she trusted him and her safety was her number one priority.

She walked over the door and waited for him to join her.

"Good day, Detective," she said, holding out her hand.

Matt took the offering and shook her hand. "Doctor Miller," he said softly as there was a light tap on the door and it immediately opened to reveal a man in his late twenties standing in the entrance with a bewildered look on his face. He glanced from one to the other before his gaze settled on Natalie.

"Henry," Natalie said calmly, her hand still entwined with Matt's.

Once more, Henry Rellet's stare drifted over Matt and down to their connected hands. Natalie followed his gaze and suddenly realised she was practically holding hands with the detective. She extradited her hand quickly as Henry spoke.

"Doctor Miller. I thought we had an appointment. Have I mixed up my days?"

"No, Henry, not at all. In fact, you're right on time," she said, glancing at the delicate watch on her wrist. "The detective was just leaving."

Natalie gave Matt a slight push towards the door.

Henry frowned. A look of concern crossed his face. "You're all right, Doctor Miller, aren't you?"

Natalie nodded. "Yes, I'm fine. Case related," she added. "Please take a seat, Henry. I'll be right with you after I see the detective out."

Henry nodded and moved towards a chair. Natalie stepped into the doorway of her office. Outside in the waiting room, her receptionist, Lara, was busy answering the phone. As with her office, the outer room was also decorated in soft tones of cream, all designed to put her patients at ease. A leather sofa was positioned by a large window and looked out over the city. From the angle, the harbour was visible in the distance, the bright sun glistening on the water. A glass coffee table sat just in front of the sofa and several recent magazines had been neatly arranged on the surface.

"Please call me when the meeting is arranged."

"I will." Matt leaned close to her and she almost stopped breathing. "And it's Matt," he told her as he handed her his card.

Natalie nodded her assent. She liked the idea of being forewarned when it came to him. She didn't want to be surprised by his presence again. As if reading her mind he gave her a wink and walked away. Natalie stood there in a trance, watching him go. When she finally realised what she was doing, she abruptly turned and went into her office where her patient was waiting.

Chapter 3

After battling with downtown traffic for an hour, Natalie finally pulled her dark blue Toyota Prius into her driveway and killed the engine. She hated driving during peak hours and usually worked her schedule to avoid the gridlock that happened every morning and evening when the nine-to-fivers were out on the road. Even with the traffic, Natalie found Harbour Bay peaceful and inviting from the first time she had found herself in the growing city at the tender age of twelve. Even in spite of the now rising murder rate, she couldn't imagine living anywhere else.

During the summer months, tourists flocked to the beach with its gold sand and perfect surfing conditions. Natalie planned to take a few days off to enjoy the season as well. Of all her years living beside the ocean she had never taken the time to stop and feel the sand between her toes. She had always been busy with other things, such as school and study or stressing over opening her own practice. Now that her life appeared to be in order she was going to do all the things she missed out on doing earlier. To take the time to really appreciate everything the town had to offer.

While Harbour Bay boasted country living it was home to around three hundred thousand people, situated on the southern New South Wales coast. It was one of Australia's larger cities and prided itself on its hominess, bringing in many families who had tired of Sydney which was just a few hours' drive north. The city was nestled against the sea-green harbour where on New Year's Eve it was lit up by spectacular fireworks, the colourful display sparkling brightly on the bay.

Natalie's own home was on the outskirts of town, in a quiet neighbourhood filled with mostly working households. A few children rode past on their bicycles. She watched one girl who had little multi-coloured tassels on her handlebars and an exuberant smile on her face. That was what childhood was supposed to be about. Fun and excitement. Not fear and pain. Natalie envied the girl for a moment. If she ever had children—and that was a giant *if*—she would make sure her children knew they were safe and loved. She would ensure they never knew terror and the uncertainty of what the next day would bring.

Natalie looked out her front windscreen at her house. She had bought the two-storey family home after her practice had first made a nice profit. She had seen the house advertised and fell in love. No other house would do after that and she had paid asking price for it. But never once had she regretted that decision.

The outside was made of a light cream brick. The trims a sky blue that complemented the deep hue of the tiled roof. The front porch divided the house from the lush green lawn her elderly neighbour generously mowed for her when he did his own garden. She had even noticed he had planted several pansies in the flower bed, giving her garden a bright and colourful makeover. She assumed he also weeded and watered the flowers for her since she never had herself, yet they seemed to be thriving. She made a mental note to do something nice for him. If she had been a culinary person she would have cooked or baked him something delicious but her skills in the kitchen were limited to microwaving.

Inside, the floors were made of blue gum timber and the walls a mocha shade, which was one the reasons she had bought the house. Everything suited her tastes to a T. She had made some upgrades when she had taken over ownership such as renovating the kitchen, main bedroom, and bath. Once a smaller room with just two windows, she had opened up the main exterior wall and had made it into a large glass door with attached balcony. From that position in the house, she could see the ocean. Once the sun went down, Natalie would leave the doors open so she could hear the sounds of the waves crashing against the sand. She found it had a soothing effect on her and after some days it was greatly appreciated.

Natalie gathered up all her file folders from the passenger seat, along with her tote, and juggled them precariously as she made her way up the path to her front door. After struggling somewhat, she finally managed to put her key in the door and opened it.

Standing inside the small foyer, all Natalie could think about was the hot shower waiting for her upstairs. She kicked off her shoes in the hallway and dumped the files and tote on the kitchen bench. Some papers slipped from a file on the way down and fell to the floor. Groaning, she bent down and picked them up before placing the loose sheets on top of the folders.

She opened her freezer door and pulled out the first frozen dinner she found. After she ripped open the box, she punctured the plastic film on top with a fork and placed it into her microwave before pressing several buttons on the front panel, somehow making the action look impressive and complicated at the same time.

Natalie made her way to her bedroom, pulling her clothes off as she went. Finally naked, she stepped into the shower. She stood under the hot water and let the heat pull the day's tension from her body.

She timed her shower just right, getting out minutes before she pruned. She dried herself and walked into her bedroom. Natalie slipped on her fuchsia coloured flannel pyjama pants and a pale pink singlet top. She walked into her kitchen and pulled out her easy-meal and a bottle of Shiraz. She poured herself a glass before returning the bottle of wine to the refrigerator.

Natalie settled herself comfortably on her sofa and dug into her dinner, the TV on, the channel tuned to some hip show. She wasn't interested in whatever was playing, she only had it on for background noise. She hated the dead silence that followed her everywhere inside the house. The large ceilings made every step she took echo eerily.

Natalie wondered again about getting an animal but vetoed the idea immediately. As much as she would like the company, the thought of caring for something other than herself gave her the chills. She had enough trouble keeping herself fed and healthy to worry about another living creature. Besides, pets need love and she just didn't think she had any to give out, having been often accused of being a cold, heartless bitch. She had shrugged then and she shrugged now. Water off a duck's back. It was just one less person she had to play nice to. Once men learned her iciness wasn't just an act, she was mostly left alone, which was just as she liked it—or at least liked most of the time. Nights like tonight she wished she had someone to share her day's activities with. Years of bottling up her emotions had left her teetering on the edge, just about ready to jump off.

She finished her tasteless meal, leaving the empty tray on her kitchen bench. She would take it out to the recycling bin later. Sitting down on the bar stool beside the island bench in her kitchen, Natalie pulled the files closer and got comfortable. She took a deep sip of her wine and waited for it to seep into her bones. After flicking through the file over the past few hours she knew she wouldn't like what was written deep within the pages. Every time she picked up Hallie Walker's file she shivered, an involuntary action she couldn't control. It was as if she somehow, deep down, sensed the evil there. The hairs on her arms lifted and goose bumps broke out all over her body.

Rubbing a hand up and down her arm, she picked up the crime scene photos of Ian Walker. Her stomach showed signs of revolting, her meal preparing to make a second showing. She closed her eyes and tried to push the image from her mind in hopes of settling her churning tummy. After several deep, calming breaths Natalie steeled herself against the horror, pain, and fear she saw in the photos. It was hard to believe the person in the crime scene photo had once been a happy family man, trying to make the world a better place.

To think of what he and his family had endured that night brought tears to Natalie's eyes and made her want to lash out at everything and everyone. How could things like that happen? How could anyone allow it? The main thing she wondered was how anyone could do those horrific things to another human being. What the hell was wrong with the person who could easily, without compunctions, wipe out an innocent family? She knew what it was like to be alone, with no help nearby and unlikely to arrive. She also knew the feeling of helplessness well, had seen firsthand someone give up their life, only to keep on living as a shell of their former self. Natalie detested above all else that such a wonderful loving family could be taken away when there were so many others out there that didn't deserve to go unpunished.

She opened her eyes and looked down at the

photos once more through watery eyes. She tried to look at them objectively as she moved on to the photos of Missy—tried to be a casual observer but she could sense the raw pain and fear emanating from the glossy prints. She thought of the twelve-year-old who had witnessed the horrendous double murder before being chased and terrorised herself. She had read earlier that had Hallie Walker not fallen into the river she might not have survived.

Natalie took another deep breath, this time not to settle her stomach. Hallie's circumstances brought about memories of Natalie's own childhood. Of the constant fear she had endured, wondering that at any time the breath she took could be her last. Knowing that just being there, living, breathing was enough reason to hide—to become invisible. Over the years Natalie had become quite good at that.

Her hand shook as she turned the page to read the police report on Missy Walker's death. She was pretty sure she had the gist of it but professionalism drove her on. There could be a vital piece of information within the report that could help with her treatment of the woman's daughter.

One thing was for certain—the case was hitting real close to home. Natalie's own personal demons had begun to rear their ugly heads. She reached for her wine glass and took another sip. She would probably need to drink the entire bottle before she would be able to get any sleep tonight.

Natalie stared down at the police artist sketch of the Butcher as described by Hallie. The sketch was detailed; the twelve-year-old had been very observant. Beside the original were many copies, each with an artist's representation of what he would look like with facial hair or clean shaven, fair haired or streaks of grey. There even was a slightly aged rendering and another with alterations that would require the skills of a plastic surgeon. Her first thought was he didn't look like a serial killer. But then again neither did Ted Bundy. He was what he was and there was no mistaking that fact. The man in the drawing was a cold blooded murderer with countless people's blood all over his hands and conscience, if he even had such a thing.

In the back of her mind under the haze of wine, she could see the night unfolding as if watching a horror film—one she couldn't fast-forward or switch off.

She could see Hallie, scared and alone running through the woods. She tripped and stumbled a few times before righting herself. The smell of blood filled Natalie's nostrils and suddenly she felt like she was being pulled inside her mind. Her hands were flailing about in an attempt to steady her swaying body as brisk cold air surrounded her. She nervously licked her lips as she looked around. She wrapped her arms around her slim body, protecting her. Large tree trunks surrounded her, almost suffocating her. She could feel her hair growing damp from the moisture in the air. Natalie made herself take a step.

Beneath her feet, branches snapped and dried leaves crumpled. The sounds echoed through the night mixing in with the sound of feet moving quickly over the undergrowth. Natalie's head snapped around, following the hurried footsteps. Up ahead, through the tree line she could a young Hallie Walker running for her life. Natalie began to follow her. The girl's head swung wildly around as she ran, searching for an escape. Natalie yearned to help her, to grab hold of her small body and hug her with all her might. To protect her and fight all her demons for her.

Natalie moved faster, tracing Hallie's movements. It was all so real. She swore she could feel the ground beneath her feet. Could smell the woods and hear the river in the distance. Above her the moon lighted her path. She reached out and skimmed her fingertips over the rough bark of the closest tree. The texture grated her soft skin causing her to look down at her fingers in surprise.

She tried to clear her head. Was she dreaming? Had she fallen into a deep wine induced sleep in the kitchen? Had reading Hallie Walker's file made her susceptible to this hallucination? Had she noticed something within the file that her subconscious recognised but couldn't compute? Was this her mind's way of sorting through the information searching for an answer? She had no idea. The questions danced about her head. All she knew was that without any doubt she was absolutely not standing in the woods. No matter what her senses told her.

Natalie watched Hallie trip and land on the mouldy forest floor and her heart broke. She stepped closer into Hallie's line of sight, the desire to intercede becoming more insistent.

"Hallie," she whispered and her hand reached

out towards the frightened girl. Hallie looked up. Her eyes wide. Her red hair danced about in the breeze. Her small body quivered in the night. She reminded Natalie of a hunted animal, which as she thought about it, she was.

Natalie looked in Hallie's liquid gold eyes and she felt cold. The girls face was as white as a geisha's. Her chest rose and fell with each tired breath. But Hallie showed no sign she saw Natalie, the girl looking straight through Natalie as if she wasn't there. Natalie frowned. She was after all a psychologist and it certainly didn't require one to decipher her dreams. It was clear she wanted to save Hallie, save her from the Butcher—from the life that would follow her from this moment on. She wondered why she couldn't.

Frustrated, she didn't notice Hallie skittering away from her. A moment later the air around her crackled and for the second time that night the hairs of her arms stood at attention. She struggled to listen and for the first time noticed the lack of sound. She could no longer hear the river or the sound of Hallie's scared footsteps or even her own movements, as if she had gone deaf.

Her heart began to pound as panic took over. Her nails dug into her palm, leaving little half-moon shaped marks in her skin as her senses were assaulted with the scent of rotten food, long forgotten. Natalie clutched at her stomach as an overwhelming sense of flight or fight came over her. She spun around and came face to face with the Butcher.

The Butcher stood before her, close enough

should she reach out she would be able to touch him. He looked towards her, their eyes meeting across the short distance and her heart stopped. He took a step closer, his entire focus on her. Unlike Hallie, he appeared to see her. All of her. His dark eyes drilled into her own. His mouth morphed into a smirk as if he could read the emotional scars inside of her and she desperately wanted to flee but her feet remained firmly planted on the ground.

Her brain moved a mile a minute, processing everything around her. Under normal circumstances, she thought, the man could be quite handsome. He was young, maybe in his early to mid-twenties. He was of slim build with dark hair and she felt a niggling feeling inside her brain that she had seen him before. Her mind raced like a computer to match the appearance with the name. He seemed so familiar, someone she should know well. Unfortunately his appearance matched around fifty percent of the population and at least five men Natalie knew personally. None of which were this man.

"I-I know you," she stammered.

"Do you?" was his gruff reply.

Natalie felt the same recognition as she had before. She was so busy studying his face, searching for what she desired the most, that she didn't see his hand thrust out until too late. A bright flash blinded her as the knife blade moved with deadly precision. A sharp burning pain pierced her stomach and she cried out. She clutched her stomach as blood poured from her wound. Tears glistered in her eyes as she looked up at the man who had taken her life.

His eyes mocked her and his lips moved, an annoying shrill echoing as it left his mouth. She almost laughed. It looked so ridiculous, such a sound coming from his mouth. Her dazed mind clawed to make sense of what was happening. None of this made any sense. She was dreaming, wasn't she?

Natalie jerked as the phone beside her continued to ring. Her eyes widened in shock. The sound of her phone matched the Butcher's last taunt perfectly. Fantastic. She had just given herself a nightmare. A very realistic nightmare, she thought, as she ran her hands over her stomach. Nothing. She let out a relieved breath. Not that she expected there to be any injuries but after playing *Alice in Wonderland* she wanted to make sure.

Natalie looked down at the sketch of the Butcher and shook her head. She had been so certain in her dream that she knew the man. Of course she had recognised him. She had been staring at his picture right before she conked out.

Natalie leaned over the bench to the relentless ringing phone and answered it. Whoever was calling her didn't appear to be giving up any time soon. She might as well get it over with so she could go to bed. It had been a long and busy day and she wanted to be fresh for her meeting with her new patient in the morning.

"Hello?" her voice sounded weird even to her. Natalie reached up to her neck and began massaging out the knots. She was scared, she admitted to herself. There was a reason she never watched scary movies. Her subconscious fitting herself into the storyline while she slept, determined to fight the bad guys and win. She knew the reason she did this. Repression wasn't working as well as it used to. A part of her deep down wanted to confront the bogeyman. Even though the idea had her scared. She knew she would never be free until she did.

Logic and emotion never went hand in hand. She may be scared but she was angry too—had been for most of her life. At those who were supposed to protect and hadn't. She had no tolerance for any abuse and often donated her time and money to violence against women and children charities.

"Hey gorgeous, what're you doing?" An exuberant male voice came onto the line.

Natalie bit back a grimace. Derek Butler—her sometimes date. He was good company and self-appointed himself as her entertainer yet she felt absolutely nothing for him. It was a shame. He seemed to be a nice enough man as far as she could tell but unfortunately he didn't entice her.

"Reading case files." Or she had been before she had been sucked into the very realistic nightmare. Even now her heartbeat had yet to return to its regular rhythm. Natalie took a deep sip of her wine to fortify herself.

"When aren't you reading files?" She heard the exasperation and underlining frustration in his tone when he asked, "What are you doing Friday night?"

Natalie found herself mentally reviewing her diary and sighed when she saw she had nothing booked out. When she tried to think of an appropriate lie none seemed forthcoming and she was at a loss. It wasn't that she didn't like him. It was that she would rather stay home and work on her many cases. Especially now that Hallie Walker's case had fallen into her hands.

She had been dating Derek—using the term dating rather loosely—for the past few months. While she enjoyed his company and found that they had many things in common she was still holding back. She was also uneasy about taking their relationship to the next level. Or *any* level. Trust had always been an issue for Natalie, in the sense that she didn't trust anyone.

She knew Derek was getting impatient and she could sense the tension in him and force of will it took to keep his passions in check. She knew he was a virile man and would soon want to become physical with her and that particular thought wasn't at all appealing to her. He should be appealing to her. Derek was almost six-foot with dark hair and eyes and was the epitome of a handsome man. The type of man women of all ages drooled over, except her.

She felt nothing. No desire, no interest whatsoever. He just wasn't what she was looking for. But then what *was* she looking for? Natalie wondered briefly at that question. She really had no idea but believed she would know it when she found it.

One thing she was sure of was that Derek was not the man for her and she needed to stop being a coward and tell him that before he did the unthinkable and fell in love with her. She could not have that on her conscience.

The psychologist in her told her to take risks, to live life to the fullest no matter what happened and not to let anything get her down. Easier said than done. No matter the situation she found herself in, her mind was always analysing, studying the human psyche of the people around her so much that she never relaxed. Some people she read like books and could see straight to their souls, others, like Derek were harder. It made her wonder what they were hiding beneath their easy smiles and laughing eyes.

"Working I guess," she said, her mind nagging at her to just end it with him. "I just took on a new client today and need to establish a rapport with her. She's a delicate case."

"Aren't they all?" Derek asked, thinly disguising his frustration. "You work all week. You should let go on the weekend. There's an event I've been invited to, black tie. Please be my date, even just to save me from going stag."

Natalie frowned. She didn't like being pressured. "Like you'd remain alone for more than a millisecond. Women unconsciously flock towards you."

Derek chuckled and she immediately flashed to earlier in the day when another man had laughed in her presence and how that little sound had affected her. She reflected on the lack of feeling his chuckle created in her, adding it to the list of things against him. "There's only one woman I want."

Natalie heard the intimate quality of his voice and wasn't about to pretend she didn't understand the meaning behind his words.

"That may be but this woman is very busy."

Derek exhaled loudly. "You need a break, baby. This case can surely wait a few days. After all, you aren't a surgeon or anything. No one is going to die without you."

Natalie stood. Her bottom numb from sitting on the kitchen stool. She felt the desire to call him a jerk. Little did he know or understand the pressures of her job. Sure she didn't need to operate on anyone with appendicitis or heart complications but diagnosing her patient's mental health was just as important. A few times she had been too late to save them. Not all her patients were like Billy. More than a few were bonafide nut-cases.

Derek must have sensed her seething anger. "Is there anything I can do to persuade you? Whatever you want, baby, it's yours. All you have to do is ask."

Natalie collected her recycling and trudged outside where she deposited in the large green bin. She didn't want anything from Derek but he had been good to her. He had been kind and patient and accepted her many flaws. He deserved more than the brush off from her.

"I'll see what I can do," she said reluctantly.

"Thanks, babe. You know this means a lot to me. I'll get you a dress. It's a real fancy affair and I doubt you'll have anything suitable in your closet."

So why are you dating me?

The question lingered in her head. Derek was all suits and martinis whereas she was cotton pyjamas and microwave dinners. They couldn't have been more different from each other, yet something about her had him coming back to her. She had no idea what that was.

"I'll see you around eight. Love you, babe."

Natalie cringed. It wasn't the first time Derek had used the *L* word and she hadn't returned the favour. She hadn't been in love before, but she knew she wasn't in love with Derek and in her heart she didn't believe he was in love with her. After all, how can you truly love someone you know nothing about? She said goodbye to him in her usual manner, the one that left no doubt as to her lack of loving feelings and hung up.

Natalie immediately put Derek and the approaching Friday evening out of her mind as she looked back at the gruesome photos laid out on her granite kitchen bench top one last time before she tucked them inside the manila folder. Her gaze fell upon the drawings Matt had mentioned earlier. Each picture depicted the night of her parents' murder and had been painstakingly drawn in black crayon, the detail so fine it could easily be mistaken for a crime scene sketch.

Natalie frowned as she came across another drawing. This one was unlike the others. She found herself staring at a cemetery. The picture had exquisite detail, each mark of the crayon so meticulously made Natalie could've been looking at a photograph. Whatever the significance of the drawing, it was clearly very important to Hallie. At first Natalie thought it had something to do with her parents but the main focus was of one particular grave. The stone was carved into a peculiar shape, one not common on gravestones. The etching was clear in the black crayon, it read:

Here lies the body of Helen Teller.

The drawing of the grave disturbed Natalie. For a brief moment she felt an unconscious pull to the picture. Who was Helen Teller? Why was she important to Hallie Walker? Natalie stared at the drawing for a full minute before she decided she was making too much of the grave. She was always looking to make sense out of things that made none. Not everything in this world fitted perfectly together with another like a jigsaw puzzle. Helen Teller was probably one of Hallie's doctors, or a nurse at Paradise Valley. She could even be a fellow inmate whom Hallie disliked. Natalie made a mental note to ask the attending nurse if she had ever heard of the woman.

Natalie put the drawings back in the file and picked up the only two photos in the file that weren't of dead bodies or of the crime scene. Both were of Hallie. The first was twelve-year-old Hallie, the second as she was now—a seventeen-year-old. In both pictures her red-brown hair was untamed and framed her oval face. The younger photo showed a happy well-nurtured child of loving parents. The other showed serious amber eyes and a solemn expression that broke Natalie's heart. She wore a light blue shirt with *Paradise Valley Rehabilitation Centre* emblazoned across the right breast. Here was the orphaned daughter of two murder victims.

Natalie felt the tears burning behind her eyes. She put the photos down and decided she had enough for the night. She had more than enough information for the interview tomorrow. She got up and went to bed, only to wake up every few hours, her tired mind hearing phantom sounds echoing throughout her house. In her head she kept seeing the photos of Ian and Missy's murdered bodies, the black and white drawings and the photo of the sad-faced girl standing all alone.

Chapter 4

Matt found himself staring down at the mutilated corpse of Marie Stanton. It reminded him of the Jack the Ripper cases in Victorian England. He only hoped they found the bastard soon. Her body had been stripped and washed, revealing the deep stab wounds marring her stomach and chest. Her skin was so pale it was almost translucent.

Matt had never liked being present for an autopsy. The whole thing brought death so much closer to reality for him, which he knew to be ironic since he was faced with death every day. He assumed he never thought of it that way before since when he was at a crime scene he was in cop mode, seeing everything from a detective's point of view rather than from a man's. When he was working a case, the people became victims, the facts of the case evidence and that was how he coped.

Seeing poor Marie on the cold stainless steel table made it so much more real. He could smell the formaldehyde lingering in the air, the solution so strong he almost choked on it. He thought about her family and how they would try to make sense out of the tragedy. He wished them the best. God knows, his family never could understand how one simple trip to the liquor store had cost them their father and husband's life. Over the years Matt had learned there were no reasons or explanations, just dumb luck at being at the wrong place and at the wrong time.

Matt looked up from Marie's body to look at the coroner, a man in his late fifties who had the poor fortune to resemble Colonel Sanders of KFC fame. His hair and beard was white and his thick framed glasses made his eyes bulge. The entire LAC called him Colonel or Sanders behind his back but to the man's face he was always, respectfully, Doctor Neil Stone.

Doctor Stone reiterated the facts to Matt, which he already knew since Darryl had given him a brief explanation. Matt was more interested to find out if there had been any fabric fibres or DNA found that had been handed over to forensics with the hope of shedding some light on the whereabouts of the perpetrator. There hadn't been any, of course. The Butcher had been at this a long time. Long enough to know it wasn't wise to leave calling cards for the police. That, or he had been watching more than his fair share of *CSI*.

Matt felt the disappointment down to his toes. They really needed a break in the case. Something to give them a new perspective to explore. He hadn't been lying to Doctor Miller when he said the case had gone cold. Try frozen. Even the tip line they had set up was yielding little results.

The Butcher was still a ghost. There was nothing the body could tell them that they didn't know already. Marie had been murdered in a parking garage on her way to her car late at night. There was no video footage. The city was too cheap to put up CCTV cameras in the dark structure. Although Matt knew that would all change now. It always seemed to take an unfortunate incident to make the purse strings open. Not that it would do any good now that the damage had been done.

Matt left Doctor Stone and Marie and made his way to the showers. The horrid scent of decaying flesh and death lingering in his nostrils made him want to gag. He nodded to a few colleagues as he walked past—some giving him a wide berth in the hallway, which only fortified his resolve to scrub down his skin with lemon juice. They all knew he had been given a shit of a case. They all knew the legend of the Butcher and Matt could see the relief in his fellow officers' eyes when he had been the one to take the lead. No one wanted this case on their record. But for Matt he didn't care because one day he would find the son-of-a-bitch and take him down.

He didn't care if it took the rest of his life to close the case so long as he closed it. He wasn't one to be concerned about his record. He wasn't keeping a tally or making bets to beat the quickest closure. He did his job. He closed cases, sometimes fast, sometimes after they'd long been cold. Matt was in it for the victims. For the families left behind and to put the scum who had hurt them behind bars. He wasn't looking for media coverage or shiny medals and commendations. He wasn't an ambitious man, completely content to stay exactly where he was for the rest of his life. He felt he was doing more as a detective than he ever could as Superintendent or Commissioner. Besides, he didn't think he could stomach the duties.

He stripped off his clothes, allowing them to fall where he stood. Naked, he stepped inside the stall and began to lather himself completely. He took his razor from his shaving kit and began removing his day old whiskers.

His eyes burned as the water touched them. He knew they were bloodshot, having little sleep the night before. His seventeen hour day had turned into thirty-one hours. After managing a quick two-hour nap, he had awoken less than rejuvenised and wishing he hadn't tried to rest. He had spent most of the night reviewing the evidence from previous cases, collected back in the nineties when the Butcher had first started in hopes of finding something to nail him—forensics having since become foremost in any investigation. But his time would've been better spent elsewhere, learning nothing new or remotely helpful.

He scrubbed at his skin with the rough brush. He felt the slight pain as it glided over his skin hard enough to almost draw blood. He wasn't fazed, so long as it removed the scent of death from his body. He let his mind drift to the case. Matt had found many things puzzling. The first was his choice of victims. Most serial killers had a pattern, something that was only theirs, an identifying mark or a signature. The Butcher only had one. His victims were all female, with the exception of Ian Walker. So far the cops who'd worked the case—himself included—had found nothing else linking the victims. It was almost as if the man chose randomly. But Matt, with his many years of training, knew that was impossible. There was no such thing as random with these men. There was always something that drew them to their victims, something that was the same with each of them. Matt only had to find out exactly what it was.

He squirted some shampoo onto his palm and then rubbed it into his scalp. He knew he was taking the time to cover all his bases. Making a real effort to look impressive. Matt thought back to the day before and his meeting with the good doctor. He shook his head in disbelief at the thought of Natalie Miller seeing him so dishevelled. Of course he hadn't been expecting such a young and undeniable beautiful woman.

When he had been told to see a Doctor Miller, the foremost expert in psychology in Harbour Bay, he had been expecting a much older and experienced woman. He found himself wondering if the doctor was married then shook his head. During his brief encounter with her yesterday he had noticed several indicators to her single status. There had been no ring on her finger. No pictures of a happy couple or any stick-figured piece of artwork displayed proudly. From the way he had assessed her office no one including the doctor would have noticed his appraisal.

He closed his eyes as he remembered how his heart beat fast in his chest. At the sudden lack of room in his pants when she had approached him. He swallowed hard at the image of her sitting on her desk, her skirt hem raising that little bit, showing off long, well-defined legs. He only hoped his observation had gone unnoticed and he hadn't been staring at her with lust filled eyes. For the first time in his life, Matt had appreciated what heels did to a woman's legs and her black stilettos were sexy as hell. He was growing hard just thinking about it now.

It only proved to him that he seriously needed a girlfriend to tend to his needs. Natalie Miller's face popped into his head, her cobalt blue eyes seducing him, beckoning him closer. It was a nice dream, he thought, as he opened his eyes and stared at the egg-shell coloured tiles covering the LAC's shower cubicles. It was also a major no-no. Besides, he couldn't afford any distractions. Who was he kidding? *She* was the distraction. He would be working with her until the closure of the case, whenever that may be. That was going to be a lot of time spent together. He tried but couldn't find the downside to that.

He shifted his mind away from trouble as he turned off the faucet and wrapped a towel around his waist. After picking up his discarded clothes from the floor he opened his locker and pulled out a fresh set. Drying himself quickly, he began to dress.

He thought about Hallie Walker. A young terrified girl who was his only real hope. He tried to have faith, to believe she would be of help but who knew how screwed up the girl had become over the years. Talking briefly with the hospital's nurses on the phone hadn't lifted his spirits. Right now he was relying heavily on Natalie Miller and her ability to get the teenager talking. Since she had pushed her last several psychologists away, he prayed Natalie was as good as he'd been told. Matt knew he was being unfair to Hallie. He could only imagine what she had gone through in her short life, but he kept seeing the bigger picture—the countless other women who would be tortured and killed by the Butcher's hand.

The Butcher, Matt sneered at the awful title. He hated the publicity the man had gotten over the years. How Matt wanted to face off with the man, have him fight a man for a change. The image of Marie Stanton flashed across his mind. He gripped the door of his locker hard, enough to leave indentations in his skin.

The Butcher was a sadistic bastard, whose only pleasure came from pain. He knew where to strike to prove fatal, making his victims survive long enough to know they were going to die and that no one would come to help them. In all his years of killing, he had only ever made one mistake and that was Hallie Walker.

Chapter 5

Matt watched as Natalie walked down the long corridor towards him. She was dressed in a form fitting canary yellow A-line skirt that came to just above her knees. Her silk blouse was a peach colour that brought attention to her high breasts, the top few buttons undone. When she moved he caught a glimpse of her lacy bra underneath. Her brunette hair was pulled tight off her face and pinned to her head in a tight chignon, the same as the day before. As she drew closer, he saw her long curved eyelashes were coated with mascara. She wore no eye shadow but her eyeliner highlighted the startling deep blue of her eyes. Her full lips shined with a light pink gloss.

He realised he was staring at her when she raised one delicate eyebrow as she stopped in front of him and he didn't move. She was wearing heels— another pair of sexy stilettos, this time in a pale pink—but still stood several inches shorter than him. She smiled up at him and his heart started to pound. *Jesus*, he thought. The woman only had to smile to send him into a coronary. Matt couldn't believe his heart was fluttering over something as simple and non-sexual as a smile.

I'm acting like a sex deprived teenager.

Matt mentally shook his head to clear it. He had to get a grip on himself before he did something stupid.

"You haven't been out much lately, have you, Detective?" she asked, her tone teasing him.

"Why would you say that?" he croaked. Surely he wasn't that transparent and resisted the urge to look down to make sure nothing was protruding, announcing to the world his need for womanly companionship.

"Well, let's see. You're very rusty with subtly if the once over you just gave me is any indication. You're as bad as my teenage patient." She shook her head and smiled ruefully.

Matt glanced away from her. "Let's just say I've been preoccupied."

Natalie nodded. "Well, you may need to make a little 'you' time."

Matt could feel the embarrassing blush rise from the collar of his dress shirt. *If only she knew just how much me time I've had lately,* he thought. Maybe if he told her the numbers she might be sympathetic. Images of satin sheets and naked skin flashed in his mind. Good God, was she right? Had he reverted back to being a teenager who has just discovered sex? He hoped not, because those years were the worst in his entire life.

"You may be right, Doc. You ready to meet your patient?" he asked, prepared to move along to why

61

they were both here. He watched as she raised herself to her full height and looked at him. He saw confidence in her steady gaze and was comforted by it.

"I am. But before we go inside I would like to ask for the police file on the Walker double homicide. The information in the hospital file is limited. I want to understand more of what Hallie experienced. To see what she saw. Can you make that happen?"

He frowned. He knew what was in those files and the idea of Doctor Miller reading them had all his male protective instincts rearing up.

"I can but is this really something you need to do? Those photos aren't for general viewing. It can give you nightmares if you let it. I wouldn't recommend them for light reading."

"Your concern is noted, Detective. But I can hardly be expected to help someone with whom I can't empathise. Please allow me access to the file."

Matt let out a deep breath and ran his fingers through his hair. He noted Natalie following the motion and wished he'd had time to have his hair cut. With his free hand he retrieved his mobile from his pocket and hit a speed dial.

"Donovan," was the almost instant answer.

"Hey, it's Murphy. I want you to get a copy of the Walker file over to Doctor Miller's office as soon as you can," he told her.

"Oh, so now I'm your secretary?" was Amelia's huffy reply.

Matt imagined her eyes narrowing and her back stiffening. Damn, she could be so prickly at times.

"Just do it, Donovan, and don't argue. You can take it out of my hide later."

"With great pleasure, Murphy, I assure you," Amelia purred and he already felt the bruises. "I'll have it couriered over."

"Thanks." He hung up and said to Natalie, "It's on its way."

"I appreciate it. I hope I didn't get you into trouble with your colleague?"

He grinned. "No, Donovan's bark is worse than her bite. She just doesn't like being treated like a woman."

"Really? I kind of enjoy it, on the rare occasion. Although I can see how in her career it can be difficult."

"It's more difficult on us than it is on her, I assure you. Shall we begin the interview?"

He motioned for her to precede him as he opened the door to the interview room. He followed her into the small, almost claustrophobic room that gave him the chills. Matt had seen more accommodating cells. The walls were covered with a soft white protective padding and the room was sparsely furnished with only one rectangle table in the centre and three chairs. Two had been placed side by side opposite the third which was currently occupied.

Hallie Walker sat quietly at the table, her hands neatly clasped together in front of her. She was a delicate girl, the table almost swallowing her up as she stared sightlessly at the wall. Her red-brown hair was pulled back into a severe ponytail and she was dressed in the blue uniform of the hospital.

Matt's heart sank. She had been his last hope.

Every other avenue had run dry. He tried to think of what this meant to the case but all he could see in his head was twelve-year-old Hallie—feisty, determined to live and get justice for her parents. He had wanted better for the girl and felt responsible for not making more of an effort to see her over the years. Maybe he could've done something to help prevent this.

"Maybe we should—" He started to tell Natalie they should just forget about it when he was interrupted by a feminine voice not belonging to the woman beside him.

"You must be my new psychologist," Hallie said, before turning her head. Her shrewd amber eyes assessed Natalie before they moved over to him. She gave him a quick look and seemed to discount him as unimportant.

He was extremely relieved. He looked over at the waif of a girl, who had not quite grown into her teenager body. She was too thin, her skin much too pale and her eyes full of pain and internal suffering. If there was anyone in need of help it was Hallie Walker.

Natalie stepped forward. "I am. Natalie Miller. This is Detective Matt Murphy."

"I remember," Hallie said coolly as he took the seat beside Natalie. "Unfortunately I haven't been lucky enough to get amnesia and all the drugs in the world can't make me forget, Detective. You were younger then."

"As were you," he added.

"But never young again," she said sadly. "It's amazing at the things you take for granted until they're all gone. What your life revolved around once ceases to exist now. What once seemed important isn't even a blip on the radar."

She glanced at each of them in turn. "But you're not here to talk about philosophy." Her voice hardened. "Let me save you some time. You're leaving with nothing. I told you all that I know five years ago. I did my part and now I'm done."

She pushed back her chair and rose.

Matt felt like a prick for asking her to do something she clearly didn't want to do and worried about her mental stability. He hated the pain he saw plainly on her face. He wished he could've seen her in the light. Back in the days before her life came crashing down around her. She fascinated him, he admitted to himself. Haunted him with her serious amber eyes. He had seen the strength and intelligence in her when she was most vulnerable and no amount of time had ever erased that sight.

"Hallie—" Matt started but stopped when Natalie touched his arm.

"I understand this is difficult for you, Hallie—"

"You know shit, lady," Hallie interrupted.

***

Hallie spat venom at the woman whose honest and caring blue eyes watched her carefully. She didn't want her to care, didn't want her to be nice because it would only hurt her when Doctor Miller decided to leave. And she would leave her. They all did. It was just a matter of time.

For years she had battled against the nightmares

and the only thing that kept those at bay were the drugs. Hallie didn't want to live the little life she had in a drug filled haze and as much as it hurt her to think of her parents, she would rather remember them than not to think of them at all. For five years she had been haunted by that night and the worst of it was that everything was a blur. Nothing retained any detail in her mind except for the fear and cold and desperation she had felt. That night was a private moment—the last time she had seen her parents alive and happy. Call her selfish but it was no one's damn business what she had experienced and how she felt about it.

"I know you hate me right now...hate us," Natalie told her. "And you have every right to, Hallie. When something hurts us, the last thing we want is to share that pain. I know that since arriving here you haven't once discussed the events that led to you being at Paradise Valley."

"And I don't intend to start now."

"Your insight—" Natalie persisted.

"What is with you people?" she demanded. "You're all goddamn ghouls. Why must I relive that night just to entertain you? Do you think it's easy for me? Because it's not, it's hard. It's not someone's imagination. It was real. Lives were taken and blood was spilt. My parents' blood." She emphasised the pointed by jabbing an index finger into her chest. "It's bad enough I have to live through it every night but during the day too? No fucking way."

"Watch your mouth, kid," Matt warned.

Hallie sent him a cold, hard glare. "Or what,

Detective? What could you possibly do to me? Look around, this is my life and will be until that son-of-a-bitch is caught or killed. Either way, I don't care."

Her bottom lip quivered and she fought to keep the tears at bay.

"You have a right to be angry, Hallie," Matt told her. "Believe me, I would be pissed too, but I'd also be looking for revenge. The girl I met once long ago was a fighter. Where did she go?"

"The Butcher killed her and left her to rot deep inside. I've been alone too long, spent too much time inside my memories dying just a little more every day." She moved to face the wall and stood staring at it with the same intensity she had when they'd first arrived. "Why now, Detective? You've had five years to catch him and nothing. What do you possibly think I could know now that I didn't know back then?"

"Perceptions change. You're older now. I had to take this chance," Matt told her.

"He's back, isn't he? Killing more innocent people. Who was she?" Hallie asked as she turned back to face Matt and Natalie.

"Her name was Marie Stanton. She was twenty-seven," Matt answered.

"Only ten years older than I am," she said, her voice filled with unshed tears. "You know what's funny—not funny ha-ha, but funny strange? I can't remember the scent of my mother's perfume but I can't forget *his* smell. Every time I close my eyes I can smell that putrid stink as if he was in the room with me."

67

Natalie shuddered. "That's because scent is one of the most powerful memory triggers. I can only imagine what you must have seen and felt. You were a brave girl."

"I was lucky."

Hallie closed her eyes and immediately her father's Fairlane materialised in her vision. The beefy car pristine, her father having washed it the weekend before. She watched as her father took his place behind the wheel, her mother climbing in beside him. She couldn't do a thing to change the events she knew were coming but her body ached with the need. Feeling useless—impotent—she made fists with her hands. Her mind rebelled at the memory as it always did but she fought it with all her might. It was the one memory of her parents that stayed with her. She had forgotten the rest.

She had been petulant all day, often complaining about being with them and not at home or at a friend's place. She hated the constant travelling that had been part and parcel of her father's career. She remembered giving her parents hell. She had wanted to be treated like an adult, to be left at home like normal children and had shown her parents her displeasure. Not in front of the cameras or the reporters that had hounded her, but when they were alone she never failed to sulk.

She shivered in response to the memory of the cold air. Tears fell from her eyes and she impatiently swiped them away. Her body shook as the memory swamped her, causing her to feel the pain, the breathlessness—the horror—and she lashed out, screaming incoherently and throwing her body into the wall as it all became too much. Her brain felt as if it was on fire. She felt strong arms wrap around her protesting body and draw her none too gently into a hard chest as her flailing arms were restrained.

"Hallie? Hallie, calm down. You're safe here. No one is going to hurt you except yourself if you don't calm down," Natalie told her as she stroked Hallie's hair. "I know it's hard for you to relive that part of your past. The pain. The anger you must feel. The guilt you must bear. But you must believe there was nothing you could do except survive."

Hallie lifted her chin and stared coldly at her tormentor. The woman who cut so deeply into her she could imagine exactly how her parents felt, shared their pain as the Butcher sliced them open.

Hallie took deep breaths as her heart raced in her chest. "I can't help you. Not with that. Nothing has changed from my original report and I will not torture myself just to give you information you already have. Now please leave."

Natalie held her gaze. "Only when you agree to let me treat you. I really do believe I have something to offer you that will allow you to have some semblance of a normal life, all it takes is a little time and—"

"Patience?" Hallie asked. "Why do you want to help me when I can't guarantee I can return the favour? All I see is fog. There is nothing but emotion beneath it. Emotion I can't control."

"Because I believe I can make a difference in your life. Because I am here for you, not for a case or a murderer, just you," Natalie said and Hallie heard the honestly in her voice. "I want to treat you. Not because of what you can give me but for what I can give you—peace of mind. No more night terrors, no more pain and no more drugs."

Hallie wanted to believe her. The night terrors had begun the night of her parents' murder and every night after she would wake up drenched in sweat, her throat hoarse from screaming. She had terrified her foster parents who hadn't known what to do with her. She had been brought to Paradise Valley for treatment and when she had not improved, had been drugged to keep her from hurting herself. Now she could control her anger, and fits like the one she had just had were few and far between. Until today when she had been pushed. She hated it when she lost control. She became another person and it scared her. She would wake from an episode strapped to her bed, her face and body aching from the abuse she had given it. Did she dare to believe this doctor, one of so many, could help her? Could she accept this doctor's help? She wanted to but she was scared of what would become of her if she did.

"But you have to be willing to meet me halfway," Natalie continued. "Together we can get you out of here."

Matt released Hallie and she bit back a whimper. She desperately wanted him to keep on holding her. It had been a long while since she had felt so comforted, almost loved—certainly cherished. But she didn't and she felt so hollow inside.

"What if I don't want to leave?" Hallie demanded, but her tone fell flat.

Natalie's eyebrow rose. "If we can make you better why would you want to stay here? You're a bright girl, Hallie, who can have a bright future. Why throw that away?"

Hallie crossed her arms over her chest. She wondered why she was bothering explaining herself. Over the years she had just ignored those who had come before Doctor Miller, but there was something about this doctor that had her spilling her guts and admitting all her dirty little secrets—or at least some of them. What was it about Doctor Miller that had Hallie reaching out, instinctively trusting her?

"Before I came here, I would wake up in a fit. It was that night again for me. I was so terrified I didn't want to close my eyes. But eventually they would close on their own and then I couldn't wake up because I was so tired and he was chasing me again. I couldn't escape."

"He killed you?" Natalie asked.

"Yes, again and again. They were so real…are so real…although they don't come as often as they used to but when they do they're awful." She shivered uncontrollably, feeling a fine sheen of sweat coating her forehead. She swallowed hard. "When they brought me here for treatment, it was the first time since that night I felt safe and I realised, so long as I'm locked inside these walls, he's locked out of them. From that moment, I promised myself that while he is still living, while he is still free, I will remain here."

"Is that why you refused help in the past? Afraid that someone would cure you and send you back out where you're vulnerable?" Natalie enquired, her eyes wide as she glanced from Matt back to her.

Hallie nodded. "They'd have just sent me on my way with a bottle of pills and the name of a psychologist. No offence, but I don't see someone like you standing between me and the Butcher."

"There are other options," Matt stated. "The police—"

"Can't help me," she interrupted. "No one can. Haven't you ever run away from a problem?"

"Yes, I have," Natalie answered truthfully but offered no examples. She sat forward in her seat. "I'll make you an offer, Hallie. Work with and not against me. Allow me to treat you without objection or resistance and I promise you I will not partition for your release until he is caught."

Hallie studied the woman sitting before her. It was strange but she believed her and more than that, she trusted Doctor Miller. Why, she couldn't understand and didn't bother trying to figure it out. She had relied on her judgment before and had yet to be steered wrong.

Hallie nodded. "Okay. Give me your best shot," she said lightly but hope was beginning to wash over her body.

"We'll start tomorrow."

Matt and Natalie stood and prepared to leave.

"I'm sorry I couldn't help you. And it's can't, not won't," she told Matt, because it was the truth. She did remember him and his compassionate eyes, how he had tried to help her. She wanted him to know that if it was in her power she would do anything to help catch the man who had killed her parents. "I remember some things with perfect clarity and others are a blur. I don't understand it but it's true."

Matt smiled sadly. "You've done more than your fair share, kid. Now it's time for me to do mine."

Chapter 6

After leaving Paradise Valley for the third time that week, Natalie headed back to the office as was becoming her routine to catch up on her paperwork and see her regular scheduled patients. She had listened to her patient's complaints, suggesting courses of action they might take that could prove helpful. No matter the case or intriguing details she heard, Hallie Walker was foremost in her mind.

Treating her could be difficult if she took the wrong approach and Natalie wondered how she should tackle the case, keeping in mind that should she step on one of Hallie's invisible boundaries a mental barrier would immediately appear and she would be screwed. Which made her job extremely hard since everything about Hallie's condition involved her parents, a subject clearly out of bounds. In the days since that first meeting she had allowed Hallie to steer the conversation where she wanted it to go, gradually building a relationship with her patient. Hallie needed to trust that Natalie only had Hallie's best interests at heart and that everything she did was solely in helping Hallie. It was a slow process but well worth the effort in the end.

Natalie understood Hallie's recalcitrance. Fear was a powerful motivator and it made Natalie sick that the teenager had to go to such depths to feel safe by seeking refuge inside the hospital. Natalie had read the evaluations on Hallie. They had all remarked at how intelligent she was. How she excelled in her classes and read the hospital's library dry until they ordered in books especially for her.

In Natalie's mind, Hallie had done remarkably well in her circumstances. Hallie Walker was strong. She had already fought and won. When most, less strong minded people crumbled in nothingness, she had plotted, executed and thrived.

Matt had understandably been disappointed at walking away empty handed but had been more concerned over Hallie than his case. He had promised she could have whatever files she wanted if it helped Hallie in any way, and promised she would receive those files she requested that day. It was obvious to her that he cared deeply for her patient and he had risen in her estimation and she found herself liking him even more. He had told her he would be around and that if anything arose he should be aware of to contact him immediately. She had agreed, maybe a little too eagerly, at the idea of seeing him again.

Natalie wiped Matt from her mind. It was dangerous to let her thoughts stay on him too long. She mentally reviewed her appointment book and told herself to inform the receptionist to book her appointments as close together as possible. The less back and forth from Paradise Valley to her office the better. Her finger clicked lightly on her computer mouse as she printed another newspaper report on the Butcher. Natalie wanted to be completely up to date with the case. *The better to know your enemy*, she thought.

Hours later, Natalie was sitting on the coffee coloured couch in her family room with a notepad resting on her thighs. The TV was on in front of her and the police tape of the interview of twelve-year-old Hallie Walker was playing. The footage was clear. It was obvious the camera was mounted high up on the wall in the interrogation room from the angle in which it looked down on the witness. Hallie sat at the table wrapped deeply in blankets, her eyes red. A mug sat in front of her, the liquid inside steaming, sending white curls of puff wafting out. Two uniformed officers sat on the opposite side of the table observing Hallie, their backs to the camera as a child advocate sat beside her.

The first officer announced himself as Ryan Garratt, senior constable. The date was August sixth, 2005, and the time was four-twenty in the morning according to the timestamp on the display.

Ryan Garratt softened his voice. Years of experience would've told him to tread carefully, otherwise the girl would most likely close up.

"Okay, Hallie, what I would like you to do is go over it again." Hallie looked at him with unseeing eyes. "Do you think you can do that for me?"

Hallie nodded slowly and recited the events for

the officers one more time. Her voice was hoarse from crying and her hair was still damp from her trip in the river. Natalie watched every movement the girl made, every nuance, and listened closely as she spoke. The more she understood about twelve-year-old Hallie, the more she could work with the seventeen-year-old version.

The on-screen Hallie started sobbing uncontrollably.

"I want my mummy."

She rocked back and forth, trying to comfort herself. Natalie had to bite down on her bottom lip to keep from screaming at the adults to comfort her. For a moment she wondered how they could be so heartless. She knew she was being overly protective. Had they actually comforted Hallie she probably would've broken down and become catatonic and then been no help at all. But the latent maternal gene in Natalie felt there was a middle ground that could've been explored. Tears burned in Natalie's eyes. She could feel Hallie's pain as if it was her own.

She replayed the footage over and over again until her emotions were raw and exposed. Natalie picked up the remote and turned her television off. There was nothing more she could learn from it. She felt the warm, salty tears silently trickling down her cheek and swiped at them as she walked out of the room.

Natalie abhorred violence and as much time as she had spent studying the human psyche, she couldn't understand why people hurt one another. How soulless did one have to be before they stopped caring about the pain they caused, or the lives they took?

She entered her bathroom and turned on the tap, watching as her bathtub slowly filled up. She added a few drops from her collection of sensual oils. It had been a while since she'd had a bath. As a child she used to love them. When her father had been alive he had joked that she had been born part fish. Natalie remembered fervently stating she wasn't a fish but a mermaid. Who wanted to be a fish when they could be something as romantic and beautiful as a mermaid? And she had wanted to be pretty.

Natalie had often thought of herself as plain or mousey or at least that was what her beauty queen of a mother had told her. Her easy-going father hadn't argued with her, allowing his daughter the fantasy of believing. It wasn't until a few years ago that she had been able to sit in a bathtub again and even now she couldn't fully relax. It had taken everything she had to overcome her fear of contained water.

She placed her mobile phone on the basin nearby and undressed before slipping into the water. The scent of rose soaked into her skin. She closed her eyes and tried not to think of Hallie, the Walkers or the sick bastard known as the Butcher. The only trouble with that plan was her mind wandered to places she had kept locked up for years.

She remembered Hallie's words from the other day. "Haven't you ever run away from a problem?"

Natalie saw the small farm house, miles from anything in her mind. The pale green paint peeling

78

from the timber having been years since it was last painted, the elements having wreaked havoc on the once pretty 1920s style house. Natalie saw herself as a seven-year-old, sitting before the vanity in her bedroom, her waist-length hair shimmering in the sunshine that peeked through the second storey window. She painted her lips with red lipstick and puckered them just as she had seen her mother do. The deep red clashed horribly with the pretty pink princess costume her aunt and uncle had given her for her birthday. It had come by post—addressed directly to her—and Natalie had felt very special to have gotten the delivery and she treasured the outfit above everything else she owned. The costume was the first thing that had been bought just for her and no one else had ever worn it. The rest of her clothes had come from the Salvation Army Store in town.

She had been in such a state of euphoria that she hadn't been listening for his truck. When she heard the screen door slam shut as he entered the house, her smile faded rapidly. She jumped up from her seat and ran over to the door, locking the door before moving across the room to crouch behind the bed.

She shook in fear as she heard her mother's voice yell, "Gary, no!" and then the tell-tale slap as his hand connected with her mother's fleshy cheek.

Heavy footsteps sounded on the stairs and she knew he was near when she heard the top step squeak when his weight sank and lifted on it.

God, no, please!

She looked over the mattress of her bed as she heard him bang on her door then try to turn the knob. His voice slurred from too many drinks as he continued to bang on her door.

"Natty, open up. Come on, baby, open up for Gary. Natty! Goddamn it, open the fucking door!"

Like hell, she thought. She might not be the smartest girl in the world but neither was she the dumbest. Natalie knew very well what lay beyond the door and she had no plans of experiencing it today or ever again.

Gary's voice went hard with anger and he started shouldering the door. Natalie watched wide-eyed as the door shuddered each time Gary hit it. The old door wouldn't be able to hold out for long. She prayed, knowing full well that there would be no answer from the almighty God, almost as if He had forgotten her. She tried to believe He was very busy and not just ignoring her. Her gaze fixed on the door, her eyes widening when it broke in two. He spotted her immediately. A hard look appeared on his angry and drunken face as he admonished her. "Natty."

Tears rolled down her face unabashed as her gaze darted around the room, hoping that for once someone would stop him or she would find an escape. Her voice broke as she pleaded with him. "No, please, please!"

He made his way towards her. She tried to dart around him. Please God, please let me make it to the door, she continued to pray. He couldn't chase her forever. He was old and drunk. He always fell asleep soon after he got home. He just had to tire himself out beating on her or her mother first. She saw the door to her room; it was closed and she could almost reach out and touch it. A feeling of relief went through her as she thought she was almost free. She screamed when his hand caught her wrist and dragged her out of the room and into the bathroom. Natalie struggled futilely against him, trying to kick out at him in hopes he would release her.

"Stop that," he growled at her as he knocked her to the floor. "When I say for you to do something, you do it!" he screamed at her, spittle landing on her cheek. He hit her again, leaving a red mark on her face. Her bottom lip quivered and she nibbled on it as she waited for her punishment. Gary was always punishing her for things, even those that were not her fault or that she was unable to control.

She knew he didn't need an excuse to hit her. Her being there was enough. He had never liked her and had only pretended to while he had courted her mother. After they'd been married all pretence had gone out the window and the real man had emerged. Natalie hadn't been surprised. She had sensed something off about him, like most children sensed the evil in adults, and had warned her mother who had been less than thrilled to hear what her daughter thought of the one man in town who was interested in a widow with a daughter and no real prospects. Her mother had refused to look at her for an entire week and it wasn't until she made Natalie promise to be a good obedient girl around Gary that she had showed her daughter any response whatsoever.

Natalie closed her mind against the horrid feel of Gary's hands on her body as he pushed her against the old fashioned claw bath tub. Her own hands clutched at the porcelain side, her little fingers sliding against the cool white ledge. It was still full from her bath earlier. She had stupidly forgotten to empty it out once she was done and was now going to pay the price.

"I'm sorry. Please! I won't do it again. I swear. Please!" she cried out. She knew there was no bargaining with him but she still tried. She also knew from experience no matter how loud she screamed her mother would never save her. No one would. She was alone with the monster of her nightmares, the very embodiment of the Devil, the Bogey Man and the Grinch in one. Even in her sleep she was never free of him.

Gary roughly pushed her head under the water and held it there as she struggled against him.

"Maybe now you'll learn," he told her, satisfaction in his voice.

She had been told from a young age that hate was a very strong emotion and that she should never hate anyone. But from the moment Gary had entered her life, she had downright hated him. Never before had she felt that way. She may dislike her mother but she didn't hate her. She was just a weak, useless and selfish person—one who had never wanted a child. She had only had Natalie to make her father happy and if there was one person her mother had loved other than herself it was Natalie's father.

Unlike her mother, Natalie's father had loved her deeply, enough that she had never felt her mother's lack of emotion at least not until he had *died and she had realised just how much her mother despised her.*

She flailed about in the water as she struggled not to breathe. If there was one thing to be said about Gary it was that he had a short attention span. Especially when he was drunk. He would soon tire of holding her head down and would proceed to the more physical.

Natalie's mobile rang, jarring her out of her horrible memory. She resurfaced from under the water and took deep breaths in an effort to calm her pounding heart.

"Hello," she greeted, her voice sounding alien even to her.

"Hey, babe, how's it going?"

Natalie frowned. Derek. She really didn't want to deal with him right now. She didn't want to deal with anyone right now. Natalie rested her arm on the side of the bath and blinked away the last vestige of her dream. It had been some time since she had last dreamed about Gary and tonight it had knocked her on her arse. Hallie and the case were dredging up memories from her past best forgotten.

But they weren't forgotten. They were only pushed back into the dark recesses of her mind. She doubted if she would ever really forget the horror she had been subjected to. Natalie wondered how she expected Hallie to make peace with the past when she, her psychologist, couldn't seem to. Really she should try practicing what she preached sometime, she thought bitterly.

Her voice was still shaky as she spoke. "Fine."

"Are you sure you're okay?" he asked.

Natalie could hear concern in his voice and wished she felt something other than friendship for him. He deserved better. She should've broken up with him a long time ago when she first knew nothing would ever develop between them.

"Yeah. Listen, Derek, there's something I need to say," she started, feeling like a heel but knowing it needed to be said.

"Okay, well, whatever you need to say you can say it when you see me. Your dress should be there soon."

Natalie frowned, her mind trying to keep up with him. She had been fully prepared to say the words that would end their relationship and here he was saying something that made no sense to her. She replayed the conversation over in her head and still came out confused.

"My dress?"

"Yeah, for the party tonight. You forgot, didn't you?"

Had they talked about a party? She couldn't remember. Obviously it hadn't captured her attention long enough to file under 'exciting upcoming events.' She stepped out of the bath carefully and wrapped a towel around her, tucking the end between her breasts and yanked out the plug. She watched, satisfied as the water drained from the tub.

"No," she lied. "Of course I haven't forgotten."

Derek made a resigned sigh. "Well, did you make other plans?"

She had plans to go to bed early, catch up on

some sleep, but she knew Derek would fight her tooth and nail until he got what he wanted. Which unfortunately for her was her.

"No."

"No drama then. I'll pick you up at eight."

Natalie looked at her sodden body in the vanity mirror. "Better make it a quarter past."

"Quarter past, see you then. Love you, bye."

She hung up without replying. Natalie didn't want to lie to him and make matters worse. At least he couldn't possibly read anything into her words or actions, never having given him anything to indicate she felt anything but friendship towards him. It should make their parting easier on him. She just had to get through this night first. At least it gave her a short reprieve where she could figure out exactly what she would say. She had been on the receiving end of a break-up a few times but never had the unfortunate task of delivering one.

Of course she had pushed them all away and had finally tired of her inability to trust and warm to them. Derek had been the only one that had seen her coolness towards him as some sort of challenge.

Natalie heard a knock at her door and trudged downstairs wondering how Derek would take her dismissal of him. Hopefully in the hours to come she could find a way that wouldn't bruise his male ego. She opened the door only seconds before she remembered she was dressed only in a towel. Oh well, the young man before her didn't seem to mind. She may have made his night by the look on his face. She flashed him a tentative smile and took the box from his hands before she shut the door on his still wide open mouth. Hopefully he was gone by the time she was ready. She didn't want to trip on his tongue.

Natalie dressed in record time. The skin tight red dress hugged her curves and moulded itself to her breasts like a second skin. It wasn't the type of dress she would have chosen herself. She disliked the kind of attention women tended to get while the clothes to skin ratio was unbalanced but decided to take a chance for once, finally listening to her own advice.

It took her a few minutes to track down a pair of red heels that would match her dress since they were buried in the back of the closet, long since forgotten. After she ran a cloth over them to get rid of the layer of dust coating them, she popped them on her feet.

She was readjusting the last strap on her shoes when she heard the knock at her door announcing Derek's arrival.

Chapter 7

He watched her from his car. Her waist length blonde hair spilled over her shoulders as she moved the green bag of groceries from the trolley to the boot of her car. She was the very embodiment of everything he hated and his hands became fists wanting to beat her down here and now. He took a steadying breath and tried to calm himself. He would get nowhere if he let his emotions rule his body. He still had so much to do. The woman in front of him reminded him of so many others who had lost their lives at his hands and so would this woman, in good time.

He had learned to be patient, not to rush if he was to exceed. In his youth he had been foolish, almost losing it a couple of times, but in the end he had been the victor and the newspapers had even given him a name: The Butcher.

He liked it. It was better than any of the other names he had been given or taken over the years. He looked down at the cover of his *Woman's Weekly*. There the blonde's face was plastered as she smiled seductively at the cameraman, coiffed and teased to be the envy of every woman who read it and every man's fantasy. It was a special edition. The nation's businesswoman of the year title was being run and she had won.

He didn't know her name. He didn't care either. She wouldn't be alive much longer for it to matter. When the timing was right she would meet her end and he would be there helping her move from life to death. He was a proficient killer and unlike others he had read about he didn't keep souvenirs or records on how many he had killed. He had his memories and no one could take them away from him.

He watched as the nameless woman got into her car and reversed slowly out of the car park. He started his car too and followed her at a discreet distance. He knew her timetable now—could tell the time and day from her movements. He had, after all, been watching for her some time now.

He could have taken the blonde back there in the parking lot. She had been alone and at this time of night there was no one out shopping. He wouldn't have been seen, but he liked the time he had with his victims. He didn't like to be rushed and he didn't want to be interrupted by someone who had just realised they were out of milk. No, best to wait. Relish the moment.

He drove past her as she pulled into her driveway. He knew she would be in for the night. A quick shower, a glass of wine and then if she wasn't too tired, a few chapters of her latest paperback. He didn't need to keep watch. He had done what he needed to do, his information correct and detailed. Besides, he had someplace to be tonight and slowed his car down for the corner. Another woman to watch. A woman who had a dark past of her own, much like his. He whispered her name into the dark confines of the car, almost a caress. Natalie.

Chapter 8

Matt had been told—and not so nicely—to go home and rest. Since he had practically moved into his desk at the start of the investigation, he had seen the sense in taking a break and coming in fresh and ready to work in the morning. He only hoped he would see something he had previously missed or somehow come up with a new avenue to investigate.

His body was far from relaxed. Beyond tired, he was standing on pure adrenaline and caffeine alone. He had been up for over fifteen hours and knew sleep was a long way off so he stopped in the gym for a heavy workout. His body protested the entire time, unused to the gruelling session he was pushing for.

He nodded to many of the officers he saw there, some he remembered from working on the street. The cops of Harbour Bay were a close lot, looking out for each other and their families. He looked over to the boxing ring and recognised Nick Doyle instructing a petite blonde. Although the woman looked like she couldn't lift a feather she certainly packed a punch, attacking Nick over and over until she was soaked in sweat.

Matt watched with a small amount of satisfaction when the blonde knocked Nick off his feet and onto his arse. She then reached out her hand to help him back up. Nick graciously took her offer then moved into a fighting stance once more. The blonde considered her options.

Matt had been surprised when Nick had first started teaching his female co-workers martial arts, believing it to be some sort of ploy to get into their pants. Not that he needed any help in that department. Buffed and tanned, Nick could easily double as a Ralph Lauren model. But, as Matt soon discovered, besides being good-looking—a blend of blue eyes and black hair—Nick also genuinely cared about his female colleagues' safety and coached over ninety percent of the female staff in self-defence. And it wasn't just kickboxing or some fancy form of karate, it was full-blown street fighting with all the dirty trimmings.

Matt had soon learned Nick was the youngest of five and the only male. He might be the class clown but he took protecting the women around him seriously.

Matt continued to watch, amazed as the blonde deflected all of Nick's attacks and he wasn't pussy-footing about either. If one of those hits got their target she would be bruised for a week, if not longer. Nick landed hard on his back again as the blonde tripped him up. He looked surprised as he went down, his breaths coming in hard and fast as he once again stood. He patted the woman on the back, his face showing he was very pleased she had knocked him down. Nick wasn't the type to worry about his ego. He may be cocky and a constant joker but he wasn't a sore loser and took crap as well as he gave it. He, like Darryl, got in and got the work done. None of them worked a case solo, neither did they take sole credit. If a case was closed, it was because of the collective powers of the LAC.

Because of their small unit, they all watched each other's backs and weren't competitive with one another, or at least not much. Nick looked up and noticed Matt watching them and gave him a wave. The blonde looked over her shoulder, interested at who Nick was waving at and smiled at him. Matt recognised her from the few times he had unfortunately been ordered to give a statement to Internal Affairs—the lower end of the police force according to most cops. No wonder she was looking to learn how to fight. She would need to be vigilant just walking in through the main door to the building. Her kind was not looked nicely upon and their presence never appreciated.

Her name was Kellie Munroe. A nice enough woman who not only knew her job and did it well but was smoking hot. Even though she looked like *Policewoman Barbie* she could be quite fierce if called upon. He had once witnessed her lose her cool and had been sufficiently awed. He watched intently as she bid Nick goodbye. Almost every male head in the gym turned to watch her leave and from what he could see, Kellie didn't seem to notice the attention she got. She was confident enough in her abilities like Amelia Donovan, his fellow detective. She dressed femininely, nothing overly attention drawing. Not that she needed it, since her entire being screamed female, but enough that she was comfortable.

Matt closed his eyes. Kellie's walk reminded him of another woman he knew. Natalie, in the few short days he had known her, had turned his entire life around. He wasn't even aware of when she had wheedled herself into his subconscious, only knew she was there and there was no way he could dislodge her. She turned him on more than any other woman ever had and he sensed his downfall. He was even kinda looking forward to it.

"Don't ever pick a fight with Munroe, whatever you do. She'll clean the floor with you," Nick said good-humouredly as he rubbed his forearm where Kellie obviously got in a good one.

Matt didn't argue. Not that he needed the warning. After that incident where she lost her temper, he had steered clear of ever offending her.

"So what're you doing here? Heard you were told to go home," Nick said, concern crossing his face.

Matt knew he looked like shit. No sleep and stress will do that to you. "On my way now. Just thought I might burn off some of my agitation. I'm pretty sure I'm too wired at the moment to get any proper sleep."

Nick nodded, understanding where Matt was coming from.

"Yeah, well, as long as you go home that's all

that matters. You're not the almighty, man. No one expects you to do this on your own. That's what we're all here for."

"I know, believe me. I'm just frustrated."

Nick grinned wickedly. "There's a cure for that. I'm sure your shrink would be only too glad to help you." His eyebrows rose and fell suggestively.

"Weren't you supposed to be doing something helpful, maybe catching a killer?" Matt demanded, with no bite to the words.

He wasn't about to touch the idea of Natalie helping him with anything other than the case. It had been a few days since he'd last seen her. He was having enough trouble keeping her out of his mind as it was without Nick putting in some suggestive alternatives.

"Matthews is working on it for now while I'm down here. Still have another couple of officers coming to kick my arse."

"You mustn't ever lack for anyone in that department. I know of a couple who wouldn't mind getting a kick in."

Nick grinned. "Don't I know it? Be good, get some rest."

Matt nodded. He was about to, just as soon as he tired himself out. He moved over to the weights and began lifting. Twenty minutes later he was heading home, the case and Natalie still on his brain.

Chapter 9

Natalie stood with her back against the wall in the darkest shadow of the room, sipping the dry wine from her glass. It was the only one she would allow herself so she took her time. Whenever she was surrounded by the unknown she was always diligent of her consumption. One drink did not incapacitate her and she was still able to make smart, informed decisions. One did not make her sluggish or haze her mind. She was always vigilant, especially during these types of events where the alcohol was flowing.

She resented the fact that for the past forty minutes she had been left alone. Not that she needed to be entertained but he had invited her. She would much rather be at home. She was still feeling raw and vulnerable after her dream and wanted nothing more than to slip into her cotton pyjamas and review Hallie's case. She was annoyed at wasting her time. She could have been working, reviewing the tapes of Hallie's previous sessions. She had already watched a few which seemed to follow the same lines. Hallie starting off antagonistic, trying to push help away and then turning for the worst when the psychologist conjured the image of the past in her mind, the girl becoming violent in the blink of an eye.

Natalie glanced around *Sweet Harbour's* conference room. This was one of the town's premier hotels. The walls were a rich burgundy that matched the dark stain of the polished floorboards. A long rectangular table covered in a pristine white tablecloth that reached the floor was against the west wall and held delectable appetisers. She had already sampled the king garlic prawns, canapés, and mini quiches and found them to be satisfactory and resisted the urge to go back for more.

Natalie tried making small talk with some of her fellow guests but the effort had been too much. She was much happier hidden away where she could observe the people around her. She found it relaxed her and spent the next few minutes reading the body language of several guests.

When they had first arrived, Derek had taken her on a lap of the room, introducing her to people she would never remember like a preening peacock as if to say *'this is mine'* and she thought that had been his intention. It explained the dress he had chosen for her. If he knew her at all, he would know it was not her style and that it would cause her some discomfort.

She had gone from a respectable doctor to Derek Butler's date and had noticed the obvious omission of her doctor status when he'd introduced her. Natalie wondered if he felt threatened by her title and successful career. Not that she could—or would—do anything about that and certainly made no apologies. She had worked hard to get to where she was and if a man couldn't be proud of her for that and supportive of her aspirations, he wasn't a man she wanted beside her. She stopped analysing Derek. It didn't matter. After tonight it would all be over.

Natalie tried to feel sad at the knowledge of the upcoming break-up but no emotion stirred within her. It only reinforced her resolve to make it final. Derek may be an attractive male but he wasn't the man for her. She wanted a man who made her heart thump in her chest. A man who made her breathless when he drew near. A man she thought of even when she was alone and made her excited at the thought of seeing him again.

Natalie gave it another twenty minutes then picked her way through the crowd where Derek was charming a small group of five. She touched him lightly on the arm, feeling the sinewy muscle beneath her hand. She felt his strength—his power—and felt scared. It was such a stupid emotion, she thought. She had spent time with Matt Murphy over the past week and she had never felt threatened in his presence. She knew without a doubt he would die protecting her before he would lift a finger to her—and he carried a gun. Natalie was amazed at her certainty when it came to Matt but couldn't fathom why her body never relaxed completely around Derek.

"I'm going to head home," Natalie informed him.

Derek frowned, either from the interruption or the fact she was leaving. "Is everything all right?"

"I'm just tired. It's been a long day."

A long week actually. Hallie's case was an emotional rollercoaster that didn't seem to stop. Yet, Natalie couldn't seem to back down. She felt a connection with the teenager that made her continue to push herself beyond breaking point.

She would've much preferred to take a taxi home, but Derek had insisted and ushered her out the door. Ten minutes later, Natalie was in the passenger seat of his black Audi driving through the quiet, late night streets of Harbour Bay.

She couldn't wait to get out of her dress and slip into bed. Natalie exhaled in relief when her house came into view. A sense of pride washed over her. It was hers. Who would've thought bricks, plaster, and glass could mean so much to her? She stepped out of his car before he had a chance to exit and she met him on the path that led to her front door.

"Thank you, Derek. I'm sorry to have pulled you away from your party."

He shrugged. "You're more important." He leaned in to kiss her. She turned her head away.

Thankfully over the past few hours she'd had time to imagine several scenarios to tell him she no longer wanted to see him. She didn't want to hurt him but neither did she want to continue their relationship, such as it was.

"Listen, Derek, these past few months have been nice but I think it best that after tonight we don't see each other again."

He shot her a look of disbelief. "Are you

breaking up with me?"

"Yes. I'm sorry. It's just not working out."

"You're just scared of your feelings for me. Don't let your fear take you away from me."

Natalie blinked. Conceited jerk. She had known he spent a considerable amount of time on his appearance but she hadn't thought him vain and narcissistic. Did he truly believe that every woman he met instantly fell in love with him and couldn't possibly accept that she felt nothing?

"Don't tell me how I feel, Derek. I know better than you."

Derek frowned in the darkness surrounding them. The street light behind him their only source of light. She had not remembered to turn on her porch light before leaving earlier and regretted the oversight.

"You can't deny you have feelings for me," he stated as if a fact.

"I can and I do. I feel nothing for you, Derek. I wish I did but I don't. Please understand."

He took an aggressive step towards her which startled her. Natalie stepped back but he advanced so quickly she didn't have time to put distance between them. He caught her about the waist and pulled her into his solid chest and before she had a chance to protest, his lips descended on hers. He took her mouth ruthlessly, forcing himself inside her mouth as he bruised her soft lips with his assault.

Natalie pushed him away. "Get off me." She wiped at her aching lips in an effort to remove his taste from her mouth. She felt violated, his invasion sickening her.

Derek stumbled but quickly righted himself. He retaliated by striking her across the face, the sound of the slap carrying in the silent night. Her eyes widened in surprise and her skin stung where he had made contact and she raised her hand to her face and touched the bruised cheek.

Fear momentarily stunned her but she soon found her voice and her tone was cold and steady as she spoke.

"Get off my property right now."

Derek's face turned contrite and moved towards her, arms outstretched as if to comfort her. "I'm so sorry, babe. I don't know what came over me." She did. He wasn't used to hearing the word no and obviously thought he could manipulate any situation. "You shouldn't have made me so mad."

Natalie froze and saw a red haze ebb at the corner of her vision. How dare he blame her for his loss of control? She saw him more clearly now then she ever had before. He had the sentiment of a typical abuser. It was always the victim's fault. How had he been able to dupe her for so long? She'd pushed the right buttons and his real personality emerged.

"Leave right now, Derek, or I will call the cops."

She produced her phone and punched the 'zero' button three times and poised her finger over the green 'send' button. Not that it would do any good if he chose to advance on her. She had felt his strength and knew she couldn't defend herself against it. She would be either dead or badly beaten by the time help arrived.

"Natty, babe," he said pleadingly, as if she would forgive him if he showed her he was remorseful. She wondered briefly how many women had fallen into that trap only to regret it later.

"Don't call me Natty." She threatened him with her eyes, which she was sure were a combination of anger and fear. "Get out of here, Derek. I won't tell you again."

Natty. She hated that name. Derek held up his hand in surrender.

"Okay I'm going. I'm sorry."

He turned his back on her and she watched him go, refusing to relax until he was gone from her sight. He peeled out of her driveway with a squeal of tyres. Natalie let out a relieved breath and her knees went out from under her. She caught hold of the side of her house to keep from falling face first and held on for dear life, the cool brick wall strong and steady against the palm of her hand. Slowly, a foot at a time, she made it to the door, despite her brain screaming at her to get to safety but her wobbly legs just wouldn't cooperate. She slammed the door behind her and secured the deadlock.

Natalie stared at her reflection in the mirror by the front door, noting her pale complexion and the fear in her eyes. She had never wanted to see that look again and as she brought her hand up to gingerly touch her cheek she noticed it shook. She had spent the past sixteen years avoiding that very situation. It frightened her that she had been so blind.

Natalie prided herself at reading people and yet Derek had her completely fooled. Had she allowed herself to become complacent? Was she so arrogant in her abilities to read another that Derek had been able to use it against her and wheedle his way into her life? She hoped not. She would need to be more careful. She had been lucky tonight and had been able to defuse the situation. Next time could be another story. She studied the bruise already forming and moved into the kitchen to retrieve the cold pack she knew to be in her freezer. She pushed aside her frozen meals until her fingertips located the hard block and after rolling the cold pack in a tea towel, Natalie pressed it to her cheek.

Hopefully it would help with the swelling.

Natalie shivered and not just from the cold pack. Derek had showed signs of having Borderline Personality Disorder. It worried her that she had not seen it before tonight. But then, she had spent little time in his company. A few hours here and there, as well as events such as the one tonight where they were never alone. Still, she thought a professional such as herself should've been able to see what lurked beneath. She would report him to the police in the morning. Her knowledge of BPD told Natalie she wouldn't be the last. Years of experience told her this was just the start for him and he would soon escalate. His actions might even kill someone one day and she couldn't let that be on her conscience.

Tears fell from her eyes as she admonished herself again and again for being so stupid. She removed a sheet of paper towel and wiped her nose before switching on the kettle. As she forced herself to go through the simple motions of making chamomile tea, her hand stopped shaking and she began relaxing. She was starting to feel calmer, more in control.

Her mobile rang and she jumped. Okay, so she wasn't completely in control yet. She checked the caller ID just in case it was Derek, relieved to see Matt's name on the display. She had programmed his details into her contact list earlier in the week and realised now she was glad for his call. Anything to get her mind off what had just happened.

She answered the phone and was surprised—and thankful—that her voice sounded so steady. She held the handset to her ear as she took a sip of the hot and soothing tea.

"Hey, it's Matt. I was just wondering if you had a chance to view those police reports yet."

Natalie remembered the stack of files she had brought home with her that she'd planned to review until Derek had called and she'd gone out with him instead. She instantly felt guilty. Hallie and Matt deserved her full attention on the case.

"Sorry, no. I'll make a start on them now," she promised.

It wasn't as if she was going to get any sleep tonight. She tossed the cold pack back into her freezer, her cheek numb.

"It can wait until tomorrow. What time are you seeing Hallie?"

"Ten. Why?"

She didn't bother asking him how he knew she planned to see her. Natalie had visited with Hallie every day for as long as her schedule would allow. He must have been advised by the hospital staff since Hallie was technically part of an on-going investigation.

Matt sighed. "I was thinking afterwards we could get together and go over them. You can give me your impressions and I can give you mine. Maybe by putting our heads together we can come up with some new leads. I could certainly use some about now."

"Sure," she said, making her way towards her stairs located in the centre of house. Moonlight gently spilled through the windows and casted tree branch shadows on her floor. She stepped carefully, afraid to spill her tea. "I take it no new developments have arisen?"

She heard the weariness in his voice as he answered. "No. It feels like I'm going around in circles and every time my phone rings I fear it's someone telling me there's been another murder, another woman I couldn't save."

"It wouldn't be your fault, Matt. No one could blame you for not trying. You've practically worked yourself to the bone to catch him, and you will catch him. I have faith that you will."

"I hope you're right, Natalie."

She shivered when he said her name. It sounded so intimate. She sat down on her bed and got comfortable, taking another sip of tea. Natalie imagined him on his own bed. Her mind had him on his back, staring up at the ceiling, maybe with his arm beneath his head. It had her wishing she could crawl up beside him and wondered what it would be like for him to hold her in his arms.

Natalie felt an ache in her heart that was almost painful. Longing. A need to reach out and connect with another human being. She was tired of silent houses and a cold bed. She hated feeling so hollow, so alone.

"Don't put too much pressure on yourself. Even the toughest elements can crack."

"Are you saying you think I'm tough?" he asked, amusement in his tone.

"Yes. Tough. Kind. Courteous. Caring. All words I associate with you."

There was a moment of silence at the other end, then, "I hope I don't disappoint you."

Natalie switched off the bed side lamp, casting the room into darkness before snuggling beneath the blankets. She imagined him beside her, his voice sending little sparks along her nerve endings.

"You could never disappoint me."

"I'm a man. It's completely possible. In fact, probable."

She laughed and felt the last bit of tension from Derek's transformation leave her. He did that. Matt Murphy. The man with the emerald eyes and kind heart that felt too much. She was surprised he didn't buckle from the weight he carried on his shoulders.

Natalie wanted nothing more than to reach out and help carry the load. That was when she vowed to help him wherever and with whatever she could. Natalie wasn't sure when the conversation shifted to music, books, and personal preferences but when she yawned she realised they'd been on the phone for over an hour. She enjoyed talking to him and if her eyes weren't so heavy and threatening to close on her she would've continued long into the night. They said their goodbyes and reluctantly she hung up.

Natalie fell asleep almost immediately and dreamed of the gorgeous detective.

Chapter 10

Detective Senior Sergeant Dean Matthews couldn't wait to finish his shift. His arse was dragging against the ground so hard he had carpet burn. The entire Detective Unit was working the Butcher case, hard. The Boss, Superintendent Alec Harris, was hell bent on bringing in the man. Who could blame him? Everyone in the LAC wanted him behind bars.

He had spent the first half of his shift tracing down useless leads that had led nowhere and during his most frustrating moment, a call had come in about a service station robbery. Since he and Donovan were the only detectives on call, they had hauled arse down to the servo and had examined the crime scene. It hadn't taken them long to track down the robbers. The idiots hadn't noticed or maybe hadn't cared about the CCTV cameras all over the property, capturing not only the robbery but also the license plate on the getaway car.

They hadn't even tried to hide, returning home to count their brief winnings. It had taken less than an hour for him and Donovan to locate the address and rock up at the house. Now back at his desk, he rubbed his face, trying to draw out the tiredness he was experiencing. He gulped his lukewarm coffee, a drop missing his lips and landing on his lemon-meringue coloured shirt. He grabbed a tissue and wiped at the splash.

"Yep, there's the end of that shirt, Matthews. No getting coffee stains out of that," Donovan said cheerfully as she placed her sunglasses down over her eyes. "The glare is bad enough alone without it being worn by a man, even a good-looking one at that."

Dean grinned. "Good-looking, huh? Why don't we discuss that further over drinks?"

The scowl he got back made had him widening his grin.

"Just try it, Matthews, and I'll make sure you can't have kids *ever*."

And she would too, he knew, which made her even more scary and entertaining. The entire LAC were always laying their shit on her just to watch her get her back up. But they had learned fast that if they dished it out they had better be prepared to get it back tenfold. Amelia Donovan was no wall-flower.

They all knew she'd had a hard childhood, growing up in the rough part of town—Dick Coleani's side of town. He was a big crime boss in Harbour Bay and while not in the scope of the mob or even the Morans, he had quite the empire and was involved in every shady deal going down.

While Donovan had escaped the life of a druggie

or stripper like most in that neighbourhood grew up to be, she still sported the attitude of someone who had to work harder than the rest to get where she was and let everyone know she was determined to do great things. Which of course she would and they all knew one day they would be calling her Boss.

She was the unofficial 'wife' of all the detectives, laying out orders and expecting them to be followed—and now, not yesterday, not tomorrow or a week from Sunday, *now*. The moment she moved in they had all felt the iron fist circling them and cutting off any freedom and pleasure they had left.

He smiled. How could he not? She was so fresh, so real it was hard not to like her. Sure he knew there were some out there, crooks mainly who would like to see the back of Detective Inspector Amelia Donovan but he was looking forward to seeing her in management. She wasn't going to be an arse-kissing bureaucrat, but instead tell them how it was going to be.

"You know you love me, Donovan. Besides, I thought you and me were going to be making babies together. I can't give you a Dean Junior if you take away the family jewels."

She sent him a stony look and he waited for it. After a second she cracked a smile before scolding him.

"You wish you could get some of me. But sorry, I only save myself for the best."

"What, the ones that last more than thirty seconds? You're setting your sights too high."

She pitched her well-used stress ball at him and he caught it easily. Her dark hair was still pulled back neatly in a ponytail and he wondered how she kept it so tidy. His dishwater blond hair looked like he had stood under a Boeing 747 during take-off.

Dean thought back to earlier in the evening and the incident that had made his night. It had been when one of the robbers had tried to escape. Amelia had chased him barely five feet before she'd tackled him to the ground and cuffed him, shoving his head into the loose gravel beneath him. When she had jerked him to his feet a few small pieces had dropped back to the ground from his face and Dean had hid a smirk. As Amelia approached him with her catch, he had spoken up, his hip resting casually against the car as he waited patiently with his own moron for her.

"Tackled by a girl." He shook his head and clucked his tongue before Amelia stuffed her catch into the backseat of their car. As he climbed in and turned the key he continued. "That's got to be embarrassing. I wouldn't know about that, but you do. So tell me pal, was it embarrassing?" he taunted.

"Kiss my arse, man," the punk sneered.

"Oh, you'll have plenty of offers for that where you're going," Dean told him and beside him Amelia chuckled.

Out of the five detectives who worked the Harbour Bay Detective Unit, he liked being partnered with Donovan the most, although he usually got saddled with Nick Doyle, the consummate joker. He appreciated Donovan's approach and they worked well together.

While Amelia wasn't tall by his and the other male detectives standards, she was strong and could tackle any one of them easy. What she lacked in size she made up with brawn. As they say, dynamite comes in small packages.

The collar certainly hadn't been worth his or Amelia's time or that of the LAC but a crime was a crime and they had a job to do, no matter who the culprit.

After they had dropped off their thieves to their cell, he and Amelia had returned to their desks to finish up their shifts. The rest of the night had proved uneventful. Amelia consulted with the media about informing the public to be vigilant during this time, for women in particular not to go out alone and to walk in sets of two or more, as well as to call crime stoppers or the LAC if they see anything or anybody suspicious. After that she had fielded calls from every idiot in the city who believed their creepy neighbour to be the Butcher.

Dean watched as she made a gun with her hand and pretended to shoot herself during a call. The next one, she mimed hanging herself and the one after that she tried to strangle the caller. Dutifully she recorded each call, jotting down any that deserved follow-up, but he knew from her expression none had come close.

Matt came to stand behind her as he entered the *Pig Pen* and looked over her shoulder. Amelia scowled at him, her beautiful face looking fierce and deadly.

"I wouldn't test her this morning Matt. She'll probably scratch your eyes out," Dean warned him.

It annoyed him that Matt looked clean and fresh, his own shirt now rumpled with multiple coffee stains marking the fabric that would have to be dry-cleaned.

Matt grinned at him as if he knew what he was thinking and he probably did. Over the years they had worked so closely they often knew what the other one thought or was about to do. In their line of work it was imperative to get along well with your co-workers.

"What? That time of the month is it, Donovan?" Matt asked innocently and quickly jumped out of the way before she could hit him or worse shoot him.

Dean shook his head sadly. "I warned you."

"Yeah, you did," Matt said as a stress ball hit the back of his head.

Where the hell did she get all these stress balls? She was always throwing them at one or all of them during her shift and whenever she did that, they confiscated the offending item but she still came up with another next time. He wondered if the officers in Occupational Health and Safety were forever giving her the balls in hope her temper might die down.

Tough luck, boys, he thought. She was a Capricorn.

"So what are you doing today?"

Matt reached down and picked up the blue squishy ball and gently tossed it to Dean who placed it into his desk drawer, adding it to his collection of already thrown balls. As he closed his drawer the wheels screeched against the runner that grated on his nerves.

"Just checking in before I go over to Paradise Valley."

Dean nodded.

"How's the doctor doing with the girl, any advances?" Amelia asked, her curiosity peaked. He had advised them all of Hallie's previous lack of cooperation.

"So far so good. Natalie keeps reading Hallie's statement to her in hopes of uncovering some latent memory. But the kid is stubborn, more so than you, Donovan, if you can believe it."

Amelia's eyebrow rose enquiringly. "Natalie, is it?"

Matt frowned. "Huh?"

"Since when has Doctor Miller become Natalie?" she asked, her shrewd eyes studying him.

"Since last night," he said stonily. Dean sent Amelia a look. Matt let out an exasperated breath, obviously realising how his last statement had sounded. "We talked on the phone about the case," he added, too quickly. "We're just working together, nothing more."

Amelia recovered first. "Better be careful, Matt."

At the same time, Dean said, "You better know what you're doing."

"I'm not doing anything," Matt defended.

Yet. Dean read the intention clear as anything on Matt's face. The doctor wasn't just a passing fancy, a one-nighter to relieve tension. Matt, he thought, had fallen hard. Shit. The moment one of them went the happily ever after route the rest of them would be expected—if not pressured—to follow suit.

Happy couples always wanted more couples around them and he foresaw many blind dates in his future.

Dean shuddered. "You're smitten," he accused.

Amelia nodded, backing him up.

Matt glared at them both. "My relationship with Natalie, Doctor Miller, is strictly professional and will remain so. I'll be on my mobile," he informed them before stalking out of the room.

Dean turned to Amelia. "What do you think?"

"He's on his way to picking out china patterns."

Damn. That's what he thought too.

Chapter 11

At nine-thirty the next morning, Natalie pulled her Prius into the visitor's car park of Paradise Valley. She gathered up her files and note pad and climbed out of her car. She looked about the near-empty lot and up at Paradise Valley, which despite its name didn't look at all like paradise.

The structure itself was huge, housing patients not just from Harbour Bay but the surrounding areas as well. The exterior was made of pale cream bricks and looked just like what it was—a hospital for less than stable individuals or a prison. Once a mental institution before the government closed them down it was still referred to as such by the locals and was the last of its kind in the country. The security fence around the property was less than inviting and certainly a deterrent for anyone with the delusion of escape.

The hospital was monitored by CCTV cameras and several unobtrusive security guards. The grounds surrounding the hospital were vast, allowing incarcerated inmates some degree of freedom. Not much had changed since her internship here many years ago, Natalie thought as she made her way to the front door and entered the building.

She had been thinking of becoming a psychologist to people like Hallie until she had chosen the private sector instead of working for the government. She had never once looked back on her decision and now she knew without a doubt she had chosen the better option. She liked variety in her work and the ability to pick and choose her patients, as well as her hours.

Paradise Valley smelled of disinfectants and the normal hospital scents that reminded her the occupants within weren't well. Today she was dressed in a plum skirt and a sky blue blouse. Her hair was pulled lightly back from her face in a loose bun. The heels of her pumps tapped loudly against the floor as she walked and the nurse behind the reception desk looked up from her computer at the sound and smiled.

Natalie greeted her politely and made the obligatory small talk as she filled in the mandatory visitor paperwork. She pinned her official pass to her clothes as she stifled a yawn. After falling blissfully asleep with the delectable Matt Murphy on her mind, her dream had changed for the worse and she had tossed and turned most of the night as she relived the terror she had felt when Derek had hit her. She had awoken, twisted in her sheets and spent the rest of the night reviewing everything Derek had said and done, trying to decipher what she had missed. She still wasn't enlightened and felt like a complete failure. How was she expected to help others when she had missed Derek's flaws even though they'd been right in front of her?

After plastering a generous layer of concealer under her eyes and packing on the foundation over the slight discolouration on her cheek, she didn't look too bad. She sure wasn't going to win any beauty competitions but neither was she looking like she had gone a round with Mike Tyson.

Hallie looked up as Natalie opened the door. She was once again sitting at the table in the stark white room, only this time she had crayons and paper in front of her and was in the middle of sketching out a drawing.

"You came back."

Natalie looked down at Hallie. The pain in her amber eyes ate away at her insides. "I told you I would. I know it is hard but you need to start trusting me, Hallie. I will not abandon you."

Natalie took the seat across from Hallie. She slid the drawing across the table so she could look at it. The picture was like the others, done in black crayon, and Natalie looked over at the various colours Hallie could have chosen. Was it an artistic choice or one of perception? Did Hallie see the world as a cold and dark place? Natalie wouldn't be surprised if she did. She had no reason to believe otherwise.

"You're quite talented. Does it help to sketch out your feelings, putting them to paper?"

"I guess. Do you really believe I'll ever leave this place?" Hallie asked, her shrewd eyes studying Natalie.

"I do. I have enormous faith in you, Hallie. It can't be easy to relive such an event. I know you think I'm being hard or unfair on you because I push you, but I only want the best for you."

Hallie leaned back in her chair. "I'm surprised you turned up. I wasn't expecting you to, even though you promised…and after last time."

When she had lost her temper and lashed out violently, Natalie recalled. She had purposely incited the response from the teenager in order to confirm her suspicions.

"I don't know why I become so enraged," Hallie confided softly.

Hallie looked scared, concerned for her mental health as she stared down at the table. Natalie reached out and placed her hand over Hallie's smaller one. It was cold to the touch. The girl jumped and her eyes rose to lock onto Natalie's. Confusion, mistrust, hope, and fear all lingered in her youthful gaze.

"It's called PTSD. Do you know what that is?"

"That's what soldiers get sometimes after they return home from war, isn't it?" Hallie replied, a frown on her face.

Natalie nodded. "Yes. Very good."

"But I don't understand what that's got to do with me. And why I get so angry."

"That just part of Post-Traumatic Stress. Anger occurs when the body is overwhelmed and unable to cope. You're fighting it now but in time, with patience, acceptance, and repetition, I'll be able to treat you," Natalie explained.

"Just like that?" Hallie sounded dubious.

Natalie smiled. "Nothing is fixed overnight but yes, it's treatable. You'll of course need counselling for years to come. But that can be provided to you as an outpatient."

Natalie looked forward to the day Hallie Walker stepped out of Paradise Valley and into the sun. She would shine so brightly. It was merely a matter of time, she thought. She was already improving. Natalie knew Hallie saw no differences in her demeanour but over the last few sessions she had changed considerably.

"You're going to keep your promise, right? They'll not release me until he's caught?"

Natalie looked over at the scared teenager sitting across from her. Her heart ached. What she felt for Hallie was beyond the professional. Hallie meant more to her than any other patient she had ever treated. Usually she didn't allow her personal emotions to become involved, but with Hallie she hadn't a choice. A feeling so deep seated in her subconscious that she didn't understand but embraced fully. Maybe it was because they both shared a violent past or maybe simply because Hallie had endured so much, yet still went on. Natalie envied her. She was strength and courage and had fought harder than anyone she had ever known—herself included.

"Or until you say otherwise. It'll be your decision. You're in control," Natalie said.

Hallie laughed, the sound falling flat. "I don't feel in control of anything."

"Which is why I brought you these." Natalie pulled a thick folder from her large white purse and

119

placed it on the table between them and took a deep breath, unsure of the reaction she was going to get. "Your parents' police file. I thought you could look at it objectively. I believe it will help you move past the fear and allow you some closure."

She had gone into work early that morning to make a copy for Hallie who now stared at the file as if it was poison. Natalie placed a palm flat against the manila folder in front of her.

"You don't have to, Hallie," she told her patient who continued to stare at the file beneath her hand with trepidation. "No one will make you. But try to take it one page at a time. Allow the facts to wash over you without emotion. If it gets too much you can just put it down."

Hallie licked her dry lips. "I'm not sure I can do it."

"You are a brave woman, Hallie. You just have to have confidence in your own abilities."

"Do you?"

"Have confidence in my abilities or yours?"

Hallie shrugged.

"I do. Yours and mine. You have overcome so much in your short life that the only thing you can do is succeed."

"Thank you. I do value your help and guidance. I'm not always appreciative and can be a downright pain in the arse. But you sticking with me means a whole hell of a lot."

"You're welcome. You remind me a lot of myself in my younger years," Natalie revealed. "Things weren't always easy for me either, granted you had it a lot harder than me. But we're fighters, you and I, and we will get through this together. I'm not going anywhere. Have faith in that."

Hallie's eyes filled with tears and spilled over on her cheeks. Her slender shoulders shook as she cried. Natalie jumped up and hugged Hallie tight, her arms reaching around protectively and instinctively. She rocked Hallie, comforting the teenager in such raw pain. How long had it been for Hallie to have someone show affection for her? It had been Natalie's experience that the hospital nurses weren't the nurturing types and her heart ached. She wanted to shower Hallie with all the love the girl should've gotten from her parents.

As she soothed Hallie, Natalie looked down again at the picture Hallie had drawn. It was of her parents. Ian and Missy Walker were all smiles and Natalie could see much of Hallie in Ian. She clearly favoured her father.

Natalie soon found herself staring down at the picture, her eyes narrowed and her mind elsewhere. She thought of other drawings done in black crayon. Her brow furrowed as she fought to find something locked within her mind, something she had noted and filed away for further assessment at a later date. When it suddenly came to her she wondered why she hadn't thought of it before.

"Who is Helen Teller?"

Hallie drew away and looked at the picture Natalie held.

"I don't know. Why?"

"Because you drew her grave once, long ago," Natalie answered.

She opened the file containing Hallie's Paradise

Valley information that Matt had given her and retrieved the drawings and laid them out for Hallie to see.

Hallie sucked in a breath at the vivid and detailed sketches. Even done in black and white it was hard not to see the blood clearly depicted on the paper. She reached out and flicked through them tentatively, studying each piece as if she'd never seen them before.

"I drew these? I don't remember," she said. "They look so horrible, so terrifying."

"These pictures are nothing but your subconscious trying to make sense of what happened. It's therapeutic. The first step in healing."

Hallie nodded and reached the last picture and stared down at the grave.

"Helen Teller," she read and frowned. "I really don't remember drawing this and I don't know a Helen Teller. Do you think maybe she was a friend of my parents?"

"It's more than possible."

"I'm sorry. If it's inside my head, it's locked away far enough that I can't retrieve it."

Natalie smiled reassuringly and squeezed her shoulder. "It's all right. I'll have Matt, Detective Murphy, look into it. If Helen Teller lived, he'll find her and what she meant to you and your parents," Natalie vowed and Hallie smirked. "What?"

"Matt, huh? Do you have a thing for our detective, Doctor?" Hallie asked as only a teenager could.

"I don't think it's appropriate for us to be

discussing this," Natalie told her, hoping to close the conversation.

"So, can I take that as a yes? He's quite good looking, isn't he? I believe the word is 'hunk,'" Hallie said with a devilish smile and a twinkle in her eye.

"Yes, the word is 'hunk,'" Natalie conceded and realised she enjoyed talking to Hallie this way. The anger and rage was gone and a jesting, smiling girl emerged. It was a glorious sight to see. So this was Hallie Walker, the real Hallie Walker, and Natalie was glad. She was a pleasure to finally meet.

"You should go for him. Life is too short to hang back. Believe me. If anyone should know, I do."

A knock on the door startled Natalie and she and Hallie turned towards it.

***

Matt entered the room and stopped when he caught sight of the identical looks gracing the two beautiful faces in front of him. He became even more intrigued as they both flushed. They were up to something. Both women wore expressions he'd seen often enough on his mother and sister's faces. He guessed they'd been discussing him and he wondered at the context.

"Detective Murphy, please join us," Natalie said as she sat back down in her seat. Gone was the surprised and guilty look, her face now serene and professional.

"Thank you."

He took the empty seat beside her and felt her

leg pressed against his. He'd had some very vivid dreams about those legs. He hadn't been able to get her out of his mind and after last night he felt closer to her than ever. Closer than he had any other woman. He hadn't felt so relaxed since the start of the investigation and that was because of her. He was surprised at how easy it had been to talk to her about everything. He'd enjoyed listening to her talk and laugh and even when she had sounded so tired, he hadn't wanted to suggest they hang up.

He'd been with women before, but none held a candle to Natalie. He wasn't sure why he felt so drawn to her, only that he did. She made him feel weak and strong at the same time. He forced away all thoughts of Natalie, which was extremely difficult as her floral perfume—a combination of vanilla and gardenias—tickled his nose as he sat so close to her. Close enough that should he stretch out his hand out, he could lay it on her thigh. He squeezed his eyes shut against imagining how it would feel. He clenched his jaw and thought about what he was doing there. When he opened them again he was composed.

"How is the case going?" Hallie asked. "I'm really sorry I wasn't able to help."

Matt stared at her across the table. He was amazed at the transformation. Hallie looked better than she had the last time they had spoken. She was still a waif, her blue uniform practically swallowing her whole but she seemed freer somehow—happier. She had gone from angry and hostile to relatively calm and agreeable. She looked like the typical teen despite the serious golden eyes. He doubted she would ever be carefree but no longer were they filled with fear or annoyance. He felt a rush of pride at her ability to bounce back. He had always been in awe of her. She showed such resilience. If he ever had a daughter, he hoped she shared the same characteristics.

"You needn't be sorry. In fact I'm the one who should be apologising. I should've found him by now," he answered.

"It's hardly your fault," Natalie mollified. "This man has made it his mission in life to disappear, to hide from authorities."

"His teeth were white, extremely white. I remember thinking it odd at the time," Hallie said softly.

Matt turned to face Hallie. Her eyes were focused inwards as she spoke, not seeing him or Natalie at the table. He froze, not daring to breathe in fear he would disrupt whatever was playing inside her head. Five years ago, when she had first given the police a description, she had been generic at best. Her youth hadn't allowed her to be very detailed. This is what he had hoped to discover, and the reason he had enlisted Natalie's expertise.

"His clothes, they were old and worn and his hair long. Longer than yours, Detective, but not by much. Those white teeth, they were sharp. Almost like a vampire's, these ones." Hallie reached up and touched her canines. "I think he also had a twitch or something. His mouth curled slightly to one side."

She looked over at them. "I've never seen him in my mind since that night, not awake anyway, and in my dreams he's always been a shadow. A faceless man."

"You're remembering. That's good," Natalie encouraged.

"Do you remember which side?" Matt asked.

"It would be his right. No, his left." She threw up her hands. "I don't know. I'm sorry."

"You did great. I'm proud of you, kiddo," Matt told her and he saw something flicker in her eyes.

"He'll never stop. Not until he's dead."

"No, he won't," Natalie agreed. "But neither will Detective Murphy."

Matt shot her a look. She sounded so confident in his abilities. Hallie glanced from Natalie to him then back at Natalie.

"I'll give it a go. I can't guarantee when. I'll have to fortify myself before I try, but I will try," Hallie told them.

Matt mentally shook his head. The Director had told him Hallie Walker was the most uncooperative and troublesome adolescent he'd had the unfortunate job of caring for. But looking at Hallie now, he thought the Director must've been talking about another girl.

He followed Natalie out of the room and together they walked back down the hallway in comfortable silence.

As they returned the visitors passes, the nurse spoke. "I've never seen her respond as she has with you. Whatever you're doing, keep it up because it's working."

"I intend to. By the way, I left a file with her. I would prefer you not take it from her. I would like for Hallie to confront her past, to accept it and hopefully heal. The file is rather graphic but I believe she can deal with them."

The nurse nodded. "Of course. I'll let the others know."

"Thank you. I would also like to start her on Prazosin and a mild anti-depressant. Can you please have the administrator sign off? If Hallie refuses to take them, just tell her I asked for them to be prescribed."

"Very well."

"I'll discuss the dosage at a later date with the administrator once I see how she goes," Natalie told the nurse.

Matt was sufficiently in awe. He had just witnessed Doctor Miller in action and she had been magnificent.

He walked her to her Prius. He had purposely parked next to her for that reason. Her long, shapely legs walked confidently in her heels and her hips swayed enticingly. His pants were suddenly tight and uncomfortable so he raised his stare from her arse and sped up to walk beside her.

Was he just sex deprived or was it something more? Natalie was an attractive woman but then so were many others, and he didn't feel this pull towards *them*. He was determined to find out. But after the case was closed. He may break the rules occasionally when warranted, but he didn't just for the heck of it, although he was sorely tempted to. He gave Natalie a covert glance. Oh yes, he was more than just a little tempted. There wasn't a single thing he didn't like about her, but he especially liked her good humour and the way she looked at him as if she too was struggling with desire.

"Would you like to grab some food while we discuss the case?" he asked, feeling another hunger start in his belly. "How much time do you have?"

Natalie glanced at the watch that graced her delicate wrist. "My next appointment is at four so we have plenty of time."

He liked the sound of that. "Follow me?"

Natalie smiled as she opened the door to her car. "Anytime."

Matt went hard in a rush. Damn, but she did turn him on.

Chapter 12

Natalie parallel parked beside Matt's police issued Holden Commodore outside a small seventies era building on Alcott. An obscure sign indicated it was *Tanner's Bar and Grill*. She had never heard of it and wouldn't have known it was there if she hadn't been directly in front of it.

She met Matt on the sidewalk and he opened the door for her. Natalie stepped through the opening and stopped to take in her surroundings. Tanner's wasn't going to make any reviews in the *Harbour Bay Tribute*. A bar was situated to the left and several flat screen TVs hung on the wall, showing various sporting events. An ATM was wedged between two doors which she assumed were the toilets from the stick figure images on each door. The right side of the room was lined with several booths and a few two seater tables were placed sporadically around the floor for those not wishing to sit at a booth or the bar.

Despite the mid-day hour, the bar was packed with men in uniform. Tanner's was apparently a cop's hangout which explained why she'd never heard of it. Not that she went out regularly but she often heard about the restaurants in town in the elevator on the way to her office and filed away the names of the ones that received good reviews for when she didn't feel up to microwaving and could pick up dinner on the way home.

"We can go somewhere else if you'd like," Matt said as she took in the bar.

Natalie turned to him and smiled. "No, this is fine. Let's get a booth."

She followed Matt towards the back of the bar to one of the last remaining booths. He nodded to several people as he passed and they reciprocated, giving her a quick scrutinising look before turning back to their drinks and sporting events.

Soft music played on hidden speakers before being drowned in a cheer that rose from the men milling around the bar. Natalie stumbled and let out a sound as she started to fall. Matt adroitly spun around and caught her easily before she fell to the rough, sticky floor.

"Are you all right?" he asked and she shivered, the heat of his hands on her body causing her a delicious chill.

Natalie nodded and looked down at her bare foot then back a few paces to where her blue pump—that matched her blouse—remained. Matt followed her gaze then bent to pick up her heel which had been glued to the floor by something she stepped in. He glanced at her and gave her a sheepish smile before he lifted her leg gently. Natalie caught hold of his shoulder to keep her balance as, like Prince

Charming, he slipped the shoe on her foot.

Natalie felt the burn of his hand on her leg and desperately wanted him to slide his hand under her skirt. Her breath caught in her throat as her mind was overrun by erotic thoughts. She blinked to clear her vision and blushed when he looked at her questioningly.

"Thank you."

He smiled, the dimple in his cheek showing. How she wanted to kiss that dimple, the man and his entire body.

"You're welcome. Take a seat. I'll go order. What would you like?"

Natalie slipped into the nearest booth, all the while chastising herself and her wayward thoughts. She was no Cinderella and while this man was delicious, he was not someone she could fool around with. Could she?

Natalie grabbed the folded laminated menu from where it had been propped up between the salt and pepper shakers and perused the list while silently willing her heart to quit beating so fast.

"Chicken burger with fries and tomato sauce," she told him.

"No salad?" he joked.

"I already have a round figure with meat on my bones so I doubt it would matter much," she muttered, then glanced up to find him staring at her in surprise. "Sorry. Something one of my patients said."

He gave her a slow once over that made her blood boil and she let out a breath.

"You don't have to worry. It's all in the right

places," Matt told her. "What would you like to drink?"

She forced herself to speak. "House wine will be fine."

One drink certainly wasn't going to affect her mental capacity and if she was survive the next hour or so with him on the opposite side of the booth she would need some fortification.

"I'll be right back."

Matt moved off to the bar. She watched him speak with a few people he knew for a moment, then retrieved the file out of her tote bag and placed it on the table, cautious of wet spots or sticky substances on the scarred wood.

She had missed him, she realised. It was crazy but after last night something had changed in their relationship. What that was, she had no idea. Somewhere between favourite all-time album and his most embarrassing moment, the tone had changed and now she was wondering where that left them. Beyond the professional and dipping a toe into the personal, testing the waters. But was that all they would be?

She knew he was attracted to her. The heat in his eyes told her that and she was definitely feeling attraction towards him. Was it possible to move forward and go somewhere deeper? More intimate? She hoped so. Obviously they would have to wait. The circumstances of their meeting and the cases they were working on were the priority. There would be time afterwards to explore the possibilities. Although, truth be told, she wasn't sure she could wait that long. He had seriously messed with her hormones.

Natalie tore her thoughts and her stare away from Matt and took another glance around. The bar, despite its grungy appearance, had a nice ambience. It wouldn't have been her first or second pick, but she knew better than anyone not to judge a book by its cover. The smells emanating from the kitchen made her stomach growl and she was thankful no one was around to hear it. She had only had a coffee and banana for breakfast and was glad Matt had asked her for lunch otherwise she was sure she wouldn't have had anything other than the protein bar that was in her desk drawer.

A minute later, Matt returned and set the wine glass down in front of her.

"Our orders will be done in about five minutes," he informed her as he sat and took a sip from his own glass. It looked like coke and she couldn't smell any of the J's—Jim, Johnny or Jack—and had been served in an official Coca-Cola branded glass.

"On the clock," he said, and Natalie realised she must have been staring intently at the glass.

"When you're not on the clock, what do you drink?"

"A beer now and again. Whisky when it's been that kind of a day."

For some reason, the idea of him drinking didn't scare her as it would if he had been anyone else. She trusted him, which surprised her. Trusted him to keep her safe and that was a big thing for her. The revelation was startling and telling.

"I can't imagine what you see day in and day out."

He shrugged. "It's not all bad. Thankfully, murders are few and far between. There are still car accidents which can be brutal, and domestic violence. They always leave a foul taste in my mouth."

She could well imagine those scenarios. Blood. Bruises. Tears. Pain.

"How long have you been a cop?"

"Over fifteen years."

She sat forward. "How do you handle the dark side of your job?"

He gave it some thought. "By focusing on the people I can help. Knowing that I have changed their lives for the better. Although I didn't do such a good job with Hallie."

Natalie placed her hands over his where they rested on the table and gave them a squeeze. "Hallie is not lost. She may be scared. But she is tough. You saw that years ago. I see that today."

"You gave her the files, didn't you?" he asked. She started to pull her hands back but Matt caught them with his own and held them there. He pinned her with his green gaze.

"I did and before you blast me for it, remember you came to me for help. That's what I'm doing. Trust my instincts, Detective."

"I do. I just don't like the idea of Hallie reading it, even if she did experience it firsthand."

"Which is why I believe reading the case would be far better than having her relive it through memories. In your files, the case is laid out plain and simple. Just facts. She can be somewhat emotionally detached which hopefully will have her remembering the night clearer. I can't guarantee that she can assist your case but it's worth the chance."

"So long as it helps her, I honestly don't care."

A young waitress approached the booth holding a tray with two plates on it. "Beef burger and salad?"

Matt indicated himself and reluctantly they broke apart. Natalie didn't miss the look the woman shot her before placing the plate with Matt's burger down in the space where their joined hands had been.

"I guess that makes you chicken and chips," the waitress stated to Natalie as she set down the plate with the chicken burger in front of Natalie. "So who's your friend, Matt?"

Natalie shot him an amused look. He had a pained expression on his face. It was clear everyone would be talking about their lunch for some time.

"Natalie Miller," Natalie introduced herself.

"Glory," the waitress said. "You have a nice lunch, Natalie, and don't be a stranger." She gave Natalie a wink only she could see before moving off back behind the bar.

Natalie blushed and turned her attention to her lunch. She poured the tomato sauce over her chips and then popped one into her mouth and looked over at Matt.

"This is a really friendly place," she commented.

"Yeah. As you might've guessed, it's a cops' hangout. Tanner, who owns the place, is a retired cop. We all supported him when he first opened and still come because it's the best food in town. I forgot that bringing you here would be like bringing you home to meet my mother."

Her stomach did a somersault. She tried to ignore the pleasure she felt at that thought. She tampered down her emotions. He had said he'd forgotten not that he was serious enough about her to declare her to one and all.

"Are you going to cop much flack?"

"Not from these guys. My own team, yes, but that's okay because we often tease each other. I'll just be on the receiving end this time."

"You don't sound too worried."

"I'm not."

Natalie wondered what that meant. But then decided to stop analysing the situation and his words and just enjoy it. She took another chip and munched. Matt reached over and stole a chip from her plate. She widened her eyes dramatically and scolded him.

"If you wanted chips, you should've ordered chips." She smiled mischievously, picked up her fork and speared a rich, ripe tomato from his plate and popped it into her mouth. He laughed heartily then traded her half his salad for half her chips.

Chapter 13

Natalie stared at the stack of files on her desk but didn't see them, her mind on Matt and their lunch together. After they had finished surreptitiously running though the file—her hand sore from writing down a copious amount of notes—Matt had walked her to her car, his hand splayed on the small of her back. She had gone breathless at the first touch and when they had stopped beside her car, she had wanted nothing more than to pull him into her body and kiss him hard and passionately. She hadn't, and he made no move towards her, much to her disappointment.

He had then delighted her by opening her car door for her. It was chivalrous and sent a thrill through her body. No one had ever opened her door for her and she found she enjoyed it. For some reason it made her feel special. After climbing into her car, he had closed the door gently but firmly and as she had driven off she had glanced back to see him staring after her.

She had to get a grip on herself and seriously

needed to stop focusing on it. She wasn't living in a fairy tale despite how he made her feel.

Natalie let out a calming breath and stared at the pile and winced. She really had to stop procrastinating. As much as she wanted to wile the day away thinking of Matt—and she could easily do so—she had work to do. She pulled down the top folder and began reading. Peter Hoffman had come to her eight months ago because of authority issues dating back to childhood. It had been a fairly simple case. One of the few she had and although she technically hadn't cured him as his was a personality trait, she felt that she had helped him deal with the issues in his life and he'd been able to move on to be a more balanced individual.

If only other cases had been as simple as that. Natalie picked up another file and scanned the pivotal information. Jerry Friday had been ordered by the courts to see a psychologist for behavioural problems. The man had been driving down the wrong side of the street and when police tried to pull him over, a four hour car chase ensued, resulting in his arrest, which he decided to resist. It led to two officers being treated in the ER for bodily harm. Police were baffled when they'd brought him in to discover that he wasn't drunk, that this was simply his normal behaviour.

In view of his aggressive tendencies, the court had issued him with an ultimatum. Either visit a psychologist and work on his issues or three to five in minimum security. Jerry chose her and she had spent a year trapped inside her office with him one hour a week until his sentence was up. Whether they had made any progress was still lost to her. Unprofessionally, she was happy to see him go.

Natalie placed Jerry's file on top of Peter's. Once she was done going through all her old files they would be taken down to the basement and archived. It was procedure to keep the files for several years before they could be destroyed.

One by one, Natalie went through the old files. She found it was kind of like looking through old photo albums and going down memory lane. She could imagine her patients before her, reciting their issues to her to solve. She could remember the problem ones or the ones she seemed to help. Others were faces lost in a crowd. She hated that but was realistic. Natalie knew she couldn't save everyone. It was kind of like war, she reflected. You pray when you go you don't lose any of your team, but in truth you knew you would be bringing some home in body bags.

It took another three hours and countless mugs of coffee to see the end of the pile and she jumped up and down rejoicing the moment the last file was placed on top of the pile to go to the basement.

Natalie leaned back in her chair, kicking her shoes off before placing the heels of her feet on her desk and dug around her desk drawer for her emergency packet of cashews. She started chewing on them as she enjoyed her brief down-time. She thought about her previous cases and then about the Butcher. Her mind always seemed to fall back to him.

Her professional brain couldn't help wonder what had brought him on this path of murder and butchery. What happened to him that had caused him to act this way? Was he abused as a child? Not that it was an excuse, of course, one she certainly didn't allow. Many people throughout the country were abused when they were children, but not all of them turned out to be horrific serial killers.

Had he started off by torturing young children or defenceless pets? Was there someone out there who'd seen his sickening behaviour and chose to ignore it? She shook her head. As much as her profession relied on getting into people's heads, she had no such desire to delve inside the mind of a murderer, even if it could help the case. The Butcher was different and she knew if she was to delve into his mind she might not return safely and certainly not without scars or psychoses.

Over her years as a psychologist, Natalie had met some colleagues who had done just that. They had ventured inside prisons around the country and some even around the world and had interviewed serial killers. Natalie marvelled at their bravery or stupidity, whichever way you looked at it. She certainly wouldn't be able to do it. She had enough nightmares in her life. She didn't feel the need to add more of someone else's. She had even tried to read a report one of her classmates had written on one of the country's worst offenders. Natalie had read the first chapter and then put it down. There had been no need or reason to subject herself to that darkness.

She sighed when she heard her computer beep, interrupting her thoughts as it reminded her an appointment was due. She opened up her calendar and looked at the name. Her mind flashed to the day she had met Matt.

She felt a shiver of excitement go through her at the thought of Matt. When she was near him, she felt a sizzle of awareness and she had found herself staring at his lips once or twice. She wondered how they would feel against her own, how he would taste. She felt her body go warm as desire flowed through her.

At that moment her office door opened and Henry Rellet stood hesitating in the doorway. Natalie pushed all thoughts of Matt, and his body, out of her mind. She had other things to think about right now and she couldn't afford to be side-tracked, even by thoughts of the very sexy detective.

She waved Henry in. Cautiously, as if half expecting something to jump out at him, he made his way towards her. He took his seat and sat poised on the edge of the plush leather chair as if at any minute he would need to run. She had noticed before that he never really did relax in her presence as much as she made it a 'calm and safe' place.

Henry was a normal enough person in her estimation. His clothes were bland—often beige, cream or an off-white. He was one of those people no one ever really noticed and if they did, tended to forget as soon as he was gone from their sights. His honey-blond hair was gelled down and brushed to one side and she wondered if even a hurricane could dislodge one strand. For some reason it looked odd on his head, not quite suiting his skin tone. His light blue eyes watched her carefully.

Natalie waited patiently. She knew Henry had his own timetable and wouldn't or at least *couldn't* be rushed. Henry spent his time talking to her about his day to day life. He had what he called a 'time consuming and demanding' job and liked to be able to relax with her as he was a different person outside her office. Most people treated her like a sounding board, someone to listen to their thoughts whether they wanted to hear her input or not. Some people just wanted to get secrets off their chests and she was their own private confessional.

"Well, I've been seeing another woman. She's just right for me," Henry declared.

Natalie nodded. Each visit he always told her he had found 'the one' only to tell her the next time the woman had left. She wondered what he was doing to push them away. She looked back over her notes and counted the failed relationships. He was in double digits now. She figured he must come on too hard and fast or smother them. There was no way he could be *that* unlucky in love.

"She's perfect. All blonde hair and blue eyes. She's definitely the one."

"What about your last girlfriend—"

She broke off trying to remember the woman's name. Natalie consulted her file but couldn't find it. Had she been having an off day and not recorded it? She was usually more thorough than this. Patients liked it when she could recall details like that at the drop of a hat. It made them feel important that someone actually cared about the small things.

As she flicked through Henry's file she realised she hadn't once recorded any of his girlfriends' names. She had, however, made a note about there being one and her occupation which she found odd. Henry might not like to name names but he had no problems with telling her what they did for a living.

She found the last '*GF*' notation and read the job title. "The hospital worker?"

Henry nodded. "She just wasn't good enough. I had to get rid of her."

Natalie frowned. She wondered what the girl had done to deserve the boot. It wasn't as if Henry could afford to be picky. He was attractive enough. His personality left a lot to be desired, but then she only saw one side of him. He had mentioned that he was different away from her office. What did she know? Perhaps he was mesmerising and assertive? Or played in a rock band.

"And how long ago was that?"

Henry smiled and she shivered. She had never seen him smile before and the small action changed his face. Gone was the affable man and in his place was a man not quite right. He gave her the creeps but he wasn't the only one.

Natalie made a note to research any treatment he might have had previously. Someone who could change their entire demeanour in a second certainly couldn't have stayed off some mental health professional's radar for long.

"A couple of days," he said nonchalantly and she watched his facial muscles mould back into the face of the man she had thought boring.

Natalie felt her eyebrow rise. He really didn't like to be alone. While as a professional she prided herself on being non-judgemental, she couldn't help it. She was human, after all, and a couple days from one woman to the next cried monophobia.

"That seems rather sudden. Are you sure it is love and that you're not rebounding? What did you say her name was?"

Natalie watched him flinch as if she had struck him. His face darkened and he visibly fought for control. The cords tightened in his throat and she thought she saw a muscle tick under pressure. This wasn't a side of Henry Rellet she'd seen before. Obviously he only liked talking about himself and not having his choices questioned or commented on.

"I didn't say I loved her. I said she's the one," he replied when he had calmed down.

She didn't comment on the fact that he hadn't answered the question about the woman's name and let it slide. She had no plans on sending her patient into a rage. Not that it didn't happen, but if she could avoid it she did. Natalie admitted she wasn't the best person when it came to dealing with male anger and the few times a patient had lost it she had cowered, stricken with fear until the building's security team had arrived and removed her enraged patient.

"Well, I'm very happy for you, Henry. I just caution you on taking things too fast. Take the time to allow the relationship to mature."

That is good advice, she thought, thinking of Matt.

Henry nodded. He sat with both feet firmly planted on the ground, his hands clasped together on his lap. It unnerved her.

"I will, Doctor Miller. She is very special. I will

take my time with her."

Henry left and once again Natalie was alone in her office. She stood and made her way to the computer and sat down in her comfortable chair with the best back support money could buy and added her notes from the day's session into Henry's electronic file. As she saved the document she looked over at the tower of files and groaned. She hated filing, and archiving her files required going down to the basement, which was something else she hated doing. She thought fleetingly to ask her receptionist to do it for her but after looking at the clock on the wall she knew Lara would have gone home some time ago.

Natalie decided against leaving them for her tomorrow. It wouldn't take much time and it would be one less thing waiting for her in the morning. As she slowly made her way to the elevator, Natalie hoped she didn't run into an Occupational Health and Safety officer, otherwise it would be her arse. She really should have gotten a trolley. She reflected as she struggled to hit the call button. After juggling her load around, she cursed her impatient self. The files were not only awkward but heavy. Before she could scold herself again, the elevator arrived and she stepped inside.

The basement was dark, with only a naked bulb giving off any light at all. She was hit full force with the dank, mouldy air that came from the unventilated room where she had several filing cabinets stored. She sneezed as she breathed in the dust lingering in the air.

Natalie quickly filed away her patient's records,

the darkness and late hour making the storage area seem eerie and sinister. When she was done, Natalie took the stairs, something she only did once every blue moon. But she usually had good reason to take the elevator, sometimes carrying armfuls of files or wearing killer heels. But she decided as a health—albeit mental health—professional she needed to set a good example. She was puffing by the time she made it to her third floor office and reflected on how out of shape she was.

Over the years, Natalie had been so focused on school and getting her master's and graduating that she had no time for other activities and then she had gone into the work force and had spent all her time and energy creating a name for herself and ensuring her business didn't tank.

Now that she was finally comfortable and settling down into a nice routine, perhaps a gym membership would go a long way. She had been quite lucky with her genes, notwithstanding her mother's faults. She was born with an athletic body and a fast metabolism so she hadn't had to spend much time watching what went in her mouth. Although in her younger years running from her stepfather was probably what had kept her in shape, she thought with a sneer.

Natalie looked at the clock on her desk. The time was just past seven. Usually, she stayed at the office until nine, always managing to find something to research, but tonight she was going to treat herself and go home early. Maybe even catch up on sleep. Natalie grabbed her purse from her desk drawer and walked over to the elevator, punching the down button. There was no way in hell she could make it down the three flights of stairs.

She thought about pouring herself a glass of wine and watching a movie or starting one of the paperbacks she'd bought over the years but never had the time to read before she headed off to bed. She had three back to back appointments in the morning and wanted to be fresh.

Natalie stepped into the elevator carriage, imagining her evening to come. She never saw the man lurking around the corner, watching her, waiting for the perfect opportunity.

Chapter 14

Natalie stepped out onto the street. Spring was in full force, the weather warmer and the days longer. In winter, she hated her building since there was no underground or close by parking, requiring her to park a block away. At night, the walk which usually only took three minutes, depending on what shoes she wore, always seemed longer. Her eyes were forever vigilant, her keys digging in her palms as she was ready to strike at any unsuspecting would-be thieves, carjackers, or rapists. Not that Harbour Bay was a hub of criminal activity, at least not the area she lived and worked in, but with the Butcher in town it would pay to keep an eye open.

Tonight, the walk was brisk and she felt her body begin to relax. Henry's reaction to her questioning still ran through her mind and she tried to make sense of it. Sure, some people got their backs up when they didn't like being told something, but this was a transformation she rarely saw.

Natalie frowned. If Henry made a change like that in a manner of seconds, like flicking on a switch, then there was something shimmering below the surface that she might not be able to treat. He had scared her and she thought momentarily about informing him she could no longer accept him as a patient as she did with all her clients that frightened her to this point, but she decided against it. How did she expect to be able to heal herself if she kept running from her own issues?

Natalie reached her car and climbed behind the wheel and automatically locked her doors. Even out of Coleani's neighbourhood, it was best to remove temptation from those who would take advantage. Natalie felt that throughout her whole life she had been fighting to stay safe, whether from Gary or some unseen force. Her safety was always first and foremost in her mind. She didn't like to be a victim and certainly didn't plan on becoming one again.

She started up her car and after a quick look out the rear view mirror, pulled into traffic. After a few minutes she was engrossed in the latest new release from Katy Perry and happily singing along.

It was a few minutes later, when Natalie glanced at her side mirrors, that she spotted him. He was driving a white sedan. It was nondescript, but she was certain he was following her. She made a few turns she normally wouldn't and wasn't surprised when the sedan kept up. He wasn't being obvious about following her but she was certain he was.

Her heart sped up and her palms became damp. Natalie couldn't see the driver, not from this distance but she was certain it was a man, his features blurred. She grabbed her phone and while weaving in and out of traffic she dialled the emergency number, triple 0. The first thought that skittered across her mind was that the Butcher had yet to be caught. Her foot stamped down harder on the accelerator on its own accord and her breath caught in her throat as her follower did the same.

The emergency operator came onto the line and shakily, Natalie relayed that she was sure someone was following her. She tried to keep the panic from her voice but in the end doubted she had accomplished that.

The trained operator immediately began giving directions on how Natalie should handle the situation, the first being finding a public place. Without endangering the other motorists on the road Natalie managed to cut across two lanes of traffic and pulled into the off-road service station, stopping at a pump. She undid her seatbelt and hastily got out of the car. At this time of night the BP was packed with travelling families and truck drivers filling up before their shift. She looked over at the entrance to see the sedan follow her in.

Natalie squeezed the phone hard. Her stomach knotted and her inner voice told her to run. In her ear, the emergency operator was encouraging her, the words going in one ear and out the other as Natalie focused on not releasing her bladder. Her gaze flicked side to side in panic as the sedan pulled to a stop at a pump across from her and the driver got out.

He wouldn't be so stupid to make a move here, surely?

No, he wouldn't do that, she thought. *You're just overreacting and what do you expect from reading too many police files lately?*

The man probably just needed petrol and following her was a coincidence, she lied to herself. So what if there were easier ways of getting there than the one she took?

Her panic became full blown and she tried to tell the operator what was happening but when she opened her mouth nothing but a squeak came out. Natalie backed away from her car, preparing to run. How she planned on doing that in three inch heels, she didn't know, but she quickly glanced at the ground, checking to see if the path was clear from where she stood to inside the service station. She could make it if she ran real fast or if she managed to find her voice, could scream and have every eye on her in a second. As much as she hated being in the spotlight, she could make an exception.

If all else failed, she could always stab him with her stiletto. The man turned around. Her eyes locked on him and refused to leave.

Derek Butler looked back at her and winked, a cruel smile curving his lips. Anger replaced fear and she remembered what she had thought the night Derek had shown his true colours. He was an escalator and he was now proving her correct. She mentally smacked her head as she remembered she had planned on reporting him to police. She had become side-tracked and then had completely forgotten about filing the report.

"Leave me alone, Derek," she said loudly so that he could hear. "It's over."

A possessive nature was a symptom of BPD, Natalie suddenly remembered. He had locked on her and no amount of persuasion would deter him. He would also want to punish her for her rejection of him. She had made several mistakes when it came to him and Natalie admonished herself for being so stupid.

He made a move toward her and she held up her phone, the display out to show she was connected to triple 0. She pressed the speaker button and Derek stepped back when he heard the operator's voice asking Natalie if she was okay.

"Stay away, Derek, trouble only lies that way. You really should seek professional help. Just don't call me," she added.

Watching him cautiously, Natalie eased back into the car, once more locking her doors and began driving. She was relieved to see he didn't follow her. She would need to be extra vigilant from now on. Derek knew where she lived and she knew he would not give up easily. She had no idea what his plan had been, but she doubted very much if she would've liked it.

After driving another three kilometres with her focus on her mirror, Natalie was satisfied that he was gone for the night. She put her phone to her ear and told the operator the situation had been diffused for now, and asked how she went about making a formal complaint.

The kind operator took down her name and address and said she would have an officer come and see her in the next few days to discuss her options.

Natalie thanked her and hung up, silently praying the rest of the trip home would be uneventful.

Chapter 15

Hallie lay on her bed. She couldn't sleep, her rest disturbed. Usually by this time she was fast asleep, running and screaming, fighting for her life. Instead she stared up at the white ceiling and listened to the restful snoring of the person in the room next to her. She looked over at her roommate. Darlene was fast asleep and Hallie wished she could join her.

Natalie had told her the cops where still operating a state-wide hunt for the Butcher but the Harbour Bay LAC—or at least Matt—believed him to be still in the area. Hallie shivered and pulled up her blankets. There could only be one reason he would stick around Harbour Bay and that was her. She was the only one to survive, the only one who could ID him. Although, she didn't know what he had to fear from her. She had given the police everything years ago and that hadn't helped. He was still free to kill.

Hallie felt like he was punishing her, keeping her in fear. Because of him, she had stayed hidden. Afraid that one day he would find her and kill her exactly like he murdered her mother. Late at night, when the world was dark and silent, Hallie felt the cold steel of his blade against her skin which only made her cower more.

The blood of the women he had killed was on her hands. If she hadn't allowed her fear to consume her, if she had fought against her mind harder, refusing to give up, the Butcher might be behind bars by now. Countless women would still be alive and she—well, she had no idea what she could be doing. Natalie was right. She did blame herself for her parents' deaths even though her logical mind told her there had been nothing she could've done to save them. She had hated herself for so long for running, for surviving.

There had been a time, during her most dark moments, when she had wanted to die. Now she was thankful she was still alive and realised just how valuable her life was, how precious *any* life was.

Her own life would never be easy. Even if she was to combat the PTSD, to finally be able to accept the past, Paradise Valley carried a stigma that would follow her for the rest of her life. She would never be normal. There wouldn't be a person alive who would not hear her name and know her history. She imagined the looks of pity and closed her mind on them. She couldn't help her past but she could change her future.

She still feared the day she might come face to face with the Butcher once more but for the first time, the very acknowledgement didn't incapacitate her. In fact she felt stronger, almost ready for the confrontation.

Hallie sat up. Sleep once more evaded her as thoughts spun around her head. Wrapping her blanket around her slender body, Hallie stood, the cold tile floor chilling her feet. She listened to the silence, only tarnished by the slight snores of a fellow inmate and Darlene's shallow breathing. She shivered again as she thought two things—that Paradise Valley was as quiet as a tomb and as cold as death.

Hallie moved towards the window and looked out at the darkness. Since her parents' deaths five years earlier she had changed a lot. She wondered if her parents would even recognise her today. At twelve she had cared nothing but freedom and independence. After years of being locked up, her basic human rights and privileges thrown out the window, she had become a shadow of her former self.

The state had provided her with books and learning tools and four hours each day she studied, which in her wacky life was the only sense of normalcy she had, providing her with a safe haven. Having been on the road most of the school year she had often been home-schooled, learning to cope without teachers and other support opportunities students got. Luckily for her she had adapted well and her studies hadn't suffered. Today, she was well ahead of others her age. Her appetite for knowledge was insatiable and only hindered by the fact she couldn't leave the hospital's grounds. There was so much she wanted to do and experience and wondered if she would get the chance.

She listened to the thunder rumble in the sky. Once the sound had scared her but now it no longer bothered her. A lot of things frightened her but that was no way to live a life. There was a whole world out there and she desperately wanted to be a part of it. With that thought, Hallie opened the file Natalie had given her and took a deep breath.

Then she began to read.

Chapter 16

Matt pulled his unmarked grey Holden Commodore into Natalie's driveway and made his way to her front door. He knocked and waited a minute before he tried again. After a few minutes he realised she was probably engrossed in her work and he moved around to the side of her house and stepped through the gate to her backyard. He spotted her right away. She was sitting at her dining table facing him. Her head was down and she was studying the papers displayed in front of her.

Her brunette hair was loose and spilled over her shoulder and she was dressed in sweat pants and a *Harbour Bay Seagulls* shirt, the local basketball team. He couldn't help but think she looked absolutely delicious.

You've got to stop thinking that way, Murphy, he chastised himself.

He stepped closer to the window, his face almost against the glass. His shadow fell over the table. Natalie glanced up as she sensed the change in light and looked in his eyes. Her eyes widened and she screamed right before her hands covered her mouth.

He jumped back from the window and waved at her. He saw the look of recognition enter her eyes and she lowered her hands, straightening out the imaginary wrinkles in her shirt as she did. She then pointed towards her front door. He nodded and she walked out of room.

Matt retraced his footsteps back to the front door and arrived just as she opened the door. He flashed her a sheepish grin before dragging his hand through his hair, feeling the shaggy length. He really needed to get a haircut.

"I'm sorry for scaring you. I guess you didn't hear me knock," he said.

Natalie shook her head and crossed her arms under her breasts before leaning against the doorjamb. "No. I didn't."

He frowned, remembering the reason he had come to her home.

"Heard you had some trouble last night."

Natalie raised an eyebrow. "Did you now? I suppose you're the officer sent with the paperwork?"

"I volunteered. Are you all right?" he asked. He didn't care if his tone was more personal than professional. He looked her up and down. He caught sight of the fading bruise, hidden beneath a light coating of foundation, and he felt a rage unlike he had known before boil inside him.

Natalie blushed. "I'm fine, Detective, thank you."

"Let me guess, you walked into a door?" he said, with a trace of sarcasm.

Natalie briefly touched her bruise which was a garish yellow. He knew in a few more days it would be gone.

"I handled it," she replied simply.

"So who's the jerk?" he demanded.

Matt pulled out his notepad. He wanted to know everything about the dirt-bag including where he could find him. He had a few ideas about teaching the bastard how to properly respect a woman. He had been livid when he'd found out Natalie had been so terrified that she'd called triple 0. His mind had leapt bounds as he feared for her safety and that sick feeling had lasted the drive over until he had seen for himself that Natalie was all right.

Natalie looked past his shoulder, her eyes unfocused. "Derek Butler. We went out a couple of times. I broke it off when I realised it would never go anywhere. My issue, not his, and obviously he didn't take it well."

She fell into silence and he wondered at what was going through her head.

"We all make mistakes," he said softly.

Natalie met his eyes. "Yes, but I should've seen it."

"Do you know how many times I've said the same words? Unfortunately we aren't perfect."

She gave him a sweet smile and his heart kicked up a notch and his stomach fluttered. He seriously had to get a grip on himself. Otherwise, before he knew it, he would have her beneath him and doing each and every thing he had fantasised doing with—and to—her. As much as he wanted that, he still had a case to solve and she was a distraction he couldn't afford.

"Would you like me to have an officer drive by?" he asked as he moved away from the idea of her stretched out in bed, waiting, beckoning to him. It could only bring trouble. "We can let our presence be known. I've found that to be the most effective deterrent."

Natalie shook her head. "That won't be necessary, Detective. He's just one man, not an army. I wouldn't even bother filing a report if I wasn't worried about the next woman he becomes obsessed with."

He frowned. "He's one of those, you think?"

Matt had dealt with men who couldn't give up the idea of one woman. Every subsequent woman was usually a carbon copy of the last and when the fantasy didn't work out they became physical. The thought of someone getting rough with Natalie had his stomach knotting painfully.

"Did he hurt you?" he asked. Steel underlined his words. He couldn't help it being heard. He was pissed off and if he ever found the man who'd laid a hand on her he would rip the man's balls off and feed them to him until he choked. "Other than your cheek?"

"No. I got rid of him pretty quick after that."

He nodded sharply and his hands became fists. He forced himself to relax. "If you see him again I want you to call me first, you understand?"

Natalie shot him a look. "I don't anticipate that being a problem anymore, but should I see him again, your number will be the first I'll dial. Happy, Mr. Testosterone?"

Matt made himself calm down and gave her another sheepish look. What had gotten into him? Well, he knew the answer to that. She was standing right in front of him, her hands crossed beneath her breasts and he wondered if she realised the action caused her breasts to plump. He knew he did. He hadn't been aware of much else since.

"Sorry, I just can't stand those who beat women. It makes me angry and sick."

Natalie smiled and patted his arm lightly. "That's because your mother raised you right."

His mother hadn't really raised him. He'd raised himself. His mother had been too wrapped up in her grief coma for active parenting. He didn't blame her. In fact he was in awe of just how much she had loved his father. Enough to never look at another man and he wondered if he would ever experience the same feeling. Hell, he swore silently. He was already halfway there. Natalie had gotten under his skin big time. He still looked at other women. He would be a fool and a liar to say he didn't. But he only ever thought of being with just one.

"Will you be okay? Would you like me to stay for a while?"

Natalie swallowed. "I would. But I think it best that you don't."

He nodded, his mouth dry. "Yeah. I agree. Call me if you need anything."

"I will, thank you."

Matt found it difficult to walk away. He was looking forward to the day the case closed for two reasons. The first being the Butcher would finally be behind bars where he belonged. The second was so that he could finally ask Natalie out. He was seriously having trouble keeping his distance.

He handed her a folded piece of paper he'd retrieved from his back pocket. "When you're done, just fax it over. The number is on top. Any questions—"

"I'll call you," Natalie finished as she unfolded the sheet and glanced down. "It all looks fairly simple and straightforward."

Matt hesitated. He really didn't want to leave her. Especially knowing there was a man out there who considered her his possession. He would get Nick and Dean to dig into this Derek Butler's background. If Natalie thought he'd do it again it was more than likely she wasn't his first.

"Goodbye, Matt," she said as walked him to his car.

He climbed in behind the wheel and started the engine. She waved to him as he drove down the street. He shook his head. That woman had seriously done a number on him. He headed back to the LAC, suddenly motivated to get some work done.

Chapter 17

"I read the file," Hallie said as soon as Natalie entered the interview room. "It wasn't easy. In fact, I felt like I was being flayed alive."

Natalie blinked at the sudden ambush. She studied Hallie as she took her seat and got comfortable. "How do you feel now?"

Hallie shrugged. Her red-brown hair rested on her shoulders and her body was poised with a quiet calm. Natalie hadn't been sure what to expect. She should have known Hallie would triumph. She was strong, resilient, and determined. If Hallie put her mind to something there would be nothing that would stand in her way.

"Fine I guess. Numb maybe. What am I supposed to feel like?"

"There is no wrong answer to that and numb is an understandable response," Natalie advised. "Did the nurses have to calm you?"

Hallie shook her head. "No. I was surprised. It took me a while but I got through it. When I first started reading, I felt sick. There was no escape. My mind couldn't retreat and I was made to accept what I read and as I did, my memory became clearer, sharper. I remember being in the foot-well of the car and hearing the brakes squeal against the road. It was like all my senses came alive."

Natalie listened to Hallie as she reiterated how she had felt each precise moment, her memory so detailed, Natalie had no issues with imagining the scene. She watched as Hallie breathed through her distress, her rage now contained and no longer tactile. It appeared to Natalie she had made the right choice, having Hallie confront that night. She had faced her fear, accepted the truth and could now move on. She was still young and the human brain had an amazing capacity to heal. It wasn't over but it was the first step forward.

Natalie couldn't have been more proud. Hallie had made such strives in their short acquaintance and her sheer will kept her going. *Much like it had that night*, Natalie thought. She couldn't wait to share the news with Matt, who would be overjoyed as well. They alone cared what happened to Hallie.

"What else do you remember?" Natalie prodded when Hallie fell quiet.

"Nothing I haven't said before. Dark hair and eyes. He was tall, about the same as my father. Strong. He pulled my dad through the window of the car like he weighed nothing."

Ian Walker, Natalie knew from the reports she had read, had been five-foot-seven and had weighed a little over a hundred kilos.

"I have the strangest sensation that I should know him. I looked at him and he felt familiar to me. But I know I don't know him. Maybe I am crazy."

"You're not crazy," Natalie told her. "I dreamt of him once and I had the same thought, that I had seen him before. We were in the forest and I saw you running. You were so scared and all I wanted to do was save you from him, from the future I knew you would have. But it was dream and I couldn't."

"But you thought you knew him?" Hallie asked, her brow furrowed.

Natalie nodded. "I did at the time. I turned and saw him. He was as close to me as you are."

"What happened?"

Natalie decided against telling Hallie the truth. She didn't want her to know she had dreamed of him stabbing her. "I woke up. But unlike you I had been looking at the rendering the police artist had drawn from your description before I fell asleep."

"I guess the same could be said for me too. I've had years of being haunted by him in my nightmares. After all this time I kind of do feel as if I know him. At least his shell." She crossed her arms over her chest. "Damn, I was really hoping I could help. You and Matt have been so great to me. I would've loved to give you something that would crack the case."

Natalie reached across the table and placed her hand on Hallie's arm.

"You have done far more than you can imagine. You gave them something when they had absolutely nothing. You keep underestimating yourself, Hallie, and you have to stop. You are an amazing woman and to think you're only seventeen. I can't wait to see what else you'll do."

Hallie blushed at the compliment. "You have more confidence than I do. It won't matter what I do. I will always be the daughter of murdered parents or the girl who spent time in a mental hospital. I could cure cancer and my past will be all anyone will remember."

Natalie squeezed the arm beneath her palm gently. "You'll overcome it as you have with everything else. Remember no one in this world is untouched. No matter how perfect their lives may seem. Everyone has experienced some kind of trauma, just in varying degrees. But it's what we do with our lives that counts."

***

Hours later, Natalie sat at her dining table, printouts of newspaper articles in front of her. After leaving Hallie, she had called Matt and advised him of Hallie's progress. As she had thought, he had been pleased if not a little disappointed that it had yielded nothing he could use. She had told him it was still early, and that Hallie's memory would continue to get clearer as each new day passed, but she had advised against getting his hopes up. There could be moments Hallie may never recollect but Natalie felt Hallie would be unlucky enough to remember with crystal clear clarity given enough time.

She had hung up with Matt and returned to her office where she had brought up *Google* and printed out every article pertaining to the Butcher. She had to find this man, now more than ever. She didn't want anything to hinder Hallie's progress, and Natalie wanted nothing more than to share the world with her, but she knew that while the Butcher still roamed free Hallie would remain locked behind the doors of the hospital. Hadn't Hallie's past convinced her of that?

Outside, a storm was brewing and Natalie could smell the rain coming on the breeze. Even in spring, Harbour Bay had a good amount of rainfall. While other cities were on water restrictions, they were still enjoying watering their gardens and washing their cars.

She had taken a shower earlier, trying to alleviate the tension in her body. It had been a hard and stressful couple of days and she was looking forward to when it was all over. She'd dressed in her warmest flannel pyjamas with a panda bear print on them and had poured herself a glass of wine to fortify herself against the horror she knew she was about to read.

The unknown man, the Butcher as the media had called him, had been active for years before the Walker double homicides or so the police had believed. Every case they attributed to him had been reopened and cross examined in the hopes of finding some evidence left behind by a young amateur but even back then, he had been meticulous.

His frenzied attacks had been quick to incapacitate so there was no DNA to be had from a struggle by the victim. But he had taken his time after that first debilitating blow. Natalie shivered.

How horrible it must've been for those women, knowing they were going to die, knowing help wouldn't come. It was the most frightening thing she could think of, spending your last few hours on earth with a monster like him. A man who got pleasure from ending lives and felt no guilt.

He was a conundrum, Natalie admitted. None of his victims fit a type, but with the exception of Ian Walker, they were all female. No two were alike, spread across the country far and wide, from both the city and outback. They were of different ages and occupations and she remembered Matt telling her the police had researched each victim thoroughly and had found no schools or gyms in common either now or in the past.

Each victim had no traits identical to another and were murdered on different days and dates which ruled out ritual killings and other patterns they searched for. She could certainly understand their frustration and was slowly but surely driving herself insane trying to find that one clue that would answer all her questions.

Natalie sat back in her chair, allowing the back to provide support and brought the sheets of paper littered on her table closer where she could reach them. She heard the thunder outside. It crackled throughout the dark sky, following the bright lightning flash and knew the storm was imminent.

She tucked her hair behind her ears and glanced at the newspaper articles her *Google* search had located. There was one that had a picture of the Senator and his wife during their happier days. Another newspaper had found a family snapshot taken just months before their deaths and had published it against a gory title.

Natalie picked up the print-out with the snapshot. The Walker family smiled up at the camera. They looked so happy. Little did they know they would soon be torn apart forever. It was a senseless murder. One that had changed the nation and not for the better. A Senator and his wife. Two people devoted to each other, their daughter, and their country.

The newspaper report had gone on to speculate it had been a political murder; that perhaps someone who had not yet come forward to claim responsibility had wanted to make a very clear statement. The police had denied that in a media release and had said the perpetrator was most likely a drifter, a transient, and the couple had been unfortunate to happen upon the wrong time and place.

The task force had closed down after seven months when it became clear the Butcher had left the state, moving on to greener pastures. He would later become the worst serial killer in the country and the most anonymous, never once seeking out attention by contacting police or the media.

Natalie stared at the family photo. Ian, a handsome man in his early forties, had been a favourite among voters. His beloved wife, a homemaker looking younger than her thirty-something years, had boosted his ratings with the family man image. Then there was Hallie, an adorable child about to embark into her teenage years, a mop of red-brown hair on her head as she smiled cheekily at the camera. Natalie's heart broke. She had held that child in her arms while she had cried for her family and mourned their loss and her own.

Natalie sat there for minutes, her gaze fixed on the family photo. She watched as it blurred before her eyes. She blinked away tears, trying to refocus. Once she had some semblance of control over her emotions, Natalie looked back at the photo and noticed it no longer held the Walker family, but a different family altogether and her hand uncontrollably shook.

The man wore a proud look, his teeth slightly crooked as he smiled towards the camera. One arm was around the waist of a blonde woman, his other resting on the shoulder of a six-year-old. There was a look of utter bliss on all their faces. A perfect family photo. But then only happy days were generally recorded in photos but the bad ones seemed to stay with you forever, without the 2D memento.

Natalie recognised the photo. She had seen it many times before. Had touched it, stroked it and even wished upon a star with it. She felt the tears fall down unbidden and she allowed herself to be swallowed up with grief, to go to a place she fought to forget. She closed her eyes remembering the farm house, the chipped paint, the screen door hanging precariously by one hinge. She had been so scared, fearful her stepfather would wake up and catch her as she folded the photo in half and tucked it into her jeans pocket. She had picked up her school bag, not filled with books that day but with clothes and a few of her worldly possessions.

She had been twelve, running away from home. Her father had passed on four years ago and in a state of despair and possible financial ruin her mother had remarried. Little had she known he was the town drunk and would often beat her when he got home from the pub.

He had drunk them out of the little money her daddy had left them and her mother had become more distant in her melancholy, opting to leave the world with pills and booze if only for a short time. When her mother had stopped being an amusing victim, Natalie's stepfather had turned on her. His so called child-rearing and discipline a world of cruel punishment. A child should never know what an adult's fist feels like, should never know the people who were supposed to protect them were the ones destroying them.

It had been after a particularly brutal beating from her beloved stepfather that little 'Natty' had decided no more. She had vowed then and there that she wouldn't allow that man to touch or hurt her again. She had lived in constant fear and her nerves were shot while she waited for her liberation day.

She had packed her school bag and had slowly descended the staircase, creeping past her unconscious stepfather lying on the living room floor. She opened the door and as it had screeched, had held her breath silently praying he would sleep through the sound. Her heart had pounded in her ears and had almost given out when he rolled over, his face to her. It had taken a few moments for her to realise he was still asleep. She had grabbed her bicycle and had ridden for hours until she came to the closest bus station where she waited, her small body filled with tension, hyped up on adrenaline for the bus to come.

It had taken sixteen hours for her to finally arrive at the Harbour Bay Bus Terminal but when it did, she thought it was the most beautiful sight in the world. She was free. She had hopped off the bus and had searched the waiting faces until her gaze had landed on her aunt's face.

She could still remember, even to this day, the sound of pleasure coming from the woman's voice when she had called out to her. She had run into her Aunt Maggie's waiting arms and she had been home.

"Well, look at you," Aunt Maggie had said, looking her up and down critically. Natalie had wished she had brushed her hair on the bus and rushed to finger comb it now. "So grown up. Your father would be so proud of you. Come on, let's go home, I bet you're tired, huh? Uncle Roger is there waiting for you."

Natalie knew she owed her entire life and future to Maggie and Roger. They had been there for her when her own parents had failed.

A thunderclap brought her out of her reverie. Her hands shook and tears were rolling down her face but she managed to keep the sobs bound within her. This was why she helped other people and never thought about her own past. Nothing good came from it and she always wound up in a state.

She put the article down as another thunderclap rolled across the black sky. Rain drops started to splatter against her large bay window that overlooked her backyard. She lifted up another newspaper clipping highlighting the details of the gruesome murders. She could see the crime scene in her head, like she had just arrived there and it was fresh in her mind. She saw the mutilated bodies. She could smell the metallic stench of blood and death. She swallowed hard to keep the bile that was threatening to surface at bay.

She took in other news clippings of the other murders accredited to the Butcher. Their crime scenes too found their way into her head. The graphic images swirled around and she swore she could smell their decomposed bodies and the coppery taste of blood in her mouth and imagined she could feel the blood warm and sticky on her body. The lightning outside flashed over her face as she struggled to the surface from the nightmare she found herself in. Her hands flailed about as she tried to grab hold of something solid in this reality. Natalie knocked over her wine glass spilling red wine all over her table, the glass smashing into tiny pieces as it hit the hardwood floor.

She grabbed the table, holding on as she waited for her vision to stop spinning. Her nails dug into the shiny table top as images flittered across her mind. She opened her eyes and looked out into her garden just as another bolt of lightning lit up the sky. Staring right back at her from the other side of the glass were the blackest eyes she had ever seen.

Chapter 18

Natalie jumped up from her seat screaming. She knocked over her chair as she got to her feet and scrambled backwards. The light disappeared from the sky, returning the world to black once more. Her heart pounded in her chest and threatened to burst through her ribcage. She placed her palm over her heart for a few seconds in a futile gesture to still it before she took off for the kitchen.

She opened the top drawer of her merle-grey granite bench top and immediately located her flashlight buried amongst her other emergency items such as candles and matches and tested the batteries. Satisfied they were in working order, Natalie made her way to the front door, collecting her car keys from the island bench on the way past. Her keys cut into her palm as she held onto them tightly. She could feel the panic button attached to her key ring and felt somewhat protected.

Armed, Natalie opened her front door and stepped out into the night. She clicked on the flashlight, the strong beam lighting her way as she slowly walked towards her backyard. She could feel the fear induced perspiration coating her skin, making her uncomfortable in the muggy air. Her street was quiet, the promise of rain keeping her neighbours inside. She could hear a dog bark several houses down and wondered if he could smell her intruder.

Lights shined brightly in the surrounding houses but no porch light came on. No one came to investigate her scream. She felt saddened by that fact and a little annoyed if she was honest with herself. What if she'd been attacked? She didn't like to think what would've happened to her if she had been. How long would it have taken before help arrived? Would anyone miss her? She was alone in the world now with no real friends and no close relatives. She barely knew her neighbours, only enough to say hello.

Natalie shrugged off her lack of involvement in her community and tried to remain calm as she thought through her situation. Panicking never helped. In the back of her mind, she knew what she was doing was stupid and dangerous and that an intelligent person would go back inside and check that all the doors and windows were locked but her feet wouldn't allow her to retreat.

She moved carefully, keeping her steps quiet and poised to run at any moment. Her nerves were raw and her body stiff with tension at what she might find, or who. She knew her imagination hadn't run away with her. She had seen exactly what she thought she saw. Natalie shivered at the memory of the cold, dark eyes looking back at her. How long had he been there, watching her, and why? She nibbled on her bottom lip as her mind came up with several possibilities, none of them good.

Natalie listened as thunder continued to rumble across the sky, crackling at the end nearby. At the same time the sky opened up and drenched her down to the bone. She cautiously walked through her side gate and moved the flashlight across the yard left to right before going over it again. Her breaths came in fast, short bursts. She trailed the light beam over the glass of the window where only days ago Matt had stood and innocently watched her. Now an unknown person had been there for God knows how long, doing God knows what.

Her body went cold as she saw the fingerprint marks glow in the bright beam of her flashlight. The bastard had his hands on her window. She looked past the smudged face outline on the glass into her home at the very place she had so recently been. Her hand shook as a shiver travelled down her spine and she nervously wet her lips. The rain pounded down on her head, running into her eyes and she blinked rapidly.

The man had pressed his face against the glass. Had been close enough to her that he could've counted the number of freckles on her nose and she hadn't had a clue he was there. Had it not been for the lightning and her glancing up at that exact moment she might never have known. She probably would've gone to bed with him watching her every move. She shivered again at the thought of that man getting his jollies watching her undress, at what he might do next. She looked down at the ground and knew he'd been there for hours. His man-sized footsteps had left an impression on the soil beneath his feet. For a second she had thought it was Derek, returning to taunt her, but after a few terrifying seconds her brain began to work through the terror and she realised it wasn't him and her heart almost failed her.

Natalie pulled her intruder's image from her memory and kept it close, reviewing his features over and over so as not to forget. She looked about her backyard to determine if anything was out of place. She wondered what she was doing. Why was she outside in the rain looking, investigating something she shouldn't be?

Natalie lost what was left of her bravery and turned around, moving fast towards her car. She pressed the button on her key ring and watched the indicator lights blink as the doors unlocked. She jumped onto the passenger seat and pressed the central lock button, hearing the delightful sound of the doors locking.

She turned around in her seat and played the light beam over the backseat and foot-well. Satisfied she was alone in the vehicle, Natalie deftly climbed over the gear shift and into the driver's seat, plunged the key into the ignition, and revved the engine as she tore out of her driveway. She didn't slow down once as she sped downtown. The windscreen wipers were working overtime swiping the raindrops away and clearing her vision. She felt the tyres buckle under her as they ran through deep puddles, the rubber leaving the asphalt for a brief second. Her stomach twisted into knots as she held on tight, her fingers curling into the leather of the steering wheel.

Natalie didn't dare take her hands away, afraid of losing control of her vehicle as she made several sharp turns. She pulled into the parking lot near her office building and forced herself to let go, almost falling out of the car in her haste to get out of the open. She took off for the entrance and ran up the three flights of stairs, not wanting to wait for the elevator, never once thinking to check if she was being pursued. Not that it mattered. She was scared and wanted to feel safe again. Rational thinking did not enter into it. After securing the doors behind her, Natalie collapsed into her chair, her legs no longer able to hold her weight and caught her breath. With trembling hands, she reached for her phone.

Chapter 19

Matt opened the door to Natalie's office and looked around. He spotted her immediately and after assessing that she was alone, he silently closed the door behind him and carried a cardboard cup of coffee over to her.

Her eyes were closed and her breathing shallow. She was asleep. Her naked feet were resting on her desk, her chair reclined. Her hair was knotted around her face and she smelled of damp, mouldy fabric. Her panda pyjamas were slightly askew and one corner of the button-up top was folded back to give him a tantalising view of a flat, creamy stomach. She looked a mess, so far removed from the coiffed and elegantly dressed woman he was used to seeing. But no matter what she wore—or didn't wear—she was still beautiful and all Matt could think of was touching her.

He stamped down on that need and focused on why he was here. He'd been out all night trying to track down any CCTV cameras in the vicinity of the crime in hopes of finding a glimpse of the perpetrator and when he had returned to the station earlier that morning, he had been told by the officer on duty that Natalie had called constantly throughout the night trying to reach him since his mobile had gone to voicemail. Stupidly he had forgotten to charge it before leaving the LAC and he'd been too busy to think of it and regretted not forwarding his calls to Darryl's mobile.

His night had proved futile once again. Frustration at not being any closer to finding the bastard bubbled to the surface and caused him to have a short fuse. He had used his siren without guilt as he cut across the morning's traffic to get to Natalie's office. He had tried to call but no one had picked up. Seeing as it was too early for Natalie's receptionist to be there, he had taken a chance that she would still be at the office.

He leaned down and whirled the coffee under her nose before gently nudging her awake with his index finger. She groaned and blinked a couple times as she looked up at him, surprise etched onto her face. Natalie rubbed her hands over her face to wipe away the last vestige of sleep and frowned. Matt could see her wondering why he was there and wondered at that himself.

"Matt?" she asked, her voice croaky from sleep.

Matt raised the cup. "Coffee?"

She groaned again. "Yes, please."

Natalie took the cup from his hands and sipped it, making another delightful sound that travelled the length of his spine to the ends of his toes. *Please*, he begged for sanity and control. *A man can only take so much.* He prayed she'd quit making noises that made him think things he shouldn't. Any longer and he wouldn't be able to hold off and might grab her and pull her down to the floor.

He watched as pure bliss passed over her face and thought she looked like she was in nirvana. Well, at least she was enjoying her coffee and he wondered if she enjoyed other things half as well. He shook his head to clear it and scolded himself for his undisciplined mind that was often wandering when he was around her. He had to be careful. As a cop he had to be vigilant at all times. One moment's distraction could cost lives. He had to get his head in the game and keep it there or pack up and go home.

He sat down on the edge of Natalie's desk as she sat up, tucking her feet beneath her chair. He watched as ten brightly painted pink toes disappeared before giving her his full attention.

"Officer Jeffries says you called last night—a lot. Want to tell me what's on your mind?"

Natalie's face paled, tension causing her lips to tighten. She clamped her hands harder around the coffee cup as if sucking the heat from it. Her eyes glistened in the light and Matt had to restrain himself from comforting her. She looked so scared and lost he felt pained. He made himself mentally take a step back. Natalie was just a consultant. He mustn't treat her any differently. He waited patiently as she collected herself and watched as her hands loosened their hold on the cup.

The process took less than a minute but to Matt it felt like a lifetime. He rested his palms lightly on his thighs as Natalie swallowed and then in a clear voice spoke.

"I saw a man at my window last night."

"What?"

He jumped off the desk so fast it gave him a head rush. He spun around to face her. He was furious to think someone had gotten close to her, someone who caused such a reaction from her. Natalie was hardly the type of woman to get riled up over nothing and she was clearly distressed. He was outraged on her behalf for the invasion on her privacy and he had to admit it, he was scared for her too. In such a small span of time, she had been hit, stalked, and now had men staring at her through the window. Something had to be done before this escalated any further. His hands became fists and hung uselessly against his thighs.

"Was it Derek?"

Natalie shook her head. "No. At least I don't believe so. It was dark but I'm pretty sure it wasn't Derek. I can't tell you who it might've been though. I only saw his face for a second. A long heart stopping second," she added. "And it was dark."

How could she be so calm? He was sweating bullets just at the thought of someone being that close to her. He took a deep breath, telling himself to relax, forcing his fists to straighten out. He flexed his hands to work out the stiffness and when he felt his voice would be steady again he asked, "Have you seen him before?"

Natalie shrugged and took another sip of her coffee. "If I had, I wasn't paying attention. I see so many people professionally and my social life leaves a lot to be desired."

The blood pumping through his veins was cold. While he hadn't had a chance yet to talk to Derek, he couldn't rule him out even though Natalie was adamant it wasn't him. Matt liked to believe it was him. Dealing with Derek would be a real pleasure, one he was certainly looking forward to. He didn't like the thought of her being in danger.

"What did he look like? Can you remember?"

She picked up her notepad and handed it to him. Matt looked down at the roughly drawn face on the paper. She wasn't by any means an artist but the impression was there.

"The only thing that really stuck with me was his eyes."

"What about his eyes, Natalie?"

"Think about the darkest night you've ever seen. No moon, no stars. Nothing. Just lifeless black wells. As dramatic as that sounds, it's the only way to describe them. I didn't even know he was there watching me until by chance a flash of lightning lit up the sky."

Matt's hand became a fist again. He could hear the fear in her voice, even though she tried to hide it. Natalie would never admit it to him but he knew she was scared and when he found the man responsible, he would personally see to it that everything he inflicted on Natalie was paid back with interest.

"You know who else has dark eyes?" he asked. He shuddered to think that maybe Natalie had a new admirer. One who would not leave roses and chocolate on her doorstop.

"Who?"

"The Butcher."

She laughed but the sound fell flat. "Why would he be interested in me?"

"Well, that's the fucking question isn't it?" he shouted. "One we don't have a damn clue about and if he has his sights on you—"

He broke off as Natalie lay her hand on his arm. "I doubt that is the case, Matt, so let's not go buying trouble. There could be a number of explanations as to my midnight visitor. The Butcher isn't the only criminal in Harbour Bay and although my neighbourhood isn't usually one targeted for burglary, we can't rule it out."

Matt stared stonily at her. She made it all sound so damn reasonable and had him looking like a jackass in a matter of minutes. He wasn't ruling anything out though. The Butcher was out there and Natalie was standing in his way to get to Hallie.

"You know, at first, I thought I was imagining it. Overstimulated brain, a trick of the light…but when I went outside, I saw a footprint in the dirt and—"

His eyes widened as what she'd just said sank in. His voice was dangerously quiet when he spoke.

"You went outside?"

Natalie frowned at his tone.

"Well, yes." She gave him a 'duh, what else could I do' look.

Stay calm, he told himself.

He gritted his teeth, reminding himself he could get in trouble if he shook her. Besides he didn't think she would appreciate being shaken. She would more than likely return the favour by bopping him over the head with something hard. If the Butcher

184

really had fixated on Natalie, she was in a mass amount of danger and for her to foolishly exit the safety of her home was more than enough to piss him off. For an intelligent woman she was being extremely stupid and he assumed she wouldn't like being told so. He would have to be careful how he phrased things, because antagonising her wouldn't help the situation.

"Are you fucking out of your ever-loving-mind?" he practically yelled at her. What the hell happened to finesse? He might as well jump right in with both feet. "You should be the one locked up inside Paradise Valley for your own safety. Jesus, haven't you ever watched scary movies? You never go outside to investigate strange noises and you never go looking for trouble."

Natalie stood up, planting her hands on her hips. Not a good sign. Matt took an instinctive step back. Growing up in a household of women had taught him when to back down or shut up or both, and right in front of him was one very pissed off woman and *he* had caused it. Natalie was really spinning him for a loop for him to miss the warning signs. He knew she was only human and did what any person would do in the situation and he shouldn't have lectured her. He was halfway towards an apology when she narrowed her eyes at him.

"And what would you have me do?" She stepped closer to him while he moved back. "Stay locked inside my house, unable to sleep for fear that a man could be looking through my windows, wondering if every sound I heard was him breaking in?"

She had a point. He wouldn't have put up with

that shit either. He looked into her angry eyes.

"Well put it that way," he conceded.

"I won't live my life in fear. No one will take my choices away from me."

Again. He heard the word even though she hadn't spoken it. He wondered what was hidden beneath the beautiful outer shell and if she would ever trust him enough to tell him. Her voice was fierce and he could see the determination in the deep blue of her eyes. She was shaken but wasn't about to let the fear rule her life. She reminded him of Hallie. No wonder the two got on so well. There was a connection between them, one he hadn't seen until now.

"Sorry. I shouldn't have said anything. I just don't like to think of you in danger. It's more than I can deal with right now."

She gave him a small nod. "I'm not totally unreasonable. I promise not to take any more unnecessary risks."

She flashed him a bright smile, melting the ice that had fallen. Matt ran his hand through his hair and took the truce she was offering. He wasn't entirely sure what had happened over the past few minutes. He had been through so many emotional changes his head spun, but he was a smart guy and smart guys didn't question or argue. They just agreed.

"So what else happened last night?"

She shrugged, looking ridiculous in her pyjamas but cute at the same time. He wondered if she knew the sight she made.

"Oh, not much. The face at the window was the

highlight of the evening." She paused. "Which reminds me, if any speeding tickets pass your desk…it would be greatly appreciated if you could push them under the rug."

He let out a long suffering sigh and muttered an explicative under his breath. "Let's go."

He waited as she grabbed her keys and put on her daffodil yellow smiley face slippers. She glared at him when he glanced down at her slippers and tried to hide a smile.

"Hey," she said and poked his ribs with her index finger. "I wasn't expecting a midnight camp out in my office, okay?"

"Didn't say anything." He held up his hands in surrender.

She gave an unladylike snort. "You didn't need to. I can read your expression."

He opened the door for her. "Yeah, well, I should at least get points for not mentioning your relaxed work wear."

He flashed an amused look at her and stifled a chuckle as she glanced down at her clothes. He watched with delight as a mortified look crossed her face followed closely by embarrassment and could only guess what was going through her mind.

She raised her head, her face tomato red, and with her back straight passed by him and out the door.

Chapter 20

Natalie watched as Matt deftly navigated past a car accident, several road works and work day traffic delays as he explained the situation to his partner, Darryl on his mobile. An hour later, Matt parked in her driveway and she was surprised to see a forensics team already on site, most likely dusting and combing her backyard for signs of her intruder. She grimaced. Her neighbours were going to love this. Matt got out of the car and bent at the waist to look through the open window at her.

"Stay here," he ordered and held up his hand, effectively stopping the argument she was about start. "Just until I have the all clear, then you and the pandas are free to go inside and change."

She crossed her arms under her breasts and glared at him. He gave her a wink before joining a group of officers that were standing beside the gate that led to her backyard. Thankfully, they had foregone the crime scene tape, but their police issued vehicles still gave curiosity seekers something to talk about. She was pretty sure her name would be on her neighbours' lips for some time after this.

Natalie sank down deeper into the seat in Matt's car. He had offered to drive her home and then back to the office once their work was completed. She hadn't argued. Her legs were still a little shaky and he had parked at the kerb of the building in a clear 'no parking' zone. She hadn't wanted to take the time to walk to her car, not that she would be able to drive once she got there. She also didn't want to be left alone even for the short drive home. She wasn't used to feeling so dependent on another person but she felt if she was to lean on anyone, Matt was the man who could easily take the load.

After a few minutes of watching the forensic team move about her property, Matt made his way towards her. She got out of the car and leaned against the closed door. She raised an enquiring eyebrow at him when he was close.

"Good news. No forced entry and all the doors and windows are secure. No one entered your house."

Natalie nodded. That was good news. She didn't like to think the creep had entered her house and looked through God knows what, touching whatever he desired. She didn't think she could deal with that degree of violation.

"And the footprint?" she asked, somewhat relieved.

Matt shook his head. "There's no footprint. It seems last night's rain worked in his favour."

He took Natalie's arm and led her to her front door, relieving her of her keys. He unlocked the door and allowed her to precede him into the house.

"What about the fingerprints? The face print?" she asked.

Matt made his way into her kitchen and started preparing the coffee maker as if he did it all the time, measuring out the coffee beans and hitting the right buttons.

Oh yes, he hit all the right buttons, she thought.

Once he was done prepping the coffee maker, he turned back around to face her. He leaned a hip against her counter. "Gone."

"Gone?"

"As in not there."

Anger bubbled up inside of her. Did he really believe she had just made all this up? That she had nothing better to do with her time than to create this elaborate story to get him and his forensic team down here to cover her windows with fingerprint dust? She was not that pathetic, thank you very much. So last night got away from her. Sure, she had been tired, scared from reading the horrific accounts of the Butcher's victims but she didn't make up the story of the face at her window and she didn't dream or hallucinate the evidence.

She crossed her hands under her breasts and once again glared at him. "I didn't make this up, *Detective*. I'm not a crazy loon out for attention." She advanced on him. "Furthermore, I find this incredibly insulting that you and all your little friends out there would think that about me—a trained professional no less."

She held up her hand signalling that she was not done. "I have a good mind to resist helping you any further in your case, Detective Murphy. You obviously have no regard for my talents at all." She covered his mouth with her hand when he looked as if he was about to speak. "But I'm not going to do that. You need help and I'm going to give it to you. I'll prove to you that I can do the job you assigned me whether you want me to or not!"

She took a deep breath. She felt remarkably better now that she'd gotten that out in the open. She looked at him, waiting for a response. "Well?" she asked, after it became clear he wasn't going to speak.

Matt raised his hand and removed her own from his mouth. She then realised she hadn't let it drop after she was done with her tirade. She blushed, her face hot. The coffee maker beeped loudly, signalling it was finished and Matt turned around and busied himself pouring the black liquid into the mugs he found hanging from a cupboard.

"Sugar, milk?" he asked, his tone conveying no emotion, his face showing none of his thoughts.

"Yes, please," she squeaked, her mouth dry. She tried to swallow but it didn't help. Natalie couldn't believe she went off like that. Of all her years keeping her cool, this one cop made her lose it so quickly—and so embarrassingly at that.

Matt nodded and added sugar and milk into each mug before handing her one. She lightly blew over the hot drink before taking a tentative sip. She met his eyes over the rim of her cup and saw laughter there. Natalie resisted the urge to hit him. How dare he laugh at her! She narrowed her eyes and contemplated throwing the coffee into his face. As if reading her mind, Matt stepped back a few paces.

"What I was going to say before your little outburst back there was, it looks as if your midnight prowler revisited you last night and removed the evidence. Forensics found some smears and a few cotton fibres on the glass."

"Oh."

Matt raised an eyebrow. "Oh? That's all you have to say. Just a minute ago I couldn't shut you up and now all you have for me is one word—oh?" he asked mockingly.

Any minute now, the blush on her face was going to burn her up and she would be a blissful pile of ash. *Yes*, she thought, *any moment now*.

"I might've said a few words, a sentence really."

"More like a paragraph, or two," he added under his breath.

"I don't do well sleep deprived and sleeping in one's office chair isn't really conducive for a good night's sleep."

He nodded as if all this made sense. "I don't believe you're crazy. Nor do I believe you made any of it up. I know you saw what you saw. You're a pretty unflappable person." He grinned at her and the dimple in his cheek appeared. "Unless of course you didn't get a good night's sleep."

"Right," she said, indignant.

"Also, I have the upmost confidence in your professional capacity."

She placed her hands on her hips. "Now you're just being a jerk."

"Just thought I'd lay everything out on the table for you," he replied.

"You could have stopped me."

Exasperated, he said, "I tried."

She threw her arms up in the air, spilling coffee. "Next time try harder."

She put down her coffee mug and stormed to the base of the stairs. At the sound of his voice she stopped and turned around to face him.

"Is there going to be a next time?" he asked.

God, I hope not, she thought. Although it had been quite fun looking back on it. She flashed him a smile. Best to tell the truth.

"More than likely," she replied and turned and ran up the stairs leaving Matt shaking his head, a huge grin on his face.

God help her, she was looking forward to it.

Chapter 21

Lara Russell looked up as the elevator binged indicating that a patient had arrived. The man wasn't dressed in Ralph Lauren. So many of them weren't. She had taken the job as a receptionist at the shrink's office in hopes of snagging a rich husband, but so far no takers. She had assumed that all Doctor Miller's patients would have some money. She had seen the invoices the accountant had left on her desk to post out and *wow!* But not one of the many men walking through the office had anything she was looking for. She wasn't picky. Young, old, handsome, ugly—who cared? It was the money that was important.

Some would say it was risky using the shrink's office as a possible dating pool, but she had it all worked out. When a suitable candidate came along, she would use the emergency key to Doctor Miller's office to go through her files, just to make sure he wasn't a psycho or anything. A girl had be sure.

But after six months at the low paying job she hadn't met anyone even close to what she considered a match. First there was the fact that most of the patients were women. If she thought she could get any money out of the hags that came through the door, she could gladly swing that way for a while but no, they wouldn't do at all.

Second, there were the little trust fund shits that found their way into the office. They would be perfect except she would have to wait a few years until she could get at their money and thirdly, all the men that came here were completely unsuitable. She had tried to flirt with them but they were either married and didn't have the balls to have a mistress, or they were gay. A complete let down. How was she supposed to get out of this nine to five hell if the Doc didn't start bringing in some fresh meat?

The man stood at the other side of the reception desk. His wrinkled shirt was untucked from his jeans and he looked about sixty. He smelled like sweat—not just any kind of sweat, nervous sweat. She smelled it all the time. Some people were just downright paranoid about seeing a psychologist.

She flashed him her five thousand dollar smile that one of her many previous boyfriends had paid for. The man's tension did not ease up. He ran his hand over his five o'clock shadow.

"Hello. How can I help you?" she asked, playing on her bubbly voice. People always underestimated a bubbly person and if that person happened to have blonde hair like she did, no one took stock of her. Unless of course they were checking her out.

The man cleared his throat. She caught the waft of toothpaste as he spoke and wondered if he'd swallowed the whole tube. She resisted the urge to step back. She had found that many patients went psycho if she made any sudden movements.

"I'm here to see Natalie Miller," the man said, his voice like gravel.

No shit, she thought. That was why he was in her office, after all. The door outside did read:

Doctor Natalie Miller BA (Hons) MPsych PhD MAPS.

Lara had no idea what it all meant and couldn't care less. Her smile remained plastered to her face as she thought the unkind words. Since she had started in the office she had trained her face to show no emotion except friendly. She always believed you caught more flies with honey than you did vinegar. Her hands stayed in sight, her fingers twitching to smooth out the creases on her face. If she kept this up she would need a plastic surgeon before she was thirty.

"I'm sorry. Doctor Miller isn't in the office right now. Do you want to leave a message?"

The man shook his head, turned around and stalked back to the elevator. She watched as he got into the next available carriage and the doors closed on his face.

Good riddance, she thought. *What a freak!*

Doctor Miller sure saw some wackos. Maybe she'd better revise her game plan.

She barely got that thought out when she saw Doctor Miller open the door that led to the staircase. Lara didn't mind Natalie. She was all right for a woman—at least for a brunette. She never looked down on her because she was just a receptionist like other people had. Sometimes she dreamed of having a practice just like Natalie's, to be in a position to command respect for once instead of at the bottom. She smiled brightly as Natalie drew near. Even from the small distance, Lara could see the dark bags under her eyes and she imagined a blackboard with 'be like Natalie Miller' written on it and then along came a piece of chalk drawing a line straight through it.

Natalie returned her smile. "Morning, Lara, any messages?"

Lara shook her head, her blonde curls floating around her face like a halo. She spent good money on hair products and clothes and makeup. Which was why she needed another sugar daddy. She was burning cash quicker than she could earn it.

"No, but a man was just here looking for you. He's gone now," she added when Natalie looked about the waiting room.

Natalie frowned. "A man? Did he leave a name or number?"

Again, Lara shook her head. "No. He didn't say anything. He just walked off."

"What'd he look like?"

"Tall, edgy. A little scruffy looking and rude," Lara added as an afterthought.

Natalie sighed. "Unfortunately, you have just described every guy I know. Thanks anyway."

***

Natalie stopped inside her office and closed the

door. She slumped against the wood. *A man*, she thought. Could it have been the same man who was at her home last night? She shook her head. There was no way of knowing since the waiting room didn't have video surveillance. Although, now that she thought about it, that was a brilliant idea and she made plans to call a security company later in the day.

She headed straight for her coffee maker. She was going to need every bean in Columbia if she was going to make it through to the afternoon.

Chapter 22

No matter what she did throughout the day, Natalie couldn't stop thinking about her late night visitor and the unknown man who came to her office the other morning. Was there a connection between the two? Were they the same person?

Matt had called the day before arranging a time she and a sketch artist could sit down and go through what she could remember of the face at her window. She wasn't particularly looking forward to the task. Every time she closed her eyes she saw his. She couldn't seem to remember much more about him except for those cold, dark eyes. Even though she had sketched a picture herself, Matt thought the artist could help her remember more details since they were trained to ask specific questions, and could even suggest some different types of looks. Matt even asked her not to review the Butcher files. He wanted a clean sketch, not wanting her to be influenced by any outside source.

She leaned back in her chair. Could they really find the man who killed Hallie's parents? It had been five years after all, half a decade, and still no one had any clue who he was. No one had ever seen him, or at least as the Butcher except for Hallie. Then there was also the small possibility that she too had seen him. The police believed him to be still in the area, that he had unfinished business and that could only be Hallie. If that was true then, the Butcher could be keeping tabs on her, waiting for the opportune time to get to Hallie. And since she was her doctor it was entirely possible she had caught his eye, and she knew what happened to people who sparked interest in him.

She couldn't stop the shiver that went through her. She would have to be careful and watch for anyone suspicious and never allow herself to be caught alone. One thing was for sure, she couldn't allow him to win, for Hallie's sake. Natalie didn't want anything to happen to the girl she'd come to care so much about.

Why had the Butcher attacked the Walkers? It was a question that had nagged at her until she thought she would scream. But then, why had he killed all those other women as well? What made them special? Did they, in some way unbeknownst to her, resemble someone important to him? Did they remind him of someone he had loved or hated? Had he just seen them and desired them or was the whole thing completely random?

That last thought was what truly scared Natalie. Sometimes you just don't know. She could deal with rhyme or reason but complete serendipity took too much control from her. She didn't like to think of chance or luck. Life was what you made it and it just plain sucked when you didn't get what you wanted out of it. For your life to be prematurely ended—well, that just bought the big one.

Natalie thought about Hallie and not for the first time wondered how different her life could've turned out under normal circumstances. She removed Hallie's file from her drawer once more and opened it. Something ate away at her that she couldn't put her finger on. Like so much of this case, it seemed to her that the answer was right in front of them if only they looked. But she along with the detectives of Harbour Bay had searched and hadn't yet found it.

She flicked through the pages, skimming the words. She had read the file enough times to know what was on each page and knew what was useful and what wasn't, which unfortunately for her, the latter outweighed the former. She reached the end and glanced at Hallie's drawings. Sometimes she forgot that Hallie was still a child. She acted so grown up all the time it was a fact easy to overlook.

She moved the drawing to look at the picture of Helen Teller's grave and frowned. Why did her brain always come back to Helen Teller? What was it trying to tell her? Of all the things that didn't make sense the picture was right on top of the list. What had possessed Hallie to draw the grave? On her own admission, she herself didn't know why. Where had she got the image? Was it locked up somewhere inside her brain, buried deep down? If so, why was it so important? What did the grave represent? Was it just Hallie's way of dealing with her parents' deaths? Of her own incarceration and fear? Questions whirled around inside her head, almost making her crack under the pressure.

Natalie sat up straighter. She could feel a headache coming on. She woke her computer up from its hibernation and waited impatiently for the webpage to load. Her fingers began skimming across the keyboard as she typed Helen Teller's name into *Google* and was immediately rewarded with three thousand results. Natalie scrolled down through the list of websites containing the words 'Helen Teller' until she found the one she was looking for. It was the online edition of the *Harbour Bay Herald*, one of the local newspapers that had been in circulation since the beginning of the last century.

She moved her mouse and clicked on the webpage and found herself looking at the newspapers archives from 1992. Helen Teller had been the Business Woman of the Year, an annual competition held for Australia's most respected and prominent business women.

"Holy hell, she does exist," Natalie murmured as she scanned the article. Helen Teller had been thirty-three and an executive at a computer firm that had revolutionised the way offices around the country worked. She was described as being very intellectual and had a head for business which had earned her company three million dollars. *Quite the accomplishment for a woman in the nineties*, Natalie thought. *More power to you.*

She reached the bottom of the article and noticed the link to another article within the newspapers archives. She clicked on the link and was brought to

1995 and the front page of the *Herald*. Helen Teller's name was the headline.

Natalie quickly skimmed the article, her blood pumping faster in her body as her heart pounded in her chest. Her head practically screamed at her like some sort of radiation detecting device that beeped louder and faster as it got closer to the source. She knew she was on the right track.

Helen Teller had been murdered, her killer never found. She had been found by her teenage son at her home in Sydney's Western Suburbs and stabbed repeatedly, her throat slit—the trademark of the Butcher. Her service had been a quiet affair closed to the public. Her son had been reported to have placed a white rose on her coffin before sobbing uncontrollably. She couldn't help but feel the child's pain and wondered what had happened to him. His name was not in the article, probably to protect his privacy, but Natalie doubted if he had grown up unscathed and felt the anger bubbling up inside her.

So many lives had been ruined by just one man. How had he managed for so long without detection? Right now she didn't care who he was or what his reason for killing was, she just wanted to find him and put him in the ground herself. She could do it, too, without remorse. This monster certainly felt none, so why should she give it?

She clicked on the photo attachment at the bottom of the webpage and her breath caught in her throat. She sat there as the minutes clicked by staring at the photo of Helen Teller's grave. She would recognise that unusual gravestone anywhere.

She enlarged the photo to read the inscription:

Here lies the body of Helen Teller.

"Oh my God," she whispered. She could feel the chill in the air and shivered. A thought popped into her mind and she shook her head at the irony. She felt like someone had just walked over her grave.

Chapter 23

Matt flipped through the photos on his desk, each one a shot of the victims. He had hit a brick wall and he knew it. He had Donovan going over any connections that the victims might have shared once more, combing through financial records, credit card receipts, and society columns. They'd been down this road before, but sometimes when cops got tired they overlooked things. Better to have fresh eyes and a new perspective. They had to know how the bastard chose his victims. It couldn't merely be chance and Matt was tired of calling the bastard the Butcher. He wanted the man's real name.

He heard muffled talking and looked across the *Pig Pen*—the nickname for Harbour Bay's second floor work area which housed the Detective Unit. He spotted Amelia Donovan flanked by the two burly men in his team. At six-foot-four and six-foot-three, Dean and Nick both dwarfed her. Dean was wearing one of his trademark light coloured shirts. He favoured pastels after an old girlfriend had bought him a peach shirt as a gift, and to spare her feelings wore it to work one day, putting up with the constant jokes and ribbing he got from his fellow workmates and in particular, his partner, Nick. Ever since then, he had worn the light shirts to prove he was man enough to wear what was considered feminine attire and still get the job done. Dean had been on the force for ten years and his face showed the wear and tear of the job. His honey-blond hair looked like it hadn't been combed for a while let alone cut, long enough to curl around his shirt collar. His chocolate coloured eyes were always serious.

Nick, on the other hand, was easy going, always one to joke in the face of a bad situation. It was how he dealt and he was so good-looking he was never without female company, though he never played the field and wasn't one to favour one night stands or count the number of women he'd slept with. He was the second youngest member of the team and had a good mind for the job.

They were a tight group, a makeshift family. They all took care of each other and watched each other's backs. None of them were in it for the glory. Only the knowledge of a case closed and a job well done was their reward. To get the bad guys and lock them away for the rest of their pitiful lives. Which was why they made such a good unit.

Dean leaned down towards Amelia and said something to her but Matt was too far away to hear. She smiled at him before slapping him with the file folder she held in her hand as they all headed towards Matt.

"So I hear you've taken me up on my suggestion in regards to the psychologist," Nick Doyle said, his dark eyebrows wiggling suggestively.

He knew his and Natalie's visit to Tanner's would eventually make it to his team but he hadn't expected it to be so fast. *Must have been Glory*, he thought. She had a thing for Nick and was always trying to put the moves on him. Unfortunately for Glory, Nick considered her much too young for him.

"Yeah, I bet she can't wait to examine your head." Dean smirked.

Matt rolled his eyes. "Things must be slow for you to be coming up to the big boys' area to bug me. We're trying to stop a serial killer here if you haven't noticed."

"So...tell me," Nick said as if Matt hadn't spoken. "What exactly does she look like?"

"Oh, about five-foot-six. Brunette hair. Cobalt blue eyes. Killer body," Amelia said, looking past them.

"Nice," Nick added.

"I'd have to agree," Dean said as his gaze followed Amelia's.

Matt frowned at her. "How the hell do you know all that, Donovan?"

Dean cleared his throat and Amelia swung back around to face Matt.

"Lucky guess, Einstein," she said, rolling her eyes as she moved away from his desk. The party quickly dispersed and Matt found himself looking at the gorgeous woman in stiletto heels fast approaching his desk. He gave her a once over—the first time with sexual interest, the second time as a police detective.

Natalie was pale and looked spooked. He stood as she reached his desk. She gave Dean and Nick a fleeting glance as they moved away.

"Did I interrupt something?"

Matt saw his colleagues puckering their lips and miming kissing in his peripheral vision. He was going to kill them. He really was. If Natalie hadn't been there, he probably would've shot them.

"No. Have you come to meet the sketch artist?" She shook her head. He sighed heavily, realising his day just got longer. "Am I going to like this?"

Natalie frowned, her brow wrinkling. "Probably not," she admitted.

Matt gave her a steady look. She certainly wasn't one to tell a comforting lie, was she? He took her arm and led her to the small kitchen area. A tiny circular table and four chairs shoved into a corner took up most of the area. A large corkboard was attached to the wall and held flyers on upcoming conferences that may interest the officers. Beside the counter was an old fridge and next to the coffee pot sat a newly procured microwave—the last one having blown up a few months ago. It had been bound to happen. It had been taken off the ships with the convicts.

"Before we get into this, I'm going to need some more coffee. Want one?"

She nodded before replying. "Yes, please."

He took a look at the sludge now congealed at the bottom of the carafe. His stomach revolted at the thought of the tar like substance and immediately emptied the contents down the sink and rinsed the pot thoroughly.

As he completed the task of setting up the coffee maker to create another batch he took another look at Natalie, his brain registering the strain around her mouth and the bloodshot eyes.

"You don't look so good. Did you sleep?"

"Yes."

He raised a dark eyebrow. She did not look well-rested. "Did you go home?"

She gave a long suffering sigh. Obviously whatever she had come to discuss was not her sleeping habits. "I'm too afraid to go home," she admitted. "And yes, I know I said I wasn't going to let the fear run my life but my body just isn't listening. Anyway, that's not why I'm here."

Matt listened patiently, waiting for her to get to the heart of the problem. "So why are you here, if not to see the sketch artist?"

"What do you know about Helen Teller?"

Matt ran through his brain, much like a computer program scanning its files as it searched for anything that contained the key words. He was satisfied when the information flowed to the forefront of his mind. "Helen Teller? She was the Butcher's first victim…as far as we know." He tacked on the last bit as he corrected himself.

She pinned him with a glare and he had to fight to stand still and not squirm. She would have made a very good interrogation officer. Pity the man who ever came home with lipstick on his collar. He wondered if she would take offence if he asked her what her secret was.

She crossed her arms under her breasts. "You failed to mention that fact when you handed me this case."

Matt fought to keep up. "I didn't see the relevance."

Natalie's eyebrows rose. "Really? Do you remember the picture of the grave Hallie drew?" When she saw him nod, she continued. "The grave was Helen Teller's."

Matt's eyes widened. His stance became very still as he absorbed that fact. "What?"

She took a deep breath, obviously preparing herself for a reiteration of text book proportions. "I was going through Hallie's file earlier, when I saw the drawing she'd done years ago. For some reason it pulled at me and I went on the Internet and looked Helen up. I wasn't even expecting anything to pop up. Imagine my surprise when something did. The article was on her murder and along with it was this photo of her grave."

Natalie handed him the printout. He glanced down at it, frowning. He looked back at Natalie who raised her hand, her index finger pointing up to the sky indicating that she wasn't done. She then retrieved another piece of paper from her purse, smoothing it out before handing it to him. When he caught sight of Hallie's drawing, he was sure his heart stopped beating. Excitement rushed through his veins. They were identical. A thought occurred to him. "Well, maybe Hallie was on the Inter—"

"No, I checked, Hallie is not allowed on the Internet."

Which would probably kill a normal teenage girl.

She was lucky she didn't know what she was missing. No Internet ultimately meant no social networking, no chat rooms or shopping online. Hallie probably wasn't even allowed phone privileges, not that the poor kid had anyone to call. They certainly kept things on a tight leash at Paradise Valley.

He shrugged, trying for nonchalance even when his body was now as tight as bow. "Maybe it is just a coincidence."

"When does coincidence turn into something else? Hallie once knew Helen Teller. How, she doesn't know or can't remember. But there's a link that you haven't found. Something you're missing."

She stepped past him and pulled two mugs from the drainer by the sink and began finishing the coffees. He noted that she put sugar and milk in both and he felt pleased that she'd remembered the way he drank his.

"Tell me everything, and I mean everything you know about the case, Matt. Maybe I can help. I want to help. Remember I have a vested interest in the end result."

Natalie handed him his coffee. He thanked her as he looked into her eyes. He could see she meant business and he would be stupid not to use her expertise. She saw deranged and sick minds every day. She knew what made them tick or at least had the training to understand the way they worked. He was right when he thought he needed new blood on the case and Natalie might just be the ticket.

He nodded slowly. "Okay."

Chapter 24

Matt's house was only a couple years old. The dark red brick one-storey was in an old well-established neighbourhood. The previous owner had knocked down and rebuilt the two bedroom, two bath house with double garage, adding the modern amenities that people nowadays couldn't do without and a low maintenance garden which with Matt's job appealed to him the most. The interior was open-planned; his kitchen, dining, and lounge were all one large room. His bedrooms, laundry, and bathrooms were down the hall towards the enclosed backyard. The walls were painted vivid red-orange, a stark contrast to his deep steel-blue carpet. His furniture was durable rather than fancy and only matched since he'd purchased a set. His philosophy was as long as it was comfortable it was fine. He wasn't about to spend his life savings on something frivolous and honestly didn't give a stuff about décor.

As a man who was used to living alone, his house wasn't up for inspection and Matt was thankful he'd run out of clean clothes that morning and had been required to pick up his discarded clothes from the floor and run them through the wash. Now, only a few empty beer cans sat on his kitchen counter, a stack of unopened mail beside them.

He wasn't a messy person nor was he a clean and obsessive person. His house was for living in and usually he didn't care about a light coating of dust or a few plates in the sink but Matt didn't want Natalie to think he was a slob. He'd seen more than one delicate nose get out of joint at his lack of housekeeping skills but for the first time he wanted to make a good impression.

Matt gave his house a cursory look, making sure he hadn't missed a sock or brief anywhere. He tried to keep things neat but sometimes the cleaning got away from him on cases such as this when he only ever came home to crash or when he ran out of clean shirts at the office. Now he was practically holding his breath waiting for her approval—or disapproval, whichever the case may be.

The smell of Chinese food wafted up from the plastic bag in his hand and made his stomach growl. After deciding that maybe Natalie could help with the case, Matt had dropped into the Shanghai Garden, his favourite takeaway, and picked up his usual order of beef and black beans with mixed rice and honey chicken and prawn crackers for Natalie.

He grabbed a couple of clean plates from the cupboard and showed her to the sofa. After sitting down on his living room floor, Natalie had taken charge of dishing out dinner and Matt had never felt better. There was something about Natalie that made him think about rainy days and cuddling up in front of a fire. Matt felt he could be himself around her and began to relax. He didn't think that she would mind his many little quirks. He liked the fact that Natalie didn't appear to be concerned when he made a fool of himself, which around her was a common occurrence.

He knew his boss would chew his arse out if he knew Matt was sharing pertinent case information with Natalie, but he was past caring. All he was interested in was solving the case. He didn't care if he had to cut deals with half the criminals in the city to do it. It was past time that the Butcher was put away.

Hours later, the empty Chinese takeaway containers littered the floor of Matt's lounge room. The sun had gone down and they were no closer to finding the Butcher than when they had first started. Both Matt and Natalie had decided to start from the beginning—to look at each case individually and from a fresh perspective.

So far, he had reviewed the same information he already knew, nothing new jumped out at him and he felt frustrated and useless. Of all his training and experience he simply couldn't find what wasn't there. He couldn't see whatever linked the victims, and the bodies were stacking up. He ran his fingers through his hair and looked over at Natalie.

She sat with her back up against his black leather sofa, opting to remain on the floor to make it easier to review the mass quantity of files. Her knees were up, providing a stand for the folder open in front of her, resting on her thighs as her eyes remained glued to the paper. She had already reviewed several files and they were neatly stacked to one side of her. The ones she hadn't perused were on the other. That was one of the many things he had discovered about Natalie that he admired. She was dedicated and he knew she would see this thing through until the bitter end, which he had no doubt it would be.

Matt watched as her lips moved but he couldn't hear anything. Her concentration was entirely on the case in front of her and he wondered if she even realised she was doing it. He doubted she was even aware he was in the room with her let alone anything else.

He caught the frown that creased her brow as her finger glided over the paper. Her head shook from side to side as she evidently tried to make sense of something. She opened one of the files she had already read and shuffled through the pages until she found the one she wanted and her finger slid down the page.

His entire body tensed as he felt something in the air. Her excitement was almost palpable. His gaze locked on Natalie and once again he saw her lips move only this time he heard her mumble.

"Promising law student." The frown deepened and she looked at the other file open in front of her. "Awarded biologist." Her voice was louder this time and she looked up at him, surprise on her face when she found him watching her intently. "Maybe these women have more in common than you think."

Matt raised an eyebrow at her statement and patiently waited for her to explain. If she had discovered something he had missed, he was more than eager to be enlightened. He watched as Natalie's head bowed and her attention drifted back to the file, her entire being absorbed into it. When she didn't look like she was going to elaborate, he spoke.

"How?" Matt asked.

Her head jerked up and she gave him a sheepish smile.

"Sorry, didn't mean to leave you in the dark. I believe their connection is their jobs," she said, as she tapped one of the folders.

"I don't see it. None of them were in the same field," he stated.

Natalie leaned forward. "True, but what I mean is that they each had a successful job—a career," she explained as her face turned thoughtful.

Matt could practically hear the gears turning in her head. She was on to something, he could feel it. She was radiating so much excitement he thought she could power a small country. He knew she didn't quite know just what yet, but it was there at the forefront of her brain and was pushing itself into the light.

He didn't know why he felt so confident about Natalie's ability but he knew he hadn't lied the other day when he'd told her he had the upmost respect for her ability as a psychologist. She had a talent and it was going to work for them.

"What're you thinking?" he asked after a long silence.

Her eyes had narrowed as she thought and her head tilted to one side. Deep blue eyes met his. "I'm thinking he's after career driven women. Look at each of the files. Marie Stanton was a medical graduate. Karen Filcher a biologist. Laurel Millard a lawyer and Helen Teller received 'Woman of the Year' because of her computer programming. There's not one menial job holder in the bunch."

Matt went through his files and watched as a pattern began to emerge. He was amazed that none of the detectives—including him—had discovered it before.

"I'll be damned."

Matt shook his head. So much for being a hotshot detective. Over fifteen years on the job and it takes this woman a few hours to find a link. Of course it was an obscure link. He looked into Natalie's eyes. "I never saw that before."

"We still don't know if I'm right," she soothed.

"What else could it be? We've been beating at a brick wall for so long. This is the first time we've come close to even figuring out this guy's motive."

Natalie frowned and looked uncertain. "I don't understand. Why would he target women because of their chosen profession?"

Matt shrugged. "I don't know. I'm not him but maybe he lost his job to a successful woman or a woman divorced him for a job. You tell me. There could be a hundred or so reasons. None of which we would ever understand."

Men had killed for a lot less, he knew that for a fact, but still a pattern was emerging and that pattern would tell them more about the Butcher than anything else. Once they knew what made him tick they would have a profile and once that got out maybe they could find this son-of-a-bitch.

"Has anything come up in the search of Helen?"

He shook his head. "Not yet. I have Donovan specifically cross-referencing her name with the Walkers." He paused. "What about Ian and Missy Walker? Where do you think they fit into all this? He wasn't a successful woman and she was a stay at home mum," he wondered aloud.

Natalie stretched out her back as she shifted position on the floor and stared at the pile of folders beside her feet.

"Suppose Ian or Missy saw something they shouldn't have? Something like Helen Teller's murder. Hallie said she thought Helen could've been a friend of her parents."

Matt digested that. "But if that was the case, why didn't they report it? The Walkers were law abiding people. I don't see Ian Walker as one to let a murderer go free."

"Unless he was protecting his family. Some men will go to great lengths to keep their women and children safe. Missy might've felt the same."

"That," Matt said, "is a possibility." One he would certainly investigate further.

Natalie stared at a spot behind his shoulder.

"The only thing that makes sense to me is that the murders were personal. Someone who knew Senator Walker didn't like to fly and would be driving home from Melbourne. He could've followed the family and pulled ahead when they stopped for fuel."

Natalie lifted a copy of the Walker family photo from the file. He thought she was thinking about the two people who had lost their lives and the one that got away.

"Hallie looks a lot like Ian, doesn't she? It must be hard for her to look in the mirror every day and see her father's face."

Matt looked over at the photo she held. "She's strong."

"Yes, she is. I've never met anyone like her before. She's a real survivor."

He glanced over at Natalie and he wondered at the type of woman she was. A strong minded one, he thought, and tough as nails. Hadn't she already proved that? She had been terrified and yet hadn't let it incapacitate her. She had fought back. Matt liked that about her. He liked everything about her.

Natalie was no timid wallflower. She knew what lurked in the darkness and understood human nature better than anyone. She would understand the demands of his job and why it was so important for him to continue on even when he was ready to pack it in. He saw the most horrific things day in and day out. Seeing human depravity and what the human race did to its own kind was sickening. If he let her, she would be there to balance the bad with the good.

Natalie leaned past him, interrupting his thoughts and the dangerous path they were heading and pulled forward one of the five cardboard boxes Matt had signed out of evidence earlier before leaving the station. She removed the lid and peered into the box marked *The Butcher, 2007-2010*.

The thirty by forty centimetre archive boxes contained the LAC's hard-copy files. If they couldn't find it in here, it didn't exist or hadn't yet been investigated. Matt moved to sit beside her and together they went methodically through the evidence until each box was empty.

Seventeen years' worth of unsolved cases covered the floor. Statements, autopsy reports, timelines, coloured photos—crime scene and general—filled each manila folder along with a catalogue of any evidence they'd found. A bloody scuff mark, a lone button, jewellery on the body. Each had been photographed and a report written about the location of the evidence in the scene.

Natalie had been right. Each victim had been successful. Proving themselves in what was in effect a man's world, many of them occupying the top of watch lists when they were alive.

His palms became sweaty. He looked over at Natalie. Her head was once again buried in a file, her hand gliding over the notepad beside her as she jotted down her thoughts. Her hair tumbled over her shoulders as she leaned down. Her long dark eyelashes fluttered against her skin as she blinked.

She was so beautiful. The type all men wanted to covet and protect and he wasn't immune to that way of thinking either. It was in a man's genes to protect women going back to the caveman era and they certainly hadn't evolved as much as scientists liked to think. The need to lock her away where no one could touch or hurt her was growing stronger by the minute.

"You know, you should be extra careful. You fit

his profile too."

Natalie sat up and frowned as she tucked her hair behind her ears.

"My midnight visitor could've been anyone," she said slowly. "But I'll still be careful."

He imagined her as she had been the other night. At how scared she had been. Matt nodded. "Good."

He made a mental note to arrange to have a vehicle drive by her house and office every hour just in case. He didn't like the fact she had a late night visitor and with the profile they were uncovering it seemed more and more likely the Butcher might try and attack her and Matt wasn't about to allow that. He had failed all the others since he had been unable to catch the man but he wasn't about to let the Butcher anywhere near Natalie. The last thing he wanted was to find Natalie's body on Doctor Stone's autopsy table. He would do just about anything to prevent that. The thought of being unable to save her scared Matt to death.

He watched as Natalie pulled out Helen Teller's file and flicked through it. The folder wasn't as big as the others. The unsolved crime had little evidence to begin with and the trail, like all the others, had gone cold. He caught glimpses of the information printed on the paper as Natalie skimmed the sheets. He recognised the detailed statement from the officer first on the scene. He had read it enough times that he probably could've recited the whole thing.

Next up was the autopsy report identical to the others except for the sloppiness of his first kill.

Even the detective working the case back in 1995 knew the killer was only starting out and wasn't about to finish any time soon. He had even mentioned that fact in his reports but unfortunately for him, he had died before he found his man. Matt however wasn't about to leave this case unfinished. He'd solve it from the grave if he had to. He only hoped it wasn't necessary.

Natalie came to the end of the folder and her face contorted with horror as she took in the crime scene photos. Matt knew what she was thinking and feeling. He had felt exactly the same way when he had first viewed the crime scene photos. The murder had been particularly brutal. For someone the media had dubbed the Butcher that was saying something. He heard Natalie's sharp intake of breath and the corresponding mutterings of revulsion before she pushed aside every photo but one and handed it to him.

Through the grainy pixels he could make out a child's birthday party. The child was a boy of twelve and standing next to the boy was a tall man. Matt squinted, the features of the man looking vaguely familiar. He pushed the photo in front of Natalie's face and pointed to the man.

"Does he look familiar to you?" he asked.

She took the photo from him and moved it back several inches from her face, her gaze zeroing in on the man. He watched as her face changed as recognition set in.

"Ian Walker," she answered. "A very young Ian Walker. I'd say mid to late twenties. Most certainly before his political career, definitely before Missy.

If he'd been stupid enough to cheat on her we would've heard about it by now."

That was true. If there was one good thing about the media, it was that the secrets they needed to know had already been printed and in the age of the internet, nothing was sacred anymore.

"You were right. There's a connection between Ian and Helen. They were lovers."

"You don't know that. They could be close friends," Natalie said.

He gave her a look. Natalie ignored him as she flipped the photo over and read the scrawl on the back:

Harry's twelfth birthday, 1994.

Matt took the picture from her and studied it thoughtfully.

"The son found her. He was only a teenager at the time. I wonder what happened to him. Looks like a nice kid."

"I'd be surprised if he wasn't locked away in a hospital. Finding that particular carnage at the place you assume you're safe would damage anyone's state of mind."

Matt nodded. "Could be useful to speak with him. There's little on the Teller murder, just a brief statement of events leading up to the discovery of the body."

He pulled his mobile out from where it was attached to his belt and dialled a number. He looked back at her as he waited for the person on the other end to answer.

"Do you think you could talk to him—if he's lucid, that is? See what he remembers like you did with Hallie?" he asked her.

"Of course but every person is different, it all depends on his mental capabilities and—"

Matt spoke into the phone, interrupting her.

"Yeah, Donovan, it's Murphy. Do me a favour." He asked her to locate Helen's son and then explained what he hoped Natalie could accomplish with a sit down. "Donovan will find him," he told her as he joined her on the floor after hanging up with Amelia. "The cops on scene barely talked to him let alone interviewed the kid. From all reports he was pretty shaken up, unable to verbalise much."

"Do you think Helen's son knows who killed her? Think maybe that's why he's not talking?" she asked.

"Why not? Hallie refused help because she was so terrified of the man. Fear can make people crazy," he said. "All I know is that the Butcher knew Helen Teller more than he knew the others. She was special to him and she did something that set him off. As you saw, the rage was barely contained."

"History has always taught us, it's the ones closest to us that suffer. Helen Teller was the catalyst. She started all this. Whatever she did to piss this guy off opened something deep inside him and instead of finding closure at her death he found his calling."

Matt nodded curtly. "Right. But we checked over and over. Double, even triple checked all our information. The original Detective talked to everyone she was in contact with."

"Clearly not. There's no record he ever spoke with Ian. If he missed him he could easily have missed someone else. What happened to Harry's father?"

"Left when the kid was two, hasn't been seen since."

"So she was all he had?"

Matt stretched out his cramped legs. "Yep. Mother was an only child and no other relative ever came forward to claim him. Wish you never offered to help?" he asked when he saw her face.

Natalie shook her head. "No. Not when I know we can catch this guy. It may be long hours and hard work but it has its own rewards in the end."

"What made you decide to become a psychologist?"

Natalie's startled gaze jumped to his. He wondered at the reaction. Surely she had been asked the question before. For a long moment he thought she wasn't going to answer.

"My stepfather was a violent man, an abuser. I still have scars, emotionally and physically. He beat me," she revealed, her voice rough with emotion. "Actually, beat is the wrong adjective. He tortured me."

Matt was frozen. Of all the things he'd thought she was hiding about her past, domestic violence had not been one of them. He felt sick at the idea of someone beating her, hurting the little girl she had once been. The thought of no one there to protect a young Natalie made him so angry. He reached out to touch her before jerking back and staring down at his hand. How many times had his hand become a fist? He wasn't an overly violent man but he got angry on occasion and lashed out. He remembered all the times he'd been in a rage in her presence and felt the blood rush from his face.

"You look like you're going to faint or throw up," Natalie said with a small trace of humour in her voice. "That's not the reaction I was expecting."

"I was thinking of all the times I lost my temper around you. I'm so sorry, Natalie."

She moved closer and placed a hand on his arm. "You don't frighten me. In fact, I felt protected…safe in your presence. Even when that vein in your temple has throbbed in anger I've never been afraid. Don't ever think that."

He studied her face. "I'm glad. I never want to hurt you, Natalie. Never."

She shivered. "I know that. I've always known that. Don't be afraid to be yourself around me. I happen to like that person and you wouldn't be him if you're afraid of scaring me. I'm tougher than I look."

His jaw clenched. "What happened to the bastard?"

"My stepfather? I have no idea. I ran away when I was twelve. Came here to Harbour Bay where my aunt and uncle lived. They gave me a home filled with love."

"Are they still here?"

Her eyes filled with unshed tears. "No. They passed on a few years ago. To answer your earlier question it was because I wanted to be able to read someone so well that I saw the person they were

226

beneath the surface, the real them."

"To see into their souls?"

"In a way, yes. Psychology is known as the study of the soul. I had thought it was a way to protect myself. But I have had my fair share of misses. Derek, for instance."

"Yeah, he was a big mistake," he said lightly.

"It was during my first year in school that I fell in love with it and can't imagine doing anything else."

Matt touched her face softly. She looked into his eyes and he became breathless at the heat he saw. His stomach flipped and desire warmed his body. He glanced down at her lips, full and inviting and wondered what it would be like to press his own against hers, to taste her. The thought alone was driving him insane.

"It's obvious you were born for it. Why would you want anything else?"

He imagined taking off her clothes, touching her naked skin. Did she feel as good as she looked? He desperately wanted to know what it felt like to have her lay beneath him, to feel himself inside of her.

"I want you," she whispered.

Chapter 25

She watched his eyes widen as the whispered confession reached his ears. His hand stilled on her cheek. Natalie's heart began to pound in her chest in anticipation. She had never felt so nervous in her entire life than in the few seconds it took for Matt's lips to touch her own. The moment their lips joined, she felt an explosion of sensation. His tongue swept inside her mouth to glide across her own. She made a satisfied sound in her throat, grabbed the back of his neck and pulled him closer.

She was sure she had never felt anything like it. Sure, she hadn't had a lot of experience with kisses and sex. Her distrust made it difficult to share something so intimate with another person but still Natalie was sure even Matt was surprised. She had felt his body tense in shock momentarily. It hadn't lasted long, barely a second, but it had been telling.

From the moment she had met Matt he had changed her for the better. He stilled her fears. He made her feel strong and powerful. He made her want him and a relationship and all the little things in between that made life worth living. In her twenty-eight years she had never felt this fire inside her before and she was curious to see where tomorrow would lead.

It was a leap of faith, she realised. There were no promises being exchanged. No words of a future. There was only desire and need and that was enough for her. For now. She may regret her impulsiveness in the morning but tonight she wanted to live.

To feel.

Natalie felt raw from exposing her darkest and tightly held secret to him. But she had never felt better than she did now. Free. Vulnerable. Alive. Not once had she ever revealed her past to anyone but she hadn't wanted to keep the truth from him. In that one moment, she had made a connection with Matt. Deeper than the turbulent emotions she was already feeling.

Natalie felt better knowing she had shared that little part of her history with him. After all, it was what had shaped the woman today. A part that was more intimate than even the act she was about to partake in. She felt naked with him, the wall she usually put up torn down by her words—her actions. She knew she was safe with him. The trust she had in him was staggering.

She didn't question or second guess herself. She jumped with both feet.

Matt moved his lips from hers and trailed kisses down her throat, his tongue leaving the skin damp. Her lips felt deliciously swollen. She tilted her head back as Matt began the ascent back to her lips. Her nails dug into his shoulders, telling him silently that she wanted more. He sat up on his knees taking her with him, pulling her into his aroused body.

Would he be a gentle lover or a ravenous one?

Natalie gave a puff of delight before melting into his body. Her arms went around his neck and held tight, her breasts crushing into his chest. Boldly, surprised by her confidence and eagerness, Natalie let her hands slowly slide down his taut chest. She removed his shirt from his pants and placed her palms on his bare stomach, feeling the muscles beneath bunch in response. She smiled at the power she exerted over him.

"We really shouldn't be doing this," he murmured in her ear as she began to unbutton his shirt.

"A little late now," she stated. They had been leading up to this since that first day in her office over a week ago, and each moment they had spent together, the fuse had gotten shorter and was now igniting in the most delicious way. "Besides, I don't think anything short of the apocalypse could stop me."

Matt smiled, his green eyes burning. "Me either. I just thought it my duty to mention that fact."

She nodded. "Duly noted."

She pushed his shirt away from his body and it dropped to the floor. Her lips were then suddenly on his chest kissing every available stretch of skin she found. Natalie had never felt so wanton before, so desperate. She never used to believe those who said sex could be mindless but now she had to admit she'd been wrong. Latent hormones were fuelling the passion she felt bubbling inside and she was enjoying every moment of it.

Natalie scraped her nails down his chest, over the light dusting of hair to his navel and below. She reached his belt buckle and began undoing it. Matt stilled her hands, an amused look on his face.

She felt like she had known Matt for years instead of just over a week. It felt right. She wanted this. She needed this. Her body was tense and screaming for release. She had never been at its mercy before and desperately wanted to ease the tight tension that had overtaken her body.

"First something of yours has to go," he whispered as he tugged on the hem of her navy blouse. She dutifully raised her arms and he removed her shirt. His gaze went to her lacy red bra and he grinned.

"Not something I would have expected from you, Doctor Miller," he said, his finger tracing the edge of her bra.

Fire ignited and swept through her body. She kissed him again, hard and unbridled, her hands on his stubbled face. Matt ran his thumb over her left nipple, teasing it to a hard peak before moving on to the right one. Natalie reached down again to his belt buckle and yanked on it hard, and as if sensing her desperation it opened in her hands. She lowered his zipper and took him into her palm. He was impossibly hard, straining for release, and she heard Matt moan as she let her fingers trail down the length of him.

His hips instinctively jerked and she revelled in the knowledge that she gave him such pleasure.

Matt reached around her and undid the clasp to her bra before pitching it across the room. He took her breasts in his palms and lightly squeezed them. She moved closer to him, unable to stand being even a few inches away. She needed the contact of his skin against her own otherwise she was liable to go stark raving mad. She kissed his shoulder, his throat, anywhere she could get at him. He chuckled as he pushed her gently to the floor and covered her body with his. Matt's hand went to the zipper on her black dress pants and slowly removed both her pants and underwear at the same time. She squirmed beneath him, her hands gliding over his muscular back and down to his buttocks.

Her body vibrated with need. Why was he taking his time? She raised her hips, grinding herself into him, his shaft resting at her entrance. She let out a frustrated breath, the apex of her thighs throbbing relentlessly, aching for his entry.

"What are you waiting for?" she huffed.

"Impatient, are we?" he replied, humour in his voice.

She bit him on the shoulder with just enough pressure to elicit some pain.

"Yes," she ground out. She wanted him inside her now.

Matt reached into his back pocket and produced a foil wrapper and promptly rolled the condom onto himself. It was a good thing he still had control of his facilities. Protection had not even entered her mind and she realised just how far gone she was. She kissed him. Thanking him and urging him on at the same time.

Matt took hold of her hips and held her still as he made his way inside her, stretching her unaccustomed body. She forgot to breathe as he filled her so completely. She felt whole. As if she had always been waiting for him to come into her life. She wrapped her legs around his waist as he began to move within her. Natalie raised her hips to meet his thrusts and soon they were both catapulting into the unknown, screaming the other's name before collapsing into an exhausted heap on the floor.

Chapter 26

The door opened beneath his fingertips. He pocketed the spare key she kept under the small frog in her garden as he slipped inside her house. It was sleek, all chrome and glass. The furniture untouched and impractical, certainly not comfortable enough to sit on but it looked great in photos such as the *Woman's Weekly* spread. He heard footfalls to his right and stalked silently towards the bedroom.

She walked past him brushing her golden mane, her body clad in only a towel. He watched her for a moment. She had no idea how close to death she was. It was amusing. Soon, her face would be so full of fear, then pain. Then there would be nothing. Her back was to him as she discarded the towel and slid the silk nightgown over her Pilate-toned body. If he had been any other man the view would've enticed him, but sex held little interest to him. His appetite was for other activities. The Butcher took a step, reached out, and grabbed her. He placed a hand over her mouth quickly, blocking any screams

she might have let out.
    An hour later, she was dead.

Chapter 27

As the early morning sun shined through the slits in the venetian blinds of Matt's bedroom, Natalie woke. She stretched out in the big queen size bed. For the first time in a long while she was relaxed. She felt so different. Somehow better. It was a silly thought but nonetheless true. She had never once let her guard down like she had last night when she'd offered up her embarrassing and painful past.

Natalie knew logically she shouldn't be mortified of what had happened to her, that it was not her fault, nor did she have any control over it but she felt it all the same as did countless other abuse victims. Her own advice always fell flat and on deaf ears. She wondered what her patients would think of her hypocritical nature. She always lectured them on the best course of action but failed to practice what she preached.

Matt had responded as she instinctively knew he would and later took her to a place she had never before visited, not once but countless times during the night. She could feel the lingering affects the vigorous activities had on her body now as she tried to move.

Natalie scooted over to the edge of the bed and wrapped a steel blue sheet around herself. Matt had left the bed no more than twenty minutes ago and she had heard him in the shower down the hall before she'd fallen back asleep. Now she could smell bacon and coffee wafting towards her from the direction of the kitchen.

Before long she found herself in the kitchen staring at Matt's back as he stood in front of the stove. He turned around when he sensed her behind him.

"Morning." He gave her a chaste kiss on the cheek. Natalie breathed deep, inhaling his scent. A combination of male, earth, and soap. Her stomach fluttered as it always did when he was near. She wondered if she would ever get used to his presence and then hoped she never did. She liked this feeling of new discovery and eagerly awaited the next.

She yawned. "Morning."

He grinned, obviously remembering why she was so tired. He looked extremely pleased with himself, as if her inability to stay awake was proof of his manhood.

Natalie couldn't help but smile. He was good for her.

"I was going to serve you breakfast in bed but you ruined that by getting up."

"Sorry," she replied as another yawn overtook her.

Matt shrugged. "No worries. You looked so damn cute asleep I didn't want to wake you."

She blushed. "Last night was the first time in days that I was at ease when I slept. I felt safe. Thank you."

For more than you know, she silently added. She watched him deftly flip the fried eggs before he turned his attention to pouring a mug of coffee for her from the carafe. He turned around and watched as she sat down on the stool by the kitchen bench. The sheet was precariously wrapped around her body and he was no doubt praying it would undo itself. If she was honest with herself, she was kind of hoping it would too. Now that her body had been awakened, she was eager to explore more, the previous night merely just a taste.

Once safely seated, Matt handed Natalie her coffee. She glanced up at him. "So is breakfast special for me or is this how you treat all your lady friends who spend the night?"

Natalie wished she could take back the words as soon as she'd said them. They had sex. That was all. They had made no promises. The afterglow of sexual release dulled and reality re-emerged. She wasn't at all good at the morning after and insecurities began to flood her mind. Natalie had been so sure she could handle last night objectively but now she wasn't so sure. She wanted more. How much more, she wasn't entirely sure.

Matt had come into her life and had flipped it upside down. She didn't know what she would do if he ever chose to leave. This feeling was exactly why she had erected that wall and kept people at a distance. Last night, the emotions had heightened her experience. Now they only served to remind her just how vulnerable and easily broken her heart could be if she allowed Matt in.

Matt raised an eyebrow. "You're special. Don't ever think otherwise. As for breakfast. Truthfully, it's been so long I can't even remember."

Natalie smiled. In just a few words he had temporarily soothed her. Later, her mind would begin to over analyse and put her back into a state again. That was when she focused on other people's problems and ignored her own. She had majored in sticking her head in the sand. *It is so much easier that way*, she reflected. *So much safer.*

"So," Matt said, rocking back on his heels. He was dressed for work in a pair of black dress trousers and a cream coloured shirt. His tie hung down his solid chest, the knot loose.

Natalie took a sip of coffee and looked at him. She was surprised at what she saw. A combination of uneasiness and sheepishness. He was obviously uncomfortable about the subject he was about to bring up.

She smiled at him in an attempt to put him at ease. "So?"

"About last night."

Natalie's heart suddenly pounded hard in her chest.

"Yes. The worst three words in history. Go on."

He grinned at her. "I just wanted to clear the air. I certainly didn't plan on it but I certainly don't regret it."

"That's good because I don't regret it either," she replied, her mouth dry from the confession.

"I like you, Natalie, and I want to see more of

you."

"I think you've seen all there is to see, Detective."

His gaze drifted over her sheet clad form. When he spoke again his voice was husky. "You know what I mean. I want a relationship with you."

It wasn't a declaration of love but that was all right. She wasn't there either. But she felt the relief immediately and felt boneless. She was afraid she would slide off the stool and become a puddle on the floor. All her insecurities washed away. He wanted her. She wanted him. It felt right—natural. She nodded, surprised at how easily she gave him the power to destroy her.

Trust. Faith. Hope.

"I'd like that too," she agreed. "There's something about you, Matt Murphy. I've protected myself for so long and yet I trust that you will keep me safe despite having no tangible proof that I won't get hurt. It scares me a little."

"And it humbles me, Natalie. Don't ever think that I don't understand the significance of you sitting at my kitchen bench wearing nothing but my sheet."

Natalie nodded and swallowed hard. Meaningful conversations first thing in the morning was not a habit of hers and she was feeling as if she'd just gone through an emotional whirlwind. She had jumped from one emotion to the next and now felt utterly drained and it was barely seven-thirty.

Matt placed the plate of fried eggs, bacon, and toast before her.

"But for now I have to focus on the case." He

leaned over the kitchen bench and kissed her on the mouth. "Just don't forget me while I'm working."

Yeah, like she had any hope of doing that.

The man's body was imprinted in her mind forever. All that sinewy muscle and taut stomach, narrow hips and huge...she was getting aroused just by thinking about him. There was no way she could ever look at him again without seeing his naked body underneath his clothes.

"After last night, you don't have to worry," she said.

A satisfied grin appeared on his face. "You don't say."

Chapter 28

Matt sank down into his desk chair. Hell, he could do with another couple hours sleep. His eyes stung from being open and only the copious amount of coffee he'd drunk was keeping them that way. He pinched the bridge of his nose. Was he actually complaining? Last night was the best thing that had happened to him in years and he was wishing he had gotten more sleep?

He shook his head. Dumb arse. He still couldn't get over Natalie's faith in him. She of all women had reason to be cautious and yet she had offered herself to him. He was scared shitless of messing it up. He didn't want to hurt Natalie but his track record with women was sketchy at best. He may have the gentle touch but in his experience someone always ended up hurt. He would give his left nut to ensure it wasn't her.

There's something about you, Matt Murphy, Natalie's words played in his mind. *I trust that you will keep me safe.*

He would too. No matter what.

Natalie was special. A unique jewel that had been hidden from the world for so long and he was the lucky bastard to have discovered it. When he'd imagined the moment they would come together he hadn't even been close. Last night had been amazing and that first kiss had thrown him for a loop. He had felt something he couldn't begin to describe but didn't question. It was all part of his feelings for Natalie. From the moment he had met her he'd been attracted to her. Physically at first. Then later, when he'd gotten to know her better, he'd wanted the whole package—scars and all.

Hell, they all had insecurities. He just wasn't good at identifying them in himself and spent little time self-reflecting. He did know he wanted Natalie Miller and cursed the case he'd been handed. He would've liked nothing more than to request leave so he could spend some quality time with the woman who had overrun his life and thoughts and figure out if they could be something more. He wasn't used to thinking long-term and had vowed not to let himself be tied down but Natalie was different. She was a kindred soul and he knew if he could ever make a relationship work, it would be with Natalie.

He had no idea why he was so adamant but he trusted his gut and it was telling him not to stuff it up. All he had to do first was close the Butcher case so he could focus on Natalie.

He found himself smiling just thinking of her.

Darryl appeared at his side. He was dressed like he had slept in his clothes and Matt wondered if his partner had ever made it home last night. Darryl's eyes were bloodshot and there was a beginning of a five o'clock shadow on his jaw.

"Been looking for you," he said in way of a greeting.

"What's up?"

Darryl looked at him and cocked an eyebrow. "Long night?"

Matt wondered if Darryl had heard about Natalie showing up at the LAC and how they'd left together. Of course he had. Nick would have gladly shared the news—him or one of his cohorts. Matt shot his partner a look that told him to drop it. Darryl took the hint.

"There was another murder last night."

"Shit."

If Natalie thought 'about last night' were the worst three words in history, Matt was adding 'there was another murder' as the worst four.

He grabbed his jacket and followed Darryl out the door.

***

The crime scene was an image straight out of *Home and Garden*. All except for the blue and white chequered crime scene tape bordering the house and the four police cars and coroner van parked out front. *The day started off so well*, Matt thought as he got out of his Commodore and took in the scene.

The inquisitive neighbours were all out taking in the sights, some talking to uniformed police officers. He watched as the local channel news van pulled up at the kerb, the cameraman immediately hoisting the camera to his shoulder and followed the made-up reporter to the best filming sight. The reporter checked her face and hair in a compact mirror before informing her viewers about the newest murder.

Matt blocked out the reporter's voice and moved into the house. He noted the same forensic team that had been at Natalie's were currently dusting for fingerprints and checking for signs of forced entry. Darryl followed behind him as they found their way to the bedroom where the activities of the night had been. The bed sheets were crushed and the comforter half hung off the bed. Two pillows lay on the floor near the deceased's hand. She looked vaguely familiar to him as his detectives gaze ran over the body of the once beautiful woman.

Her blonde hair was spread out from her head covering the carpet and she was in an almost foetal position, her hands out wide from the torso. Her night clothes were drenched in blood as was the carpet surrounding her. Matt could count the stab wounds from where he stood and noted it hit double digits. Her throat was exposed and her head had almost been severed from her neck.

It was a ghastly sight and he struggled to keep his breakfast down. Even a seasoned detective like himself found it hard at times and he was sure his skin held a slight green twinge. He wasn't embarrassed. He was slightly thankful to still have that reaction. It told him he could still be shocked and sickened and that the day to day shit he saw hadn't desensitised him. Matt figured there would be nothing worse than to look down at the victim and feel nothing.

She had fought. The clock and bed side lamp had been knocked from the small table by her bed. Two of her manicured nails had been broken and Matt hoped she had gotten a piece of her killer. Not that it would do them any good if they had nothing to match it to.

Just you wait, you bastard, I'll get you. I promise you that.

Matt stepped back, away from the body. He could smell the stench of blood and excrement and the always distasteful flavour of the body as it began to ripen and decompose.

He moved around the house taking notes. The doors and windows had not been forced. Matt doubted if she would have let the man into her house at this time of night. From the profile they had created, he certainly wasn't the type an attractive woman like the victim would've been having an affair with. Matt assumed he had copied her key or found her spare.

The rest of the house was untouched, the massacre contained to the bedroom. He had been alone with her for some time and Matt knew she hadn't died quickly and it certainly hadn't been painless. He knew how she must have suffered and how scared she must have been. He once again declared to find the son-of-a-bitch.

Darryl walked over to him. "Thirty-eight stab wounds, can you believe it? The bastard is escalating. Two murders in just over a week. He's never killed so close before. He's gotten comfortable here."

Matt was angry. He wanted to lash out. He felt impotent. He was no closer to finding the killer and now the bastard was taunting him with his kills as if to say 'look what I can do and you can't stop me.'

"I have to make a phone call."

He started to walk away. Darryl spoke. "Calling your doctor lady?"

Matt nodded curtly. "Something you want to say, Hill?"

Darryl appeared to consider the question before shaking his head.

"No, I think you already know what a dumb arse idea it is getting involved with her right now so I'll let you be."

Darryl walked off to ask the forensics team a couple of questions. Matt stepped outside the house. The sun had set since he had last been outside and it felt rather eerie to be standing at the site of such a violent crime, the victim still inside. It was rather like being at a cemetery at night. He felt the chill go down his spine.

Matt thought about what Darryl had said as he dialled. Yes, he knew how much he had fucked up when he had spent the night with Natalie. But looking back he knew he still would've slept with her. He would take the shit thrown at him for doing so and any reprimands also. So long as Natalie was there when it was all over was the only thing that mattered to him. He heard the phone ring in his ear and knew she wasn't going to like what he had to say.

Chapter 29

Natalie looked about her bed, at the files spread across it. She had taken all the folders with her when she had left Matt's house earlier. She was determined to break this case. There was something nagging at her in the back of her mind. Something she had overlooked. Something that when revealed everything would make sense.

She tapped the closest file with her fingernails, impatiently. Something wasn't right. She felt cold. Frustration welled inside her at not being able to grasp what it was that her mind was screaming at her. She thumped the mattress with her fist, losing her temper. Natalie knew she was missing something. A pivotal piece to the puzzle.

She pulled her laptop closer and typed Ian Walker's name into *Google*. Over a million results appeared. He seemed to have gotten more famous— or rather, infamous—dead than he ever had alive. She scrolled through web pages dedicated to his career before moving on to the blogs about his death.

She found it interesting that he had known the first victim, Helen Teller, and that Ian and Missy Walker had died because of that association. She wondered what exactly that relationship entailed. The most obvious being a sexual one, despite what she'd said to Matt about being close friends. She had read somewhere that Ian had married Missy in 1994, not long after they had been introduced. Which had also been the same year of Harry Teller's birthday party when Ian had most likely been dating Helen. A year later, she would be dead.

Natalie wondered at the timing and opened up Hallie's file and read her DOB. Ah, the good old shotgun wedding. Ian Walker was a man of principal and an illegitimate child was certainly off the cards. Natalie found it interesting that he dumped the smart business woman for the homey type. *Better for his campaign and image*, she thought.

Her concentration was shot to hell when her mobile phone rang. She answered promptly, having promised her patients she could talk whenever they needed.

Matt's voice came clear through the speaker. "Natalie."

She smiled. Memories of the previous night and morning once more returned to her. She felt as giddy as a school girl. It was another new experience. "Detective. What can I do for you?"

Had her voice been flirty? Was she even capable of sounding flirty? She hadn't thought so.

"There's been another murder."

With those four few words her mind cleared. She

sat up straighter on the bed. "Oh God," she whispered. "Who was she?"

"Her name was Linda Cavanaugh."

Linda Cavanaugh. The name didn't ring a bell, thank goodness, but a sadness welled up inside her. Once again a senseless crime. Another woman's life cut short because of the sickness inside one man.

"Let me guess…she was successful, driven, and accomplished?"

"Yeah. Apparently 'Woman of the Year' just like Helen Teller. The vote came in a couple of weeks ago. I'm going to be at the LAC all night if you need me. Where are you?"

"At home."

"Don't go anywhere."

She hadn't planned to and told him so. She hung up and looked out her bedroom window. Night had fallen some time during her growing frustration and the moon outside glowed brightly in the sky. She noticed it was a full moon and shivered. Somehow it made everything feel so ominous. *A lot of crazies will be out there tonight*, she thought. But then again, weren't there always?

She tried to catch her last train of thought before the phone rang and silently cursed Matt for making her lose it. She blushed at the memory of him making her lose it the night before and mentally cleared her mind. She had to stop thinking about him. At least until this case was put to bed.

She picked up the photo of Helen Teller and Ian Walker. She wondered at what Helen had done that had set the man off. Had he been pissed that Helen had chosen a schooled man like Ian Walker over him? Had the Butcher had a long history of losing out to more sophisticated men?

But if that was the case why was he killing women? Shouldn't his rage be focused on successful men? She moved on from the many unanswered questions and continued to stare at the photo. She blinked then frowned. Was she imagining things? She looked closer at the image of Helen Teller and her heartbeat kicked up.

She glanced at her notes, taking in the date the photo had been snapped. *No, it couldn't be*, she thought. But somehow it made sense. As much as this case made any sense. She brought the photo closer. Helen Teller was undeniably pregnant. Her belly protruding out, only partially hidden by her son Harry's head. Natalie searched her notes. She didn't remember reading anything about another child and at that late in the pregnancy she wouldn't have been able to abort it. Had she given birth to a still-born?

Her head ached as she thought too much. A million more questions whizzed around her head, some taunting her at not seeing the significance. She knew she had seen the answer somewhere. Her subconscious practically screamed at her. Somewhere inside her head was the answer. She had solved the case. Now if she could only work out what she knew.

It was like having someone's name on the tip of your tongue, desperate to get it out. She was so preoccupied with digging deep into her brain that when she heard a sound coming from downstairs, she thought she'd let her imagination run rampant.

251

But after listening for a moment, she heard the sound again. This time her brain registered and interpreted the noise.

Natalie's blood ran cold. She was no longer alone. Someone was in the house. She jumped off the bed. Her already pounding heart was painful in her chest. She went down on her knees and stuck her hand beneath her bed, her fingers searching until she wrapped them around the wood of the baseball bat she had been given by her aunt for protection. *Much safer than a gun*, Maggie had said. *You won't be able to shoot yourself by accident.* Natalie wasn't sure she believed in the philosophy now. She would much rather have her fingers wrapped around the cool metal of a pistol.

Her privacy—her home—had been invaded. She was angry and she was scared. She hated the volatile emotions emanating from her. She gripped the baseball bat and slowly moved down the stairs. Her eyes scanned the lower floor for any signs of the intruder.

The lights were off. It had been her way to help save the earth and she regretted the decision now. She didn't like the unknown shadows lurking in her once safe home. Where once she would've thought nothing of walking through the shadows, she now avoided them. Natalie tried to calm her rapid breathing. She didn't want to alert the intruder that she was there. She would need all the surprise she could get and stuck to the darkness of the staircase, ducking low so as not to walk in the moonlight from the drawn curtained window.

Natalie reached the bottom step and cautiously

moved away from her only defence. She had never realised how impractical her furniture was. There was nothing to hide under or behind. Nothing she could easily move to barricade herself inside if there was a need to. It would be something she would correct in the morning, she told herself, and then instantly thought about how long it was until morning. Too long. She should just make a break for it. But her purse and keys were upstairs where they had landed after her struggle with the file folders. Natalie had just balanced the purse on top of the pile, the contents spilling when it had toppled over.

She should turn around and go back upstairs, grab her keys and shimmy down a drainpipe or something into the back garden and then get in her car and high tail it out of there. What was she, sixteen? Shimmy down a drainpipe? She would be lucky to manoeuvre out of the window without being caught.

Natalie decided to take a stand. This was *her* house. Once a sanctuary against the harsh world. It had taken her years to turn the house into a home for herself and she could feel the anger bubble inside of her. How dare he destroy that for her?

With renewed resolution she moved toward the kitchen having decided that was where the sound had come from. She recognised the sound of the stool by her island bench scape against the wood floorboards. She had done it enough times to remember the distinct sound.

A dark shadow moved up ahead and her heart damn near stopped. She'd been half hoping she was just overreacting. That maybe it was a neighbourhood cat or something. It had happened before. But now she knew that was not the case. This shadow was at least five-foot-six and was endowed with a stocky frame.

Natalie stepped forward and realised her mistake as she passed through a beam a light causing her shadow to be reflected on the floor by the intruder's feet. The voice that came out of the darkness overwhelmed her. She had heard it before over and over in her head. The origin of her nightmares was here now inside her house and she was awake. And alone. The voice wafted to her, almost eerily. Her analytical brain told her that wasn't so. She was just too scared to be able to distinguish between her waking reality and her nightmares.

Gary moved into the light, closer to her, and Natalie's hand tightened painfully around the handle of the bat.

"Hello, Natty. I've been trying to find you for a very long time."

Natty, always Natty with him. She heard his name for her and her vision went red. Pain, humiliation, and a torrid of other emotions whirled inside her. She spat out at him. "And now you have. So you stalked me?"

Gary's face showed confusion. "No...I," he stammered. "Sweet Natty."

Again Natty came at her. Flashes of her past flew across her memory. The beatings. The torture he inflicted on her. The fear of an eight-year-old girl. She could feel the pain on her cheek as if he had only just hit it. The mark burned her skin and made her hand shake violently.

Natalie watched him move closer and closer toward her. Her brain was in chaos and she felt like she was spinning out of control. She was a little girl again trapped inside a woman's body. But that's what she was, a woman. No longer did she have to take his hurtful words and watch helplessly as he beat her mother and turned on her when she was unconscious. No longer would she be chased through the house and when caught made to suffer unspeakable brutality.

No, she was a woman now, with an adult's strength. Granted it was not much against a man of his size. But she felt the adrenaline pumping through her bloodstream, making her feel all powerful. As if she could take on Hercules himself.

Gary stepped once more towards her, holding out his hands as if he wanted to embrace her. She looked into his eyes and held up the baseball bat. She struck him in the head once, dazing him. She hit him again and knocked him to his knees and then a third time rendering him unconscious.

"Don't. Ever. Call. Me. Natty," she screamed at his prone form.

She felt exhilarated. She had defeated the monster of her past, the very embodiment of her childhood nightmares and adult memories. Never again would he follow her where she went and haunt her.

She stepped away from the lump of man on her floor. The adrenaline had begun to wear off and the bat felt heavy in her hands. Natalie let it drop to the floor when she was no longer able to hold onto it.

The sound of the bat hitting the hardwood floors echoed through the silent house. She could feel the shakes take over her body and tears gathered in her eyes. Tears of joy and tears of sadness. She was beginning to feel relaxed once more when out of the silent house came two words that stopped her heart.

"Poor Gary."

Chapter 30

Matt took the stairs up from the autopsy room. Doctor Stone announced what everyone had already known, that Linda Cavanaugh had died from wounds inflicted on her body and throat by persons known. The weapon used had matched that of the weapon used on Marie Stanton and every last one of the Butcher's other victims. The blade was from a large hunting knife with a serrated edge. The type that if enough pressure applied could cut through bone. Matt shivered at the thought. It was bad enough the knife cut through tissue and veins, he didn't like to think of bones being cut as well.

Matt walked through the building towards his desk. The small area the detectives had been assigned was unusually quiet. Each of his team lost in their own thoughts about how they were unable to stop the beast from killing another innocent woman.

Matt sat down in his chair, slapping the autopsy file onto his desk. He rubbed his hands over his face. Darryl stepped over to him, his face a mask of stone allowing no emotion to show. Each man dealt with the situation differently. He was pissed and didn't care who knew it. Darryl was happy to hide his emotions.

"Boss man wants to see you."

Matt looked up at Darryl and over to the enclosed office of their boss. The glass walls that allowed the Superintendent to oversee his employees had the blinds closed. Never a good sign. The Boss only closed them when he was in conference with someone and that someone was usually getting ripped a new arsehole.

"Any idea why?" Matt asked. Forewarned is forearmed.

Darryl shook his head. "Probably wants to talk about the Butcher case. It's the only thing anyone around here can talk about."

Matt nodded, stood and straightened his clothes before laying a hand on Darryl's shoulder in camaraderie. *Better get this over with*, he thought. He didn't need an ulcer burning in his stomach while he dwelled on what the Boss wanted. He had better things to do. If he was about to be chewed out then so be it. He deserved it. He should've caught the bastard already.

He approached Superintendent Alec Harris's office and knocked briskly. He heard the Boss's growl from the other side of the door. Since it wasn't actually a spoken reply, it was up to Matt to interpret. He opened the door and slipped inside, closing the door firmly behind him.

Superintendent Harris was a large imposing man, well above six-foot with greying hair. He would've been a handsome man back in his day, and after thirty years on the force it was common knowledge that he was looking forward to retiring in a few years' time. He was also looking forward to closing the Butcher case before he left. Alec was a man who never liked to leave anything unfinished and Matt knew there was no way Alec would ever retire with a man like the Butcher still at large.

Alec's ice cold blue eyes watched him as he sat down in the visitor's chair and stretched out his long legs, waiting for Harris to speak. His gaze roamed the office. The walls were covered with commendations and awards from over the years. A couple of trophies sat on the small table to the side. Alec Harris was a hard arse but he was a good cop in his day and a fair boss, sticking up for his officers when needed and hanging them out to dry when they deserved it.

He spotted the picture of the Superintendent's wife on his desk. Caitlyn Harris was a lovely woman, who it was whispered throughout the halls of the LAC had quite the lawless past. No one in the LAC could understand how a woman like Caitlyn could bare to live with a cankerous old man like the Boss. She was everything he wasn't—kind and sweet, loving and gentle. He assumed that opposites attract and knew Harris loved her more than anything. Their marriage had lasted over twenty years, resulting in one rebellious daughter, Sophie, who was the spitting image of her blonde haired, blue eyed mother.

"Heard there was another murder last night," Harris said, his voice a deep baritone.

Matt nodded. "Yes, sir."

Superintendent Harris frowned. "The Butcher?"

Matt gave a curt nod. "Yes, sir."

"Must have been some sight. Seen some of those crime scene photos myself. Horrible stuff." Matt sat patiently waiting for the meeting to come to a point. He didn't need to wait long. "How *is* the case going, Murphy?"

"I'm working on a new lead. Focusing my attention on the first victim, Helen Teller. I believe there is more to be learned from her murder than originally thought."

Harris nodded. "And your psychologist agrees with you?"

Matt refrained from commenting on the use of *his* psychologist. He wondered just how much Harris had heard. He shouldn't have been surprised. Alec knew everything that was going on inside his walls.

"Yes, sir. We discussed it in detail."

That wasn't all they did but again he didn't open his mouth.

Harris gave him a long hard look. "I know you're doing all you can, Murphy. It's a hard case and I wouldn't want to be in your shoes. Whatever you need, you've got it, understood? The whole LAC is at your disposal."

Matt nodded, appreciative of the support. He knew he needed help and wasn't afraid to admit it. "Thank you."

He stood and started toward the door. "Murphy?"

Matt turned around. "Yeah."

"I need your head clear and focused, understand? I don't care what you have going on with Doctor Miller. I just need to know it's not going to affect your work."

Matt stared at his boss. Alec could make most of the cops in the building shake in their boots, but not him. He respected Alec and knew the man respected him. They had been on the same team before Alec had been promoted and had worked side by side. Alec knew what Matt was capable of and knew he got results and he would on this case too. He just needed time.

"You know me better than that."

Alec gave an almost imperceptible nod. "I do. But then I've never known you to blur the lines between personal and professional. She must be some woman."

Matt raised a dark eyebrow. "That's it?"

"What more do you want?"

"I was kind of expecting a punishment. I messed up. I got involved with a consultant. I knew better. It was unprofessional but I don't regret it and would do it again in a heartbeat."

"I'm hardly one to thrown stones." He glanced at the picture of Caitlyn.

"One day, Boss, you're going to have to tell me that story."

Alec smiled. "One day."

Chapter 31

Amelia Donovan hated to be the person who collected the research and made calls. She wasn't by any standards a passive person. She was a go-getter and an arse kicker. But she did the work without complaint—or at least verbal complaint. She had kicked the printer once or twice when it had decided to jam. It soon fell into line like everyone else around the office who had all decided it was easier to be with her than against.

She had big dreams. Ever since she'd been sixteen she had been hell bent on getting out of her neighbourhood and making something out of herself. Now she was slated to take over as Superintendent after Harris left and she was on top of the moon. Not that she let anybody else know just how excited she was about her soon-to-be promotion. But for now she was paying her dues, being a copy-maker and all-round gopher. Besides, Matt was primary on the case and no one really wanted that title. The Butcher was a ghost. But Amelia had faith in her team. They were all good detectives. They had to be or they wouldn't have been hired.

She took the last sheet of paper off the printer and stapled it into the manila folder. She moved towards Matt's desk. The new guy was preparing to leave. He could use the rest; they all could. She and Hill had been on call last night and between tracking down leads, they had been sent out to deal with a couple of rambunctious little twits who decided after a few drinks to have a punch up. They were now in the drunk tank sleeping off their decision. She was looking forward to catching a few hours herself. She had begun to ripen having worked up a sweat diffusing the situation between the two boys and as soon as she dropped off the file was hitting the shower.

Darryl nodded to her as he walked past, his eyes already half closed. She let out a deep breath as Matt's in-tray became visible and placed the folder onto his already precarious pile. Grabbing her purse she made a beeline for the showers, passing Matt on the way.

"File's on your desk, Murphy. I'm outta here."

***

Matt nodded and said goodnight. He picked up the file Amelia had left as he sat down. His eyes bulged as he read the court document. *Damn, Donovan is good*, he thought. The document was a formal agreement between Ian Walker and Helen Chance, AKA Helen Teller, dated seventeen years ago.

263

Matt was still reeling at the web of lies spinning out of control when he read the next sheet and felt like swearing. Harry Teller had disappeared not long after his mother's funeral. He'd never shown up at his foster home and had gone completely off the grid after collecting his inheritance. It was almost as if he had died when his mother had. He had no address or job, no bank account or tax refund.

Matt wanted to kick himself. They should've thought about the boy earlier. No, not the boy—the man. He would be well into his twenties by now. To think, a murderer at age thirteen. He lifted up his phone and tried to call Natalie. He was absolutely certain they'd just cracked the case and she was the first person he thought of to share the news. His stomach flipped when both her mobile and house line rang out. She had promised him she'd be careful and take no unnecessary risks and he'd called her only an hour before. She had been at home and quite happy to stay there once he told her about the newest victim. With his heart pounding in his throat he grabbed his keys and took off towards the exit.

Chapter 32

Natalie spun around to face the man and her breath caught in her throat as she watched the figure all decked out in black come forward in the light. His face was not covered. He was *not* a common burglar no matter how he was dressed. She looked into cold dark eyes and shivered. She swore the devil looked back at her.

"Stepfathers haven't a chance with you. You know dear old dad only came to apologise to you. I believe it's all part of his twelve-step program and you had to kill him," he scolded.

Natalie darted a look at the still figure. Blood gathered on his head where the bat had connected and tears spilled over onto her cheeks. Her body trembled and she couldn't do anything to stop it.

She knew tonight was the night she would die.

"Do you know who I am, Natalie?" he asked. His dark black stare bored into her.

She tried to look away, to look at anything but him, but those obsidian ovals kept her there. Natalie attempted to calm herself. She could feel the fearful sweat coat her skin and endeavoured to level her voice as her brain tried to deny what her eyes saw.

"Henry Rellet."

The eyes and hair were different but she still recognised him. No wonder his honey hair had looked so off on him. He had obviously been wearing a wig—not to mention contacts—in her company.

Henry Rellet AKA the Butcher smiled coolly at her, as if she was some child who'd just answered a question correctly. He looked so far removed from the man who had sat in her office that for a second she wondered at him having a twin. Only then did she remember his transformation a few days before.

"And before that?"

Natalie trembled. She was going to die. She saw it all clearly now. That one piece of the puzzle she'd known she knew. That one damn piece that would make everything fall together neatly.

Henry screamed at her. "And. Before. That?"

Natalie could feel the tears threatening to spill out. She blinked them back, her voice quivering as she spoke.

"Harry Teller. Helen Teller's son." *How had she missed that?* She wondered. Rellet was the reverse of Teller. It was almost as if he was asking to be found, deliberately taunting her.

Harry Teller nodded enthusiastically. He was enjoying himself, enjoying tormenting her. Natalie pleaded with her feet to work as Harry looked about her kitchen, his gaze settling on her knife block. Natalie didn't wait around for what would evidently come next. She took off running towards the door.

Harry moved quickly, as if he was a panther and she his prey he wanted to toy with before ultimately killing. He grabbed hold of her and jerked her back by her hair. Natalie screamed and struggled, her arms flailing about wildly as she tried to free herself. His hands tightened painfully around her.

She could see it so clearly now. How he would move around the country unnoticed like a nomad, stalking his victims before killing them. He'd be out of town before the body was discovered, except this time—this time was different and she shuddered thinking about why. Her thoughts suddenly left her as she was pushed back into the wall. Her head bounced off the drywall as she was unprepared for the shove and pain erupted in her head.

"No, Natalie. That ruins everything," he admonished.

He produced a roll of duct tape from his clothes and taped her wrists together. She could feel the sticky residue tugging painfully at the small hairs it found there. He glared at her as he pushed her onto the stool in her kitchen. He made a show of revealing his knife, allowing the moonlight streaming through the window to flash across the stainless steel blade.

"Is it pissing you off that I'm not begging for my life?" she asked calmly.

He sneered and arrogantly said, "You think that's going to work? I know you're scared of me, Natalie. I can smell your fear from here."

"Of course I'm scared. I'm bound defenceless while you have a knife," she shivered at that. "But I'm not going to give you the satisfaction of hearing me beg. You know it's not really sportsmanlike to bind my wrists. Are you that intimidated by me that you need to handicap me?"

That's nice, Natalie, stroke the bear.

Pissing off the sadistic killer standing in your kitchen waving a knife about was not the way to ensure a long and healthy life. Harry smiled, flashing his blindingly white teeth and Natalie caught sight of his exceptionally long canines.

"I'm told your life flashes before your eyes when you're about to die. Do you see your life flashing before your eyes, Natalie?"

She resisted the urge to gulp. "A lot of things are flashing before my eyes. It's hard to pinpoint a certain event."

But she could see her life clearly. Splashing around the bathtub pretending to be a beautiful mermaid. Her beloved aunt and uncle. Her home. The office she had worked so hard to obtain. Matt's green gaze smiling at her. Matt kissing her. A tear spilled over onto her cheek.

"Tell me, how does it feel knowing I could've ended your life at any time? During any one of those useless sessions? Did you even realise all those women I told you about were my many conquests?"

Natalie felt the blood leave her face. Her mind raced as it fought to remember every word he'd ever said. No wonder he never used names during their sessions and she thought about the hospital worker and her mind flashed on Marie Stanton. Then only days ago the blonde he was raving on about. She immediately knew that Linda Cavanaugh had been a blonde and she felt sick to her stomach.

"You killed your mother, didn't you? Tortured her like you've done so many others, like you plan to do to me."

"She was a horrible woman. She made me love her and gave nothing in return. I did everything she ever wanted but it was never good enough. I tired of being second fiddle to her work and her men."

She felt his rage at his mother. It was palpable. Natalie wondered if when Harry looked at her if he was actually seeing her or Helen. She guessed he saw his beloved mother. The woman who had inadvertently brought about so many deaths. Natalie saw it in her mind. How it had been for little Harry Teller, the neglected boy longing for his mother's love and approval? But eventually the hatred for his mother rose and grew into an adolescent revenge.

"Do you know what she'd do to me if I was less than perfect? She'd beat me, burn me and lock me away in the cupboard. She used me as a prop, so others would think how wonderful, how maternal she was."

Natalie understood him all too well and it made her sick. She swallowed back the bile that rose in her throat. She had experienced an almost identical childhood to Harry. How close had she been to losing her path as he had done? Had it been the fact that her father had been there for a time to give her love and later her aunt and uncle? It was scary to think that she could have easily shared the same fate as Harry. It was scary what changed a person so completely that they turned into cold-blooded psychopaths.

Harry had been so isolated from love and she felt for the boy. She didn't want to be sympathetic but her heart ached for him. The child. She didn't feel anything but anger to the man.

"Did Ian know?"

Harry's dark glower bored into hers and she refused to show any emotion. His mouth twisted in amusement. "She couldn't hide it. It was her nature to seek and destroy me until she once again needed me."

Natalie closed her eyes for a moment. She knew Ian hadn't said anything. Reports of abuse would have arose during the murder investigation. She shuddered. The pregnancy. Hallie. Ian and Missy raising her together. Helen had bought Ian's silence with their baby. Harry had suffered because Ian had wanted to protect his daughter. Harry had killed his mother because she was incapable of loving him. He had resented the fact that she chose work over him and probably projected her failings as a mother onto all those unfortunate woman—on her.

Natalie watched as Harry paced the floor in front of her. She let her gaze drift about the room looking for a weapon or something to help her remove the duct tape. She hated the thought that she was about to die because Harry saw her as an unfeeling, career driven woman. She wasn't.

"You killed Ian because he knew the truth and had done nothing to help you, didn't you? You punished his daughter, your half-sister, for something she had no control over."

Natalie remembered the reports she had read about the Walkers, how they were such a loving family. The perfect unit, Hallie had everything Harry always wanted: someone to love him. It must have eaten away at him for years seeing his little sister in the newspaper surrounded by such happiness.

Eventually the abuse and lack of emotion in his household had led to murder. The crime scene photos flashed before Natalie's eyes and her breathing stuttered. She could see the bloody and mutilated body of Helen Teller lying on the floor. The blood that had seeped out of her body dried on the wood, marring the boards. She watched as the murder played out before her eyes as if a movie. A thirteen-year-old Harry stabbing his mother with a kitchen knife again and again before moving the blade to her throat. At the power he found, the lust of the kill.

Harry grabbed her shoulders hard and she could feel his fingers digging into her skin. She bit her lip so not to give him any pleasure at hearing her pain.

"When I'm done with you, I'm going to her," he promised. He must've seen her sceptical look because he moved closer to her until their heads were almost touching. "Don't believe me? I've seen her sleeping at night. She looks so much like Ian, don't you think? I plan on taking my time with her. You're nothing compared to her. An entrée to the main course and I plan on ripping out her heart."

She shivered at his tone. He was anticipating the meeting with sick interest. Natalie thought about Hallie and how truly defenceless she was in there. Hallie thought she was safe. She wasn't. She was vulnerable. Natalie felt the anger rise in her, the need to protect Hallie stronger than her fear. "You will never get to her," she vowed.

Chapter 33

Matt felt useless. He tried calling Natalie's number again only for it to go straight to voicemail. His entire body was ice cold and he couldn't help seeing the murdered body of Linda Cavanaugh and then before his eyes she wasn't Linda anymore but Natalie. Her perfect skin marred by stab wounds, her throat slit ear from ear.

He couldn't shake the fear that thought brought him. He pressed down harder on the accelerator, the Commodore running through the red light narrowly missing a car turning. The idiot had the nerve to honk his horn at him and Matt resisted the urge to flip him the bird. Did the guy not understand that a life was on the line? People these days just didn't care unless of course it was happening to them. That was the one thing he hated about being a cop. So many people were in it for themselves and everybody else be damned. It was the reason the human race was going down the shitter.

His lights were flashing almost psychotically as he drove. He had refrained from using the siren since he didn't want to alert Harry Teller to his presence before he was ready. He'd seen enough hostage situations go belly-up because the cops had rushed in without taking their time to assess their options. Without doing recon he could be signing Natalie's death warrant—if she wasn't dead already. He prayed he would make it in time. He'd lost his father because of a two-bit punk. He wasn't prepared to lose Natalie. Especially now that he'd only just found her.

I love her.

The thought appeared in his head out of nowhere. Matt knew it to be true. There was no way he could deny it, even if he so desired which he realised he didn't. He loved her and didn't care who knew. He'd never met a woman who could turn him on with just a look. One who could make him laugh and exasperate him to the point that he was about to lose his sanity. One who was not just beautiful but smart as well. He needed her.

He had known that when he found the right woman he would fall hard and here he was about to lose her. With him only now realising the depths of his feelings. He should've realised that first day in her office that she would become important to him. Maybe he'd loved her from the moment she had looked up at him and become breathless. She was a part of him and if he lost her, he doubted that his heart would ever recover. Not that he would want it to. Not without Natalie to fill it with love.

Matt turned the corner fast and he was glad for the tactical driving course he'd been required to take, manoeuvring his car like it was *Bathurst 1000.*

He would be at Natalie's house soon. Perspiration coated his forehead as he fought to keep control of the vehicle at the high speed. Only another five, maybe ten minutes to go.

Please let her be okay.

Chapter 34

Harry gave her a cruel smile. One that sent chills racing down her back. Natalie kept her back straight, her gaze unwavering as she tried to act more confident than she felt. She may have promised to keep him away from Hallie, but what hope did she have? She was bound and defenceless and he was sure to tire of her soon and kill her. *That gives Hallie a few hours*, she thought. She had read the police reports. Stab wounds in the double digits. That took time. She tried not to imagine how much that was going to hurt.

Natalie wished she'd caught the signs earlier. If only she had remembered to follow up on the behavioural change of 'Henry' when she had the chance. She blamed herself. Had she been paying closer attention she should've been able to see what lurked beneath that forgettable exterior. If she had, tonight certainly would've gone different. Instead of being held captive, she could've wiled away the time waiting for Matt to call.

Matt. They had come so close last night to

figuring it all out. She had no doubt that given time he would get to the same conclusion she had. He was a brilliant detective. He would work her murder. She just had to figure out how to ensure there was enough evidence to lead him straight to Harry. She trusted him to see that she got justice and that Harry burned in Hell for his crimes. She only hoped it was before he got to Hallie.

They had to protect Hallie.

Natalie felt the cool blade tease against her arm. She froze, her breath catching in her throat making it hard for her to breathe. Tears rolled down her cheek, Natalie no longer able to hold them back.

"I can see your fear now. You know what's coming, don't you? The pain. The begging. You're going to be thankful when I cut your throat."

The image was sharp in her mind, just as he had planned. Years of training and patience went out the window. She could no longer be understanding and non-judgmental. She was going to die and the last thing she would see was Harry Teller, her murderer. Natalie felt the fear the other women must've known and felt a kinship with them. They hadn't deserved to die, just as she didn't.

She lashed out. "You're nothing but a sick demented fuck who should've been institutionalised at birth. I bet your mother was glad when you ended her life. You freed her from your paltry presence."

Abruptly, Harry moved and in a blink of an eye his knife was against her throat. She could feel the cold steel of the blade biting into her flesh and the warm trickle of blood running down from the point of the knife. She cried out, fear temporarily paralysing her.

"Will you be as glad when I remove you from this earth?" he snarled.

Natalie quickly assessed the situation. Her training told her to continue to anger him. To push him over the edge. He got off on fear and she was feeding him. She struggled to mask it.

"If it means not having to deal with your pathetic life any longer, then yes. Do it, Harry. Kill me."

She would rather a quick death than a slow and drawn out one.

Harry's mouth curled in distaste. She knew the night was not going according to his plan and she smiled. She felt oddly disjointed from the world. The knowledge of death creeping closer was surreal. She felt the odd need to laugh. Hysteria— she knew the symptoms immediately.

She didn't fear death. The only thing she thought about was Matt. She was thankful she had the chance to meet him. She was glad she had overcome her fear and allowed him into her life. The time she had spent with him was worth every moment of pain she had ever experienced. She loved him with her entire heart and felt another tear fall, just one. The last one. A tear for Matt.

She loved him. Why hadn't she realised that before and why now when she was about to die did her heart decide to tell her? In a flash, she knew. Her knee came up and rammed into Harry's groin. He cried out in pain and dropped to his knees to clutch at the family jewels. Natalie shot up off the stool. Her feet barely touched the ground before he grabbed her ankle hard. His hand, like a manacle, sent her hurtling towards the floor. Her knees and elbows connected with the wood panelling, bringing about a numb tingle in her joints as they absorbed the shock. Harry moved over her. Pain was etched on his features. There was lust in his eyes and rage emanated from his pours.

He reached for his knife, once again moving it towards her. He raised it, preparing to plunge the blade into her body. Natalie started to shake uncontrollably. She bucked beneath him, hoping to knock him off balance.

A sound of wood cracking had them both looking up towards the kitchen door that led to her back garden and the world spun as she was hoisted to her feet by Harry's easy strength. As her vision cleared, her gaze found Matt standing in the ruin of her doorway. His service weapon, a Glock 23, was aimed straight at Harry. The look on his face left no doubt whether he would shoot to kill.

Dazed, she realised her new position. She stood between Matt and Harry, acting as Harry's shield. Her back was against his chest and his knife at her neck. Harry spoke first, his voice cold and commanding.

"Drop it, Detective. Drop it or I drop her."

Matt held his hands up in surrender and dropped the gun on the floor. He kicked it away. "Let her go."

"No," Harry screamed. "I'll never let her go. She's mine." He turned his body to the side and faced her, she assumed so he could look into her eyes as she died.

Natalie could feel the knife against her skin, his

hand under her chin when Matt dropped to a crouch and pulled his concealed weapon from the ankle holster and shot Harry. The bullet sliced through his neck and embedded itself in the wall behind them. Natalie brought up her hands instinctively and wrapped them around her neck to protect herself, the backs of her hands taking the brunt of the cut from the blade as Harry fell to the floor. She felt the sting of the knife as it opened her flesh.

The room smelled like death and cordite. Natalie took a few steps back. Not once taking her eyes off Harry, she promptly collapsed on the floor as her legs gave out. Tears of relief and pain blurred her vision. Sobs echoed throughout the room as Matt moved toward her. His gun never wavered from the body of Harry Teller. He kicked the knife away and stared down at the body for a moment before he turned his attention towards Natalie.

Matt knelt beside her and pulled out a small knife from his back pocket and cut the duct tape. He yanked it away from her skin, leaving it red and agitated. He put his hand under her chin and moved her head gently so he could look in her eyes.

"Are you okay?" he asked, concern making his voice husky. She slowly nodded, then launched herself into his arms and held him tight.

Matt hugged her back. His arms were like steel around her as if he planned to never let her out of his sight again. She could hear sirens outside, still some distance away.

Natalie sniffled. "Thank you, thank you. I was so scared. I thought I was dead. Thank you," she repeated, the last few words inaudible as she sobbed.

He stroked her back, comforting her. "It's okay. It's all over. You're safe. It's okay. You're all right."

She pulled away from him and looked up him through mist. "Thank you," she whispered.

Matt nodded. "You're welcome."

She smiled at him, tears falling off her long lashes to roll down her face. Matt gently swiped them away with his thumb. In the next minute her eyes widened and Matt paled in response.

"Oh God, Gary." She got to her feet and on wobbly legs, moved towards the unconscious man on her kitchen floor some feet away.

"Who's Gary?"

Natalie knelt beside Gary. "My stepfather." She felt for a pulse, nodding when she found it steady. "He's still alive."

"I'll get some water."

Natalie glanced up at him. He didn't sound happy about it. But then she knew he was remembering what she'd told him about the man. She watched as Matt walked over to the sink and started looking for a glass. She was glad he was here, for more than one reason. She shivered at the memory of being so close to death as she shook Gary. She tried to push it from her mind.

"Gary? Gary?"

Gary groaned and started to lift his head before stopping abruptly and promptly replaced his undoubtedly aching and concuss head on the floor.

"Natalie?" He sounded dazed. "I suppose I deserved that."

Natalie shook her head. As much as she wished all those years ago to hurt Gary like he had hurt her, the reality was less than brilliant and certainly not as gratifying as one might've hoped.

"I'm sorry. You were just at the wrong place at the wrong time."

Matt brought back a glass filled with water and handed it to Gary. Natalie caught the dark look on his face. Her self-proclaimed protector was ready to attack should she give him the word. She felt her stomach flip. *Of all the things to get mushy over*, she thought.

"Here's some water."

"Thank you," he said to Matt before turning to her. "I just came here to apologise to you for my behaviour when you were a little girl. I was an alcoholic. I know it's not an excuse but I wanted…needed you to know that I'm sober now. Have been for five years," he added proudly.

"Congratulations," she replied and meant it. Had it not been for alcohol she had always thought he would've been a half decent man.

"I quit after your mother died. I finally saw myself in a mirror and realised I didn't like the man I'd become. Look, I know I don't deserve it but I was hoping that sometime in the future you might forgive me."

Natalie looked deep inside herself. "I already have, Gary."

It was the truth, she realised, only having admitted it to her herself at that moment. Life was about the future, not the past. Nothing good ever came from holding onto painful memories.

"You have?" he asked, somewhat dubious but also hopeful.

She smiled. "Yeah, I have."

Gary's eyes misted. "Thank you. I'm going to be in the city for a while and I'd like for us to get together and have some lunch. When my head doesn't feel like someone's taken a baseball bat to it, that is."

Matt raised an eyebrow and glanced down at the bat, close by where she'd dropped it. She caught his gaze briefly before smiling at Gary.

"I'd like that."

"Great, lunch. It's a date," Gary said, as the ambulance and several of Harbour Bay's police cars pulled up outside the house, the red and blue lights streaking through her blinds.

Natalie groaned as she realised she'd have to move. If she thought the forensics team visit had been on every one of her neighbours' lips, she was about to go down in infamy as the worst neighbour ever after bringing a serial killer into the street followed by every member of the police force. Not that she wanted to come back to this house. She had loved it but now it was filled with bad memories and all she would be able to remember was how it had felt in those last few moments when she'd thought she was going to die.

She shivered. She never wanted to feel that way again.

"All clear, Darryl," Matt yelled out to his partner, and Gary shuddered.

The man she assumed was Darryl entered through the front door, followed closely by a woman and two men she vaguely remembered from her visit to Matt's office. They each wore bulletproof vests over their clothes and had their guns drawn. She shivered at the knowledge of how serious the situation was. Natalie watched as the four of them stepped gingerly into her house as if they expected the entire Manson family had taken refuge inside instead of one very dead serial killer.

She found it quite humorous. She was probably still a little hysterical but the image made her lips twitch. She glanced over at Matt. He smiled at her and for a second it seemed as if they were the only two people in the room.

He straightened. "We need to get you both to the hospital."

Natalie glanced down at her hands. They were bloody and stung painfully. Matt motioned for a paramedic with his finger before reaching down and helping Gary to his feet. Together they started their way towards the approaching paramedic.

Matt grabbed hold of Natalie's arm. "See you soon, okay?"

She nodded and looked up into his eyes. They were full of pain. She could see him warring with indecision. She knew that he wanted to go with her but his duty was first to his job and the case.

"I know. It's okay," she said. "I'll be all right. Go do whatever it is you do. I'll see you later."

He stared at her for a long moment before reluctantly turning away and joining the other detectives in her kitchen for debriefing. Natalie blinked back tears and tried to be strong. She was hanging on by a thread. But she knew he had a job to do and accepted that. At least logically. Emotionally she was a wreck.

Natalie turned her back to Matt. Her dependency on him didn't surprise her but it did worry her. She wasn't used to needing people. Natalie made herself take a step then another. Soon, she was out in her front yard. Red and blue lights flashed brightly and a young uniformed cop was cordoning off her house with crime scene tape. It was something out of a nightmare. She heard her name and saw the waiting ambulance, Gary already tucked safely inside. Her entire body numb, Natalie started towards it.

Chapter 35

Matt watched Natalie's dead gaze drift about his house as if seeing it for the first time. He wished she would say something, anything, to let him know she was going be okay. Since picking her up from the hospital she had been quiet and it was scaring the crap out of him. He had carried the conversation, barely pausing to take a breath, afraid of the silence he knew would follow.

Matt understood that whatever she had experienced with Harry hadn't been pleasant. It would've been terrifying. He cursed himself for not figuring it out sooner. It had almost been too late. Harry had had the knife against her throat. The image would never leave him.

He wanted to share her pain, her horror and fear. He wanted to hold her and help her to heal, if only she'd let him. She had almost lost her life. He would never forgive himself for that. He was the one who had drawn her into this nightmare and he wondered if she blamed him. Why not? He blamed himself. He could feel her pulling away from him and desperately tried to bridge the gap.

He had explained in the car ride home that she would be required to make a formal statement about the previous night's events and that he had requested they wait until tomorrow. After all, what did it matter? Harry was dead. Her statement was merely a formality and would be used in his review by Internal Affairs to prove the use of deadly force was warranted and necessary.

He wasn't concerned. Again, it was merely a formality. If there had been any issues in him discharging his weapon, Alec Harris would've already suspended him. He would've been relieved of his badge and firearm until a decision was made.

Natalie sat perched on the edge of his couch, her bandaged hands in her lap. Thankfully the cuts were shallow and would not cause permanent damage. They would heal in a couple of weeks. If only mental trauma was as easy.

She was pale and looked so lost. It broke his heart. He longed to go to her but was unsure if she wanted him to. She had made no action that told him so, or otherwise. From the moment he had shepherded her out of the hospital and into his car, she had made no sign that she was even aware of his presence.

Matt hated this. He hated feeling so damn useless. She had to be drowning in thoughts and emotion. Her house, her once safe haven, had been taken from her and now he had brought her here, a place she barely knew. He only wanted what was best for her, and he wanted to be close enough so that he could keep an eye on her for his own peace of mind. Almost losing her had made him realise just how important she was to him.

Matt wondered if he should've taken her to a hotel. Perhaps she would be more comfortable in a neutral place. He glanced over at the suitcase by his front door where he'd dumped it before going to pick Natalie up from the hospital. He had filled it with clothes and toiletries from her house. As it was now a crime scene, she wouldn't be able to enter it for some time. Not that he thought she'd ever want to again. At least not for a while with the memories so fresh in her mind.

Had he made a big mistake? He watched Natalie stare silently at the wall of his living room. Had he been presumptuous to think she would want to stay with him?

"I'll take you to a hotel," he blurted out.

Natalie turned to face him. "Why?" she asked, her voice as fragile as she looked. "Can't I stay here with you?"

Matt let out a deep breath and felt some of the tension leave his body.

"Of course you can. I just thought you'd be more comfortable in a hotel."

She shook her head and glanced down at her bandaged hands.

"No. I want to stay here."

"Okay. Can I get you anything?"

A smile tugged at the corner of her mouth but it seemed the effort was too much for her and it slipped back into a frown.

"I'm fine, really, Matt. I'm just tired."

He cursed himself for not following her to the

hospital. He should've handed the case over to Darryl. Except he knew he couldn't have. He was point and it was his job to finish up the case and complete the necessary paperwork, including his statement. Still, all that didn't matter when it came to Natalie. Last night must've been awful for her and he wondered if she had gotten any sleep or if nightmares had kept her awake. He moved closer to her but stood far enough away that he didn't crowd her.

"Did they give you anything to help you sleep?"

Natalie nodded. "Yeah, but I don't want to take it. I'm afraid if I do I won't be able to wake up. That if I dream I will be trapped."

She stood and paced the room. Her feet dragged, her head stooped, and he smelled the antiseptic lotion the nurses had lathered her cuts with beneath the white gauze bandage.

"You need to rest."

"I know."

He moved over to her and placed his hands on her shoulders, effectively stopping her then gently guided her to the hallway that led to the bedrooms. He was about to direct her to the spare room when she headed straight for his bedroom. He followed slowly, completely bewildered at what to do. He wanted to help her but didn't know how or where to start. She was fragile. Did he treat her as such or did he act as if everything was normal? What did she want him to do? She was hard to read.

Matt watched from the doorway as she got comfortable on his unmade bed. Natalie closed her eyes and inhaled deeply. He could imagine what she was smelling. He hadn't had a chance to change the sheets since their night together. Natalie opened her eyes and looked at him. There was so much emotion in those blue pools that he almost fell to his knees.

"Natalie?"

She patted the empty spot next to her, silently telling him she wanted him with her. Matt gladly crossed the small space dividing them and stretched out beside her. He pulled her into his arms gently, careful not to bump her hands. She rested her head against his chest and he could feel her warm breath through his shirt.

Her shudders shook them both as she began to sob loudly. Matt held her tighter in the comfort of his arms and kissed her head. He didn't speak. There were no words, only actions. She cried for hours, each tear breaking his heart. He couldn't believe how much he loved her. There would never be a day for the rest of his life that he didn't and someday soon he was going to tell her. But not tonight. He could wait. Tonight was about healing. For Natalie to purge herself of the fear and vulnerability she had felt at Harry's hand. Matt only hoped she felt the same about him.

Natalie hiccupped and Matt felt her relax beside him. He listened to her soft breathing that told him she was asleep and for a long while he simply watched her sleep. When he could no longer keep his eyes open, Matt snuggled against Natalie, inhaling her scent and allowing himself to drift off.

Chapter 36

Natalie sat in the interview room of Harbour Bay's Local Area Command. The four-storey, L-shaped, light mud brown imperious structure overlooked the sea-green harbour and farther out to the Tasman Sea. Originally it had served as a convict barrack and had been converted in the seventies for the growing police force.

The grounds were immaculately manicured, the grass trimmed and lush. The hedges were clipped and the garden was filled with a bright cornucopia of coloured pansies as if somehow trying to distract attention away from the monstrosity of the building.

Natalie tried to remain calm. It wasn't as if she had anything to worry about. She hadn't done anything wrong but still she felt nervous. She didn't think she was ready to talk about that night. Matt squeezed her shoulder and she jumped. She had forgotten he was there in the room with her. Natalie wasn't sure how. Since the moment he had picked her up from the hospital the day before, he hadn't let her out of his sight. She loved him all the more for it. She liked being someone's number one priority for a change but she didn't lie to herself and admitted that it wouldn't always be like this. Matt's job was very important and she knew if she wanted to be with him she would have to share him.

Natalie smiled at his reflection in the two-way mirror on the cream coloured wall then dropped her gaze to the charcoal grey floor. She was a coward. In the past twenty-four hours, Matt had been so patient and kind to her, yet barely any words had passed her lips. Least of all the most important ones.

She remembered how Matt had held her while she'd cried the entire night. He had been so compassionate, so tender. He had given her the strength to go on. She had been so lost, so afraid, and then he had folded her in his arms and she had been found. Natalie wondered if Matt had any idea how much his presence in her life had changed her. Probably not. Men weren't known for deep contemplation.

She was definitely in love with him. Now all she needed to do was tell him. Her stomach fluttered with apprehension and not from the approaching interview. She had never once put her heart on the line and Matt had the power to crush it into a million pieces. She could only hope he was feeling even a smidgen of the same for her. They could work with that. The thought he might not be on the same page made her more afraid than when she'd been trapped with Harry. This was what she'd hoped to avoid all those years.

The door to the interview room opened and cut

off all her troubled thoughts. A tall man with a crew cut stepped in and she recognised him from the night before last. The night when Harry had almost killed her. He had been one of the detectives who had stormed her house. He was dressed in a sharp suit minus the jacket which she guessed was probably resting on the back of his office chair. His serious brown eyes met hers.

"Doctor Miller, I'm Detective Sergeant Darryl Hill."

He shook her padded hand more gently than she'd expected. She watched as he shot Matt a frown as he sank into the chair opposite her. Natalie felt her stomach clench painfully and was glad she had refused the breakfast Matt had served her. Even the coffee was souring in her belly.

Matt took the seat beside her and she caught the brief guarded look the other detective gave him. He obviously didn't like the fact Matt was sitting in on the interview. She wondered why. Surely he was the best qualified person since he had been there to witness some of the evening's events.

But then, what did she know?

"Thank you for coming down here today, Doctor Miller. I understand you'll be wanting to get this over with." He paused briefly, looking again at Matt. "For certain reasons, I have been asked to conduct this interview due to the nature of your involvement with Detective Inspector Murphy."

Natalie blushed, mortified that Detective Hill knew about her and Matt's night together. Who else knew? She shot Matt a dark look. He stared back at her with a stony expression, his jaw clenched. When she left this room, was she going to see the sly looks on his colleagues' faces? The idea gave her pause and had her nibbling on her lower lip anxiously. Matt's green gaze held hers and her breath caught in her throat.

No man who had treated her so kindly and sweetly would ever laugh with his buddies over a conquest. It had to be the exceptional circumstances of the case that would've had an honourable man like Matt providing such personal information. Still, that didn't answer her question about how *he* felt and Matt certainly wasn't offering his feelings to her which left only one option. She was going to have to ask him. She internally shuddered. The very idea had no appeal whatsoever.

His eyes told her without words that it had been necessary and she sent him an infinitesimal nod to say she understood. She wasn't exactly thrilled that their relationship, such as it was, had become common knowledge. She'd barely had time to process how she felt let alone sharing what was an incredible and ground breaking night for her with anyone other than Matt. But she understood.

Natalie turned her focus back on Detective Hill who was still speaking. Her mind fought to catch up with the conversation while piecing together what she had missed. To her immense relief it clicked inside her brain so she didn't have to ask the detective to repeat himself. He wanted her to recount the events of that night as she remembered them with as much detail as possible.

"Please take all the time that you need, Doctor Miller. If you require a break let me know."

Natalie nodded. She was grateful Matt had chosen to stay with her. He was the only one keeping her together. His sheer presence empowered her.

Natalie listened as Darryl spoke formally for the record, identifying himself, her, and Matt. He read out the time and date and stated it was her official statement in regards to the events involving the Butcher.

Natalie waited for her cue, then obediently began reciting the facts as she knew them. The call from Matt. How they'd talked about Linda Cavanaugh's murder. She couldn't bear to call Linda 'the victim.'

Her voice was stiff but her recount precise as she relived hearing the noise downstairs and how frightened she had been. Gary's return. The baseball bat. She grazed lightly over their past to give context to the wrong assumption she'd leapt to and why he'd ended up with a concussion.

She felt Matt give the bandaged hand resting on her thigh a comforting squeeze and she forged on. Detective Hill listened intently and gave Matt the occasional glance. After a while his features blurred and she was drawn into the memory of that night as if she was once again there. The man coming out of the shadows. The fear she had felt at that moment.

"He was my patient. I spent time alone with him in my office," she said, her voice sounding disembodied even to her. "I didn't know who he was at the time. He used a fake name and a disguise. I learned then that he'd been toying with me."

"How so?" Detective Hill questioned.

She wet her lips. "He mentioned women in his sessions. Occupations but never names. He found that amusing, to tell me all about the women who had come before me. He wanted me to know there was no hope."

"You talked to him?"

Natalie nodded. Her free hand came up to blot away the tears that rolled down her cheek, using the bandage as a tissue. She made herself take deep calming breaths when she felt the cool blade against her neck again and told herself it wasn't real. She was free. She was alive. Matt had saved her. Just like he had saved her from herself.

"I angered him purposely. I knew he was enjoying my fear so I tried not to show it. I taunted him, pushed him to the edge. I know it was silly but I was pissed off when I thought I was going to die."

She felt Matt's hand tighten painfully around her own and she knew he didn't like the reminder of how close she'd been to dying. If his shot had missed the mark—she didn't want to think about it.

"You were extremely brave," Detective Hill commented.

She hadn't felt brave. Even now she was shaking from fear.

"I'll be right back with your statement. Detective Murphy, may I have a word?"

To Natalie's ears, the request sounded more like an order. Apparently it had to Matt's ears also as he stood. Natalie bit down on her lip to stop from making a sound of protest. He was her rock. If he left her now, she was sure she'd shatter.

"I won't be long."

Natalie put on a brave face and watched as he followed the other detective out. She felt as if he was walking out on her and stamped down hard on her insecurities.

By the time Detective Hill returned alone, her hands were wrapped around a mug of coffee a uniformed officer had brought her. In the short period of time, her brain had bounced from Matt, to Harry and Helen and the lives that had been destroyed to finally land on Hallie. She really needed to see the girl and tell her everything she'd discovered over the last few days. Hallie would need her, would count on her to be there.

Hallie deserved so much better than the raw deal life had thrown her. But it was what a person did with it that showed their character. Hallie could've easily given up but she'd chosen to fight. Natalie admired that. She admired Hallie. She was fierce and independent. Courageous and determined. The girl had fought so much in her short life. Natalie never wanted her to do so again. From that moment on, Natalie wanted to fight for her. She wanted to protect and nurture. She wanted to shower Hallie with affection and opportunities.

Detective Hill slid a manila folder across the table to her. Natalie flicked through the pages and saw that her words had been transcribed onto paper.

"Is Matt going to be in trouble?"

"For shooting Harry Teller or for getting involved with you?" the detective asked.

Natalie swallowed hard. "I doubt anyone is worried about Harry."

The man shrugged. "It depends on the Boss."

"I see."

"He knew what he was doing, you know," the detective said. He continued when she raised her eyebrow. "About getting involved with you, I mean. He knew the score ahead of the game but it didn't stop him."

She thought about that. Yes, Matt had known the score and still he'd slept with her, even though he could have been suspended or even relieved from the Butcher case. She desperately wanted to know what was going through his mind. Why were men so hard to read?

Natalie turned her own mind to the file and skimmed through the document. With heartfelt relief she picked up the ball-point pen that had placed on the table for her benefit and neatly signed her name on the dotted line. She was glad it was all over. She felt raw. Her time with Harry wasn't something she wanted to dwell over.

She hugged herself, suddenly cold. "What about Harry?" she asked, remembering Detective Hill's earlier question. "Surely it would be considered a necessary course of action?"

Natalie thought her life had been turned upside down by Matt but it appeared she had brought havoc into his. In their short acquaintance he had risked his career by being with her, and had shot and killed a man to protect her. Matt was probably regretting the day he'd met her.

Detective Hill's face was a mask of stone. The expression similar to the one she'd seen on Matt's face once or twice. "An investigation has been opened. Internal Affairs will determine the outcome."

Internal Affairs. Natalie didn't like the sound of that.

"They cast judgment despite not being there to witness the events?" she asked, harshly.

"Matt's statement, and your own, will be sufficient evidence for them to be able to make an informed decision. I wouldn't worry, Doctor Miller." He stood. "You can wait for Matt at his desk if you like. He should be done soon with the Boss."

Her eyes widened. The Boss. Had she gotten him into deep trouble? Was he about to be reprimanded? What was the Boss likely to do to him? Surely he couldn't be fired? He was a damn good detective and he loved his job. What had she done? Her stomach knotted.

Natalie worried at her part in whatever punishment Matt received as she followed Detective Hill through the building towards the Detective Unit. He led her to Matt's desk, which as she'd noticed previously on her last visit was slightly messy though she felt no need to clean it up. A person's work space was private and she knew she would be mad if someone cleaned up her desk, moving things they shouldn't. She thought a messy desk was a happy desk and she always seemed to find whatever she was looking for amongst the clutter.

The bull pen—or as Detective Hill had called it the *Pig Pen*—was a large area and occupied most of the second floor of the building. In addition to the open-area pen, there were two interview rooms, a kitchen, two large conference rooms and two sets of toilets that took up the rest of the space. There were no cubicles, the desks each set a meter apart and lined facing one another like a classroom, Matt's on the end. Of the ten desks, five were empty and the other four desks looked identical to Matt's.

Natalie gnawed on her lower lip as she sat down in the chair to wait for Matt. She had made a complete mess of everything. If he lost his job, would he end up hating her? How could he not? He loved his job and did it well. She would certainly hate someone who cost her the job she loved.

The door at the end of the hall opened and Matt along with a gentleman in his late fifties stepped out of the office. Natalie felt herself suddenly standing, her feet moving of their own accord as if she was a passenger not the driver.

As she approached, Matt turned towards her. His eyebrows furrowed as he looked at her face but he stepped forward and placed a hand on her lower back.

"Superintendent Alec Harris, Doctor Natalie Miller," he introduced.

Alec held out his hand and shook her own. "A pleasure, Doctor Miller." He glanced down as he felt the bandage and quickly released her hand. "I'm so sorry."

Natalie dismissed Alec's dismay. "I'll heal. I figure I got off easy. The night certainly could've ended much worse."

Alec's cornflower blue eyes were solemn. "Yes. How are you holding up?"

"Better, thanks to Matt. He has been my rock

through all of this." She caught the look Alec threw Matt. She wet her lips nervously and to her mortification tears sprang into her eyes. "Please don't punish Matt. He doesn't deserve it. He is a good cop and an even better man."

"Natalie," Matt said softly.

Natalie ignored him and focused on Alec. "Please," she forged on. "He loves his job more than anything. You can't take that away from him. I could never live with myself as I was the cause. He killed a man for me."

"He did, and the investigation will prove he had no other choice." Instant relief filled her. "But he also broke the rules," Alec pointed out.

Her previous elation evaporated. "By sleeping with me, you mean?" Desperately, she continued, "It wasn't his fault. I instigated that night." She heard Matt release a deep breath and Alec's eyebrows rose. Natalie blushed. "It was my choice. He shouldn't suffer because of me."

"He made his own decision and must accept the repercussions."

Natalie's heart stopped and she felt a hot tear roll down her cheek.

"Alec, stop," Matt ordered. His tone was authoritative and her damp eyes widened.

Alec chuckled. "I'm so sorry, Doctor Miller, but your face was priceless. I couldn't help but have some fun."

She frowned. "He's not to be reprimanded?"

"No. You were a consultant. Not that we encourage that sort of behaviour but it's not as if you were a witness or a victim, at least not at the time," he added, once again glancing down at her bandaged hands.

Natalie let out a relieved breath and went limp. Matt drew her against his body. She went willingly.

"So he's not going to lose his job?" she clarified. She wanted to be clear on that point.

"No," Alec said kindly. "You have a good one here, Murphy. Don't let her go."

"I don't plan to."

"No, I don't think you will."

Natalie heard ringing in her ears. Her relief was palpable. Matt wasn't going to be punished for his indiscretion with her.

"There's one more thing I'd like to discuss with you, sir, if you have the time," Natalie said as she snapped back to reality.

"I'm at your disposal, Doctor," Alec said and she heard the humour in his voice. He sounded as if he was enjoying himself.

Why should he not? Her face was burning. She would've loved to have melted into the floor but what she had to ask was much too important to allow her embarrassment to have control.

"I would like your support in removing Hallie Walker from Paradise Valley and into a stable home. I assure you, she is no danger to herself or others."

"Do you have a home in mind?"

"Mine," she replied firmly, as if the matter wasn't up for discussion. It wasn't. She had made up her mind. "Hallie is a good girl. She deserves a chance."

"Of course. I'll advise them immediately. Good

luck. I have a teenager and they are not for the faint of heart. Though, I think you'll do just fine."

Natalie nodded. "Thank you. I appreciate your assistance."

"Any time, Doctor Miller."

"Natalie, please."

He acknowledged her with a nod before excusing himself.

"Hope you know what you're getting into. You're going to have your hands full with that one," he muttered to Matt on his way back to his office, snickering with amusement.

Natalie froze. She had temporarily forgotten Matt had been there. She slowly turned to face him and smiled when she found him grinning at her as he rocked back on his heels in that adorably annoying habit of his.

"I know." She had made a fool of herself. Her embarrassment was still fresh. But she would do it all again if it saved him from trouble. Her gaze dropped to the carpet. It matched the floor of the interview room, she noted. "I'm sorry I interfered. I just couldn't stand the thought of you losing your job because of me."

"Natalie?"

He placed a finger beneath her chin and raised her head. She slowly made eye contact, afraid of what she might see. His beautiful eyes looked back at her kindly.

"Yeah?"

"I love you more."

Her heart stopped beating for a moment then began to pound. He loved her? She was overjoyed.

He loved her. She couldn't believe it. Her euphoria dimmed as she replayed his last words and her eyebrows furrowed. He loved her more? More than she did him? How could he possibly know that?

"What?"

He tucked a strand of hair behind her ear. "I love you more than my job."

Her breath caught in her throat. "You do?"

Was she dreaming? She had to be dreaming. It seemed like a dream.

"How could I not?"

Her face broke into a smile. He loved her. How could she ever have doubted that? It seemed so fast. They hadn't know each other long, but it felt right. She felt a connection only people who have known each other for years had. Matt was special. The only one for her. Her entire life, she had been waiting for him. He was the only man she could trust with her heart, her body, and everything in between.

"I love you too," she declared. Her heart was so full. She was afraid it might burst.

Matt drew her closer then lowered his head even as she raised her own. Their lips met and she felt his love as he poured himself into the kiss. His tongue swept against her own and she felt the corresponding desire low in her belly. She kissed him back, matching his passion until she was no longer burning from embarrassment but from something entirely different and she was more than happy to be consumed by it.

The kiss ended all too quickly for her liking but then she feared if they'd continued he would've been lifting her up onto one of the nearby desks and the idea wasn't at all unappealing.

"Later," he murmured, obviously reading her thoughts.

Several cheers and wolf whistles came from her left and she heard Matt swear. He turned her slightly and this time she definitely wanted the floor to swallow her whole.

"Natalie Miller, I'd like you to meet my team. Amelia Donovan, Nicholas Doyle, and Dean Matthews," Matt said. "You already know Darryl."

"You owe me fifty, Doyle," Amelia said and held out her hand.

Epilogue

One Year Later...

The wedding was a small, intimate affair. Natalie had invited Gary, and he'd wished them the best as he handed over a gravy boat. Alec Harris had brought his wife Caitlyn, both looking as much in love as if they'd only just met. Their daughter, Sophie, a perpetual troublemaker, had disappeared behind a thick hedge the moment she'd arrived. Her date, a young constable by the name of Cade Watson, awkwardly followed her.

Natalie, dressed in a beautiful ivory dress with small pearl beads down the back, looked about the botanical garden which served as both the location for the ceremony and reception. A buffet had been set up to her right, catered by Jed Tanner. His daughter Glory happily played bartender and Natalie was thankful she had so many friends to make her wedding a day to remember.

Matt wrapped his arms around her waist and kissed her naked neck as they looked about the gathering. Her hair had been pinned to one side with a white satin clip, curls tumbling down past her shoulder. She felt like the beautiful princess her father had often said she was. A moment of sorrow filled her as she thought about how he and Aunt Maggie and Uncle Roger hadn't lived to see her so sublimely happy. She hoped that they were looking down on her today and sharing this wonderful day that she'd been too scared to think was possible.

She was still haunted by her memories of that night with Harry but slowly over time the horror had dimmed slightly. She knew she might never get over it, the trauma too great, but she was coping with the help of Matt and Hallie. She wasn't sure what she would do without them and hoped she never found out. She loved them both dearly.

Amelia had slowly warmed to her, and looked uncomfortable in her formal wear. She'd opted for dress pants and fuchsia shirt rather than a dress, the colour blending well with her mocha toned skin. Amelia had taken her role as bridesmaid as if headed for the firing squad and had shared the duty with Matt's sister Kendall.

The three groomsmen, Darryl, Dean, and Nick had accepted her into their lives as Matt's girlfriend and she had begun to think of them as the overbearing brothers she'd never had or wanted. They were even over protective of their 'niece' Hallie, not that they needed to be. Matt had that covered. Whereas a normal teenage girl would yell and scream, Hallie seemed to enjoy it, even when it exasperated her. Natalie was pretty sure Hallie secretly relished in the fact that someone cared enough to put restrictions on her. Thankfully, she was a sensible girl and never gave them cause to worry much.

Each of the men were dressed smartly in their suits and she was sure every woman in the room was busy undressing them in their minds, despite their married or underage status. Everyone, she thought, except herself. The men might be handsome but they didn't hold a candle to her Matt. He was the most gorgeous man alive, inside and out.

Of all the horror that had come from Harry's presence in their lives, he had least brought them all together. Without the Butcher, Natalie would never have met Matt or Hallie and her life would never have changed for the better.

Matt's mother and sister had welcomed her and Hallie into the family with open arms and for the first time in years she had a family again. She felt as she had those long ago days with her aunt and uncle, and before her father had died.

Matt had proposed at a nice romantic Italian restaurant down near the promenade. The candle on their table had flickered in the warm breeze as they sat outside and she'd smelled the water in the bay nearby. Children had laughed as they'd run ahead of their parents as they made their way down to the beach. Fishermen leaned over the pier and sat on the end of the dock hoping to catch their dinner. The sun had begun to set, glowing red in the distance just over the horizon and Matt had reached into his pocket and produced a diamond ring as he'd knelt beside her.

Her breath had caught in her throat as he looked in her eyes and asked her to marry him.

"When I first met you, I was blown away. You're smart and beautiful, kind and giving. I wonder every day how I could be so lucky to have you love me just as I love you," Matt said and her heart swelled in her chest even as tears rolled silently down her cheek. "When I look into the future, all I see is you. I don't want to live without you. I love you, Natalie Miller, with all my heart. Will you do the honour of being my wife?"

Natalie had smiled and replied adamantly. "Yes."

She'd learned later that Hallie had helped pick out the ring, a simple gold band with a solitaire diamond that she couldn't have loved more. Natalie glanced over at Hallie who was dressed in a strapless magenta maid-of-honour gown. Her hair was bundled on the top of her head in a fancy up-do. She sat giggling with Sergeant Robert's daughters and Natalie was glad she was so happy.

Natalie remembered the day she and Matt had gone to collect her from Paradise Valley. It was a day she would always look back on fondly. Not only had she gained a daughter but it had been the day Matt had declared his feelings to her. They had gotten in the car after she'd been introduced to his team and she'd had another moment of anxiety. She hadn't once thought to ask how Matt felt about her decision to remove Hallie from Paradise Valley and bring her home. She'd felt awful, considering her home at that moment had been his.

Natalie had turned in her seat and had apologised

profusely.

Matt had smiled and told her to relax, that he'd known her intentions the moment she had asked Alec for support and thought it was a great idea. Natalie had been immensely relieved.

She had found Hallie staring out the window. The sun streaked through the glass and made the red of her hair burn bright. Hallie had turned when she caught Natalie's reflection in the glass and smiled, the smile fading when she'd noticed Natalie's hands were bound in bandages.

"He hurt you," Hallie declared and the tone of her voice suggested she didn't care for it.

Natalie looked down at her hands. "Barely grazed the skin."

"Is he really dead?"

Natalie nodded. "He isn't coming back, Hallie," she promised. "Have the police been to see you?"

Hallie nodded and Natalie wondered how much Hallie had been told.

"Yeah. I know everything." Tears shimmered in her eyes. "How do I look at myself in the mirror knowing I'm related to that monster?"

Natalie moved towards her and knelt in front of her. Her bandaged hands rested on Hallie's knees. Natalie's heart broke for her and the pain she was feeling. It was too much for a teenager who had already lost everything in the world she held dear. Her life had been ruined because of a few bad decisions others had made.

"By knowing that you're nothing like him."

A tear spilled from Hallie's eye and rolled down her cheek. Natalie wiped it away with the linen of the bandage on her hand.

"How could they have kept it all from me? Missy wasn't my mum. Do you think they planned on lying to me my entire life?"

Natalie shook her head. "I don't know, Hallie, and I don't pretend to know how you're feeling. But I do know family isn't always blood. Love can come despite any familial ties. Missy was your mother in every way that matters. She loved you with all her heart."

Hallie sniffled. "What happens now? With me, I mean," she added.

"How would you like to get out of here?"

Natalie felt a moment of apprehension. What if Hallie didn't want to go with her? Maybe her presence would constantly remind Hallie of this place and things best forgotten. How could she not have thought about that before? She'd been too wrapped up in her own feelings; she hadn't bothered to think of anyone else. The idea of never seeing Hallie again hurt. The girl had burrowed deep into her heart and she feared it might break. But she would comply with what was best for Hallie. It had to be about Hallie. Always.

Hallie smiled. "For a couple hours?"

Natalie shook her head. "No. Not for a couple of hours. I was actually thinking along the lines of…" She shrugged. "A lifetime, maybe?"

"Are you being for real right now?" Hallie asked, her voice low. Natalie nodded. Hallie launched herself at Natalie and hugged her. "Hell yeah."

In that moment Natalie had realised she had everything she could possibly want. "Come on, then. Matt's waiting in the car."

The three of them had fit together like pieces of a jigsaw puzzle. Hallie's adoption papers had been signed months back. Despite her only being a few months from eighteen, she and Matt had wanted to officially make her their daughter. Hallie had come a long way from the teenager she'd met at Paradise Valley. She had easily adjusted to her new home and life and had opted to continue her schooling at home with the help of a tutor and was exceeding both Matt's and Natalie's hopes for her.

The music died down and she was handed a champagne glass while Matt raised his own glass and toasted to her, his wonderful daughter and to his friends and family. Natalie's eyes filled with tears at the lovely sentiment. Vanity at having her make-up ruined had her blinking them back. She couldn't possibly love him more.

Matt then turned to his groomsmen. "You're next, boys."

He drank from his glass and everyone followed suit except for the three men. Dean, Darryl, and Nick all looked at each other, something akin to fear in their eyes.

"He's joking, right?" Nick asked.

Amelia grinned at them, obviously relishing in their discomfort. "I don't think so."

Dean shook his head. "Nope. Not happening."

"I like my bachelor status. No woman is tying me down just yet," Darryl added.

Natalie gave them a dazzling smile. "You say that now. But just you wait and see."

Acknowledgments

I'd like to thank the fabulous and talented team at Limitless Publishing, my editor, Rosa and good friends Leonie, Michael and Jason for their continual support and encouragement. I'm grateful to all. I'd also like to say thanks to you, the reader. I hope you enjoyed Not Forgotten as much as I did writing it. Matt and Natalie were my first and will always hold a special place in my heart.

About the Author

Camille Taylor is an Australian author who resides in the Nation's Capital with her small dog. She was the typical 90's kid and was raised on Goosebumps, Roald Dahl and Paul Jennings. In her teens she began reading the Queen of Crime, Agatha Christie and in later years found Christine Feehan, Janet Evanovich and Julie Garwood.

She started writing at sixteen and enjoys spending time with her family, doting on her nieces and nephews, writing the many stories floating about her head and working on her genealogy where she can trace her heritage to England, Scotland, Ireland and Russia.

Her other interests include, anything creative— such as scrapbooking and drawing and has travelled across Western Europe, New Zealand and the UAE, after spending a year living in London. She's also dabbled in tae kwon do.

Facebook:
https://www.facebook.com/CamilleTaylorAuthor

Twitter:
https://twitter.com/CamilleTaylorAu

Website:
https://camilletaylorbooks.wordpress.com/

Goodreads:
https://www.goodreads.com/author/show/7791241.
Camille_Taylor